T0196011

Feline deadly this Christmas...

Whisker Jog, New Hampshire, celebrates all things Christmas, and few things are more beloved than the town's annual holiday cookie competition. Lara Caphart, who runs the High Cliff Shelter for Cats with her Aunt Fran, is waiting for the green light for a brand-new category: pet-friendly cookies. But when the woman filling in as a last-minute judge dies after sampling someone's Santa-themed treat, Lara's recipe for healthy cat snacks will have to be put on the back burner.

The victim, Gladys Plouffe, was the town's roundly despised former home economics teacher. The chief suspect is the mother of Lara's best friend, who was hellbent on walking away with the bake-off's cash prize. Cryptic clues from beyond the grave only deepen the mystery, pointing to a cat with striking blue eyes—a cat who bears an uncanny resemblance to Lara's mysterious Ragdoll. As Lara begins a dangerous game of cat and mouse, not even her significant other may be able to stop a perfectly clawful killer from getting away with the purr-fect crime...

Also by Linda Reilly

The Cat Lady Mystery Series

Escape Claws
Claws of Death
Claws for Celebration

CLAWS FOR CELEBRATION

A Cat Lady Mystery

Linda Reilly

LYRICAL UNDERGROUND
Kensington Publishing Corp.
www.kensingtonbooks.com

Lyrical Underground books are published by
Kensington Publishing Corp. 119 West 40th Street New York, NY 10018

First Electronic Edition: December 2018
eISBN-13: 978-1-5161-0418-5
eISBN-10: 1-5161-0418-8

First Print Edition: December 2018
ISBN-13: 978-1-5161-0421-5
ISBN-10: 1-5161-0421-8

Printed in the United States of America

For Mom

Acknowledgments

To my editor, Martin Biro, and my agent, Jessica Faust, I owe you both a world of thanks for getting the Cat Lady Mysteries into the hands of readers.

And to my husband, family, and friends, I couldn't have done any of this without your unflagging patience and support.

Claws for Celebration
Cast of Feline Characters

Twinkles: An orange-striped tiger cat with big gold eyes, he's only now beginning to experience the joys of reading.

Ballou: A black, short-haired feral with an adorable white 'stache, he might just be succumbing to the charms of a sweet little tortie.

Munster: This orange-striped male, the unofficial greeter of all human visitors, is a favorite of the kids on "read to a cat" Sundays.

Dolce: Long-haired, solid black, and as sweet as a Christmas cookie, he's found his permanent cozy spot curled up in Aunt Fran's lap.

Snowball: This pure white sweetheart with one blue eye and one green eye loves to view the world from shoulder height; and while she has yet to find her *fur*ever home, she's become a household favorite.

Butterscotch: This skittish marmalade male never warmed up to his rescuers, but the sweet sound of a little boy's voice might just be the secret charm that rocks his world.

Valenteena: Alias "Teena," this tiny but regal-looking black-and-white cat with a heart-shaped marking under her chin is vocal and demanding, but all she really wants is to be loved...and fed.

Purrcival: This endearing boy with the kaleidoscope markings is learning to challenge the pushy Valenteena by finally putting his *paw* down!

Nutmeg: This sweet tortie with a half black/half gold face has quickly woven her way into the heart of the toughest guy in the shelter!

Blue: This stunning Ragdoll cat that only Lara can see has a penchant for pointing out clues to mysteries both past and present. Will the secrets of Blue's spiritual backstory finally be revealed?

Chapter 1

"Lara, I need your help," Sherry Bowker said. "I think my mom is about to commit murder. Someone has to stop her, and I've decided that someone is you. You're the one who's had experience with this murder gig. You're the perfect gal for the job."

"What? Me!" Lara Caphart huffed out a breath. "I beg to differ, Ms. Bowker. What you call experience was more like bad luck. *Really* bad luck."

Over the past year Lara had encountered two different murderers. She'd come out of it with her life intact but had no intention of performing any encores.

"Yeah, you *say* that," Sherry said darkly. "But there's something about you. You have a knack for latching on to killers. I don't want my mom to be one of them. Think of it as murder in reverse."

Lara groaned. "I do *not* latch on to killers. Not intentionally, anyway." She went back to the task at hand, namely, untangling a lump of matted fur from Purrcival's silky neck. The sweet-tempered cat with the kaleidoscope markings had a knot that just wouldn't quit.

They sat cross-legged on the floor in the large parlor of the Folk Victorian home in Whisker Jog, New Hampshire owned by Lara's Aunt Fran. Eleven months earlier, the house had officially become the High Cliff Shelter for Cats. Lara and her aunt had already rescued several cats and placed them in loving homes. The shelter's current feline community consisted of Aunt Fran's own three furbabies, a feral male, and four kitties that were rescued over the summer.

"First of all," Lara said, smiling at what she hoped was her friend's grand exaggeration, "I can't picture Daisy Bowker killing anyone, let alone killing David's mom. Second of all—"

"But that's just it! She's been doing things *so* out of character lately. Even David has noticed it." A slight flush tinged Sherry's cheeks. "He's worried that *his* mom is becoming a bee in *my* mom's bonnet. He doesn't know how to stop his own mom without hurting her feelings."

Sherry had been seeing David Gregson for about five months now and still wore the glow of having found the so-called perfect man. Lara thought it was way too early in the relationship to make that assumption. Still, she was happy for Sherry's newly minted romance. She hadn't seen such joy in her friend's eyes for a very long time.

Lara liberated the furry knot from the soft-bristled brush and wrapped it in a paper towel. She kissed Purrcival's head and released him from her grip. He rubbed his face on her chin, then padded away to score some extra love from Sherry. Sherry took the cat in her lap and stroked his mat-free fur.

Sherry groaned. "It's all about the cookies, Lara. Mom and Loretta each got an email three days ago. They're both finalists in the Whisker Jog Annual Cookie Challenge. I'm so bummed. I was praying Loretta wouldn't make the cut."

"Okay, well that doesn't sound so bad," Lara said. Except she knew that Daisy was putting all her hopes on winning the contest this year. She'd placed second three years in a row. This year she had her heart set on winning the thousand-dollar prize from the sponsor, The Bakers Thryce Flour Company. As for Loretta, Lara wasn't so sure about her intentions. She didn't really know the woman.

Sherry sank her fingers into Purrcy's soft fur. The cat closed his eyes and purred. "You don't get it, Lara. Lately, Loretta's been copying everything Mom does. Last week she got a new hairstyle that looks suspiciously like Mom's. Short in the back, longish on the sides, with a single blond streak. She's like, you know, almost stalkerish!"

"That only means she admires Daisy," Lara pointed out, though the image of a woman in her fifties copying another woman's hairdo gave her a slight chill. "You should be happy."

"I should be, but I'm not. It means she's competing with Mom. I'm not sure *what* she's competing for, but she's in the flippin' cookie contest. I didn't even know she'd entered, and now she's one of the thirty finalists!" Sherry pulled a strand of her raven-black hair into her mouth and chewed the ends. Lara hadn't seen her do that since grade school.

"I hear you, Sher. And I'm not trying to dismiss your feelings. But trust me, Daisy won't do anything crazy, even if David's mom is driving *her* crazy."

"Maybe not," Sherry said grimly. "But you'd better be there. Just in case." Her shoulders sagged. "Unfortunately, there's one more thing that will *not* make Mom happy."

"Uh-oh."

"Yeah. Uh-oh. I just found out this morning that Gladys Plouffe, my old home ec teacher, is going to be one of the two judges. She's a last-minute sub for the music teacher, who fell down the stairs two days ago and broke both her ankles."

"You mean...the Plouffeinator?"

"You remembered," Sherry said dismally. "And you never even met her!"

"I remember you telling me about the abominable Miss Plouffe," Lara said. "Among other lovely names, you called her a witch of a...well, you know."

"She tormented me in school, Lara," Sherry said. "Gave me Ds for no reason except that I couldn't, *to save my life,* thread that stupid sewing machine. Back in the day, Mom had more than a few screaming matches with her. I'm dreading Mom finding out that she's a judge."

"Does the...does Miss Plouffe still teach home ec?"

"She did until a year ago. Finally, *finally* the witch retired. But she had clout in that school, Lara. No one's really sure why." Sherry's eyes took on a glazed, faraway look. "I can still see her, sitting alone in her room chomping on a ham sandwich. She never ate lunch in the teachers' lounge, probably because none of them could stand her. I can't think of one friend she ever had in that school."

"Maybe she has dirt on someone," Lara joked.

Sherry didn't smile. "Has to be something. Anyway, you have to be at that competition next Saturday to keep a close eye on Mom."

"Sher, I think you're overthinking it, but I'll definitely be there. I mean, who loves cookies more than I do?"

Sherry gave up a tiny smile. "Probably only Santa Claus."

* * * *

Lara hadn't told anyone, but she'd tried entering the contest herself. Not with people cookies, but with cat cookies.

Cookies for cats, that is.

The yearly cookie event was sponsored by The Bakers Thryce, a privately owned flour company founded at the end of World War II by one of Whisker Jog's most beloved entrepreneurs—Holland Thryce. The business flourished until Holland's sons, Tate and Holland, Jr., joined the company. It wasn't long before all three had a falling out. Tate left with a bitter taste in his mouth, while Holland and his elder son continued with the business. Not long after Holland, Jr.'s son, Todd, was born, he and his wife died in a boating accident, leaving the child in the care of his grandparents.

As for Holland, who'd long since rolled out his last mound of cookie dough, his legacy thrived. His grandson, Todd Thryce, had carried the company into the twenty-first century by stubbornly refusing to go public. He'd also moved the company's offices to a prestigious New York address.

None of which meant anything to Lara. It was the cookies and the contest she cared about.

She bit her lip and frowned. The letter she'd received ten days ago from the company was signed by Thryce's personal assistant, Alice Gentry. Lara's suggestion that a pet-friendly cookie category be added to the lineup was soundly, if politely, denied. "You may enter cookies that *look* like cats," Ms. Gentry had crisply stated in the letter, "but not cookies that are *for* cats."

The letter went on to say that if such a category were added, there would be no fair way to judge the entries. They couldn't exactly ask the judges to taste cookies made from tuna, pumpkin, and boiled chicken livers.

Lara had to admit, they had a point. But that got her brain cells fired up. She came up with a way the cat cookies could be judged...and encourage cat adoptions at the same time. She only wished she'd thought of it before she sent off her letter to the company.

There was one more thing she could do, she decided. The contest was held each year in the gymnasium at Whisker Jog High School. In the opposite wing of the school, in the cafeteria, those who didn't make the cut could offer their cookies for sale. The proceeds went to the local food bank.

She sat at the kitchen table and booted up her tablet, the scent of cloves and cinnamon wafting around her. Aunt Fran had made a pot of mulled cider. It simmered on the stove, making the room smell heavenly.

For some reason, the internet connection took forever. After what seemed like several minutes, Lara tried to pull up the Web site for the cookie competition. Another long wait. When the site finally came up, she smiled.

"You look intense," Aunt Fran said, coming up behind her.

"Ach!" Lara jumped. "I didn't even hear you. You're quieter than a cat sometimes, you know that?"

Her aunt winked at her. "The easier to spy on you, my dear," she said in a mock evil voice. On her shoulder, a small white cat with one blue eye and one green eye perched contentedly. The cat peered around the kitchen, her pink nose lifting at the scent.

Lara smiled and held out her arms to the cat. Snowball leaped softly onto her lap and rubbed against her snowman-themed sweater. Lara bent and kissed the little feline's soft white head. "What do you think about this?" Lara asked her aunt. "What if I make my cookies for cats and sell them at one of the tables in the school cafeteria? According to the Web site, there are three tables left, and they're up for grabs. It'll only set me back ten bucks for the day."

"Go for it," Aunt Fran said. She pulled two Santa-shaped mugs out of her cupboard and set them on the counter. "You might start a whole new trend."

Lara tapped at her tablet. The connection was slow, deathly slow. It took a few minutes to get to the page where she was able to reserve a table. Aunt Fran set a mug of spicy warm cider on the table, behind Lara's tablet. "Thanks," Lara said distractedly. "Now I'm having trouble getting onto Google. The Wi-Fi's acting wonky. It has been all day."

Her aunt sat down adjacent to her. She wrapped her hands around her own mug and then took a slow sip.

"What are you trying to find?" Aunt Fran asked.

Lara grinned. "Cookies for cats. I want to find a recipe that I can tweak and make into my own. It'll be so much fun to experiment."

"You've only got another week," her aunt warned.

"Don't remind me," Lara said wryly. After Thanksgiving was over, the days leading up to Christmas seemed to fly by on speedy little reindeer hooves.

"Darn." Lara scowled and swiped at her tablet. The Wi-Fi was definitely acting up. Finally, she set aside her tablet and pulled her mug closer. The moment her lips touched the warm cider, she felt a smile creep across her face. "Yum," she said, after taking her first sip. This is positively scrumptious."

"Thank you." Aunt Fran looked pleased.

"You know what? I think I'll go to the library. I'll bet they have a book or two on pet-friendly recipes. Plus, I'll get to see that adorable Santa scene they set up every year."

"Sounds like a plan," Aunt Fran said. "When you were a kid, you loved that display. I used to have to drag you out of there before we got locked inside the library."

Munster chose that moment to stroll into the kitchen. An orange-striped cat with big gold eyes, he was one of the original feline residents before Aunt Fran began taking in rescues. A lovable darling, he looked miffed at the sight of Snowball nestled atop Lara's flannel-lined jeans. He promptly turned up his nose at her and plopped onto Aunt Fran's lap.

Lara laughed. She drank the rest of her cider, then said, "And I have to let you go, Snowball, so I can pop over to the library." She gave the white cat one more kiss and set her gently on the floor.

Across the table, a sudden movement caught Lara's eye. A fluffy, cream-colored cat with chocolate brown ears sat gazing at her. Her eyes were the bluest Lara had ever seen on a cat. The Ragdoll cat blinked once, then rested her chin on the table. A sure sign that Lara was on the right path.

You want me to make those cat cookies, don't you? Lara asked silently.

The Ragdoll—Blue—blinked again. In the next instant she was gone.

Chapter 2

The moment Lara stepped into the children's reading room of the Whisker Jog Public Library, she felt like she was seven again.

Against the far wall, beneath a towering window, was a long table covered in glittery white felt. Lumpy in spots to look like real snow, it was the setting for a scene depicting Santa and his merry helpers preparing for that yearly sleigh ride across a darkened, star-studded sky.

Nine reindeer—Rudolph in the lead—were harnessed to a wooden sleigh painted cherry-red. The sleigh was piled high with miniature packages, each one so intricately wrapped that Lara could almost believe there were tiny treasures inside. A detailed Santa made from felted yarn tottered toward the sleigh, his arms loaded with even more gifts. A pink-cheeked Mrs. Claus shuffled behind him, holding out his thermos for the long night ahead. Behind the sleigh was Santa's workshop—a log cabin of sorts. Through the windows, the faces of the elves could be seen as they toiled at their toy-making tasks.

"I loved this when I was a kid," Lara told Ellie Croteau, one of the library aides. "I used to stand here for hours after school, drinking in every detail. At least it seemed like hours."

With a world-weary smile, Ellie scooped a book off the floor. "I guess it is rather cute. Me, I'm not much of a Christmas person. My favorite time of year is when the holidays are over. Then we can put all this crap away for eleven months."

Lara smiled. She felt sorry for people who didn't enjoy the trappings of the holiday season. The woman no doubt had her reasons. Lara wasn't in a position to judge. She was grateful that her own childhood had been infused with a love of all things Christmas.

"Anyway," Ellie said, "you got here at just the right time. The third-grade reading group left fifteen minutes ago. I thought my eardrums were going to burst from all the chatter and the squealing."

The room is *for kids,* Lara wanted to point out. Instead she flashed another polite smile at the woman. *Enough of this,* she told herself. She'd come here to research cookies for cats. Time was a-wasting.

In the main room of the library, Lara peeled off her fleece jacket and sat down before one of the computers. Things were quiet today. A teenage boy with a mop of black curls and earbuds stuck in his ears sat at the monitor next to hers. If he noticed her, it wasn't obvious.

Lara rubbed the chill from her fingers and skimmed them over the keyboard. Within a few minutes, she discovered there wasn't a lot to choose from. Recipe books for pet treats weren't exactly burning up the bestseller lists. She could always order a book, but that would mean waiting for delivery. She wanted to start experimenting with cat cookie recipes right away.

A few minutes later, she landed on what she hoped would be a useful guide. *Treats for Your Cat* had a glossary of recipes that looked promising. The copyright date was 1989, which happened to be one year before Lara was born.

It's a sign, she told herself.

A flash of cream-colored fur darted across the keyboard. Lara was so startled that she took in a sharp breath.

As quickly as it appeared, it was gone.

Blue.

Lara smiled to herself, then shot a glance at the teen. He looked completely unaware that she'd even sat down beside him. Either way, he wouldn't have seen Blue.

Only Lara could see her.

* * * *

"You've attracted a crowd," Aunt Fran said, grinning at her niece.

"No kidding." Lara giggled. "The scintillating scent of salmon does it every time."

Of the eight cats in the household, five danced around Lara's ankles as she stood at the kitchen counter. Valenteena, the small black-and-white female with a heart-shaped marking under her chin, issued a long, exaggerated meow. Her theatrical cries were the reason Lara had dubbed her the shelter's drama princess.

might do their testing on her and figure out what I did. It was innocent, I swear to God. I was only trying to help. But my future would be over.

The saddest thing was the cat. Heart attack, they said. A peaceful passing, just like her owner's. The cat was old, 17. They said she died of a broken heart, but I know better. She died trying to protect her owner. I know. I watched. They found her furry body stretched out on the bed, one sweet brown paw resting on her lady's cheek. Such a sad but peaceful passing, everyone said...both the woman and the cat. But I know the truth. That precious, beautiful cat with the big blue eyes—I saw her spirit leave. I saw her float off to take care of a new life.

I sound crazy, I know. But I need to make this confession. I hope someday the killer will confess. Even if that woman was old and mean and spiteful, she had the right to die on her own time. On God's time. Lord forgive me for keeping this a secret. I do not have any choice.

Her hand shaking, Lara went over to the kitchen table. She dropped heavily onto a chair, then set the note down in front of her. She read it again, her heart nearly bursting out of her chest. The opening sentence gripped her by the throat.

Exactly one week ago today, I watched someone commit murder.

The date of the letter—March 9, 1990.

Lara was born on March 2, 1990. Exactly one week before the letter was written.

Chapter 3

"Think it'll snow later?" Lara asked her aunt.

They walked along the sidewalk of Whisker Jog High School, toward one of the school's two front entrances. A white banner announcing the Whisker Jog Annual Cookie Challenge had been strung over the doorframe. The lettering was large enough to be seen from a distant planet.

"I hope it holds off," Aunt Fran said, her arm looped through Lara's. "If it snows before this event is over, we'll all be slip-sliding home."

In September Aunt Fran had had her other knee replaced, and she was walking better than ever. Lara knew she didn't want to risk falling and undoing the surgeon's work.

"Do you think Kayla will be all right on her own?" Aunt Fran asked. "She's never handled adoptions by herself."

"She'll be fine," Lara assured her aunt. "Adoptions have to be approved by us, so no one's walking out with a cat today. She just has to serve tea and snacks and bring the cats out, assuming anyone even shows up. I'm guessing most people are either holiday shopping today or attending the cookie competition."

Lara took a deep breath and surveyed the school's grounds. She'd never gotten the chance to attend Whisker Jog High, as her family had moved to a suburb of Boston when she was only eleven. It had been a traumatic time in her life. She'd felt as if her idyllic existence had been ripped out from under her and replaced with a strange new world.

During those weeks and months after the move, Lara had been desperately lonely. She'd missed Sherry, and she'd been miserable without Aunt Fran. She'd sent each of them a card, but only Sherry responded. Aunt Fran had ignored her, or so she'd thought.

Only recently had Lara learned that Aunt Fran had written her loads of letters. Lara's mom, Brenda—now Brenda Caphart-Rice—had seen to it that Lara never received them. She'd had the post office return them as if Lara didn't exist. As for Lara's dad, if he'd been aware of her mom's deceit, he'd never let on. Mild-mannered and devoted to his family, Roy Caphart died from colon cancer seven years earlier, devastating Lara.

When they reached the front door, Lara swung it open and held it for her aunt. She was stepping into the school lobby behind Aunt Fran when a reflection in the glass caught her eye. She turned and saw a gleaming black limo pull up in front of the school.

"That's interesting," Lara said. "Someone just arrived in a limo."

"A limo? I hope it's George Clooney," Aunt Fran said.

Lara laughed.

They followed signs to the cafeteria. The tables had been arranged in three rows, with room enough between each row for people to browse and shop. Lara located her table, number thirteen, at the end of a row near the entrance to the kitchen. She set down the bag she was lugging, then peeled off her jacket.

The past week had drained her. Between her shelter duties, finishing up a rush art project for a client, and trying out different versions of the cat cookie recipe, Lara was wiped. And it was only nine in the morning.

She'd enjoyed the art project tremendously. A woman who'd adopted one of their kittens over the summer had asked Lara to paint a set of Christmas cards for her. As a watercolor artist, Lara couldn't refuse the request. Each of the thirty cards was an original—signed, of course, by Lara. The client paid dearly for them. Lara's earnings went to the fund she'd started to help people cover the cost of lifesaving veterinary procedures for their pets.

The letter in the library book still haunted her. She hadn't been able to put it out of her mind. If the letter was genuine, that meant the murder had happened on the day Lara was born. That alone was unsettling. Add to that the deceased, blue-eyed cat that left her body to care for a new life, it made for a disturbing story.

So far she hadn't told anyone about it, not even Aunt Fran. After the cookie contest was over, she'd show her aunt the letter. Maybe her aunt would have a suggestion for how best to approach Chief Whitley. For sure he'd scoff at the part about the spirit of the cat. But Aunt Fran would instantly recognize the date—Lara's birth date.

In the past the chief had cautioned Lara not to meddle in crime-solving. But this was a murder long past, so his warning didn't apply, did it?

Twenty-eight years was a long time. Was there DNA testing back then? Could the police get any fingerprints off the letter, other than Lara's?

"You've got that daydreamy look again," Aunt Fran said.

"Sorry. You know how my mind wanders."

Her aunt studied her. "Are you okay? You've been quieter than usual the past few days."

Lara shoved a strand of her curly, copper-colored hair behind one ear. "Yeah, of course I'm okay." She forced a grin. "Today's the day I introduce Lara's Cat Nips to the world. What could be more exciting?"

"Well, I hope you make plenty of *dough*," Aunt Fran said and winked. "The food bank will be very grateful."

Aunt Fran removed her coat and scooped up Lara's jacket. "I see a coat rack over in the corner. I'll hang these."

"Thanks." Lara plunked her shopping bag on her assigned chair. One by one, she removed the cellophane bags and set them in rows on her table. She left enough room for her sign, which read: *Lara's Cat Nips. Yummy Treats for Finicky Felines. $3.* The bags had tiny snowflakes on them. They looked so cute with the fish-shaped cat cookies tucked inside. She'd tied each bag with a length of red twine to give them a festive look. The shelter cats had given a resounding "paws up" to the most recent trial recipe, so Lara had gone with it.

A woman setting up a table nearby strolled over to check out Lara's offerings. "Those are for cats?" she asked.

"They sure are," Lara said. "Tested and approved by the residents of the High Cliff Shelter for Cats."

"Really?" The woman looked uncertain. "You're sure they're safe for cats to eat?"

"Positive. But I understand your hesitation. I made these myself and tested them on our own cats. All the ingredients are listed. You'll notice on the label they should be kept in the fridge. After a week, pop them in the freezer. You can take out a few at a time, as you need them."

"Sold. I'll take two packages." The woman pulled six dollars from the purse attached to her waistband and handed the cash to Lara. She grabbed two packets of Cat Nips. "Thanks. Gotta run. There's some commotion in the hallway. I wanna check it out." The woman turned and fled as if a grizzly were chasing her.

"Uh...yeah, sure. Thanks." Lara stuck the cash in the zippered pouch she'd brought, then glanced toward the cafeteria entrance. A glut of people filled the hallway. They chattered in low tones, trying to see over each other's heads. Now she really *was* curious. A familiar head bobbed among

Sherry rolled her eyes. "That sounded like Mr. Lumpkin. I can't believe he's not retired yet. He was a hundred when I was a freshman." As the crowd filtered through the doorway, Lara sneaked another peek at Gladys Plouffe. The woman was moving into the gymnasium with the bearing of an army colonel, clipboard in hand. From her expression, someone might have thought she'd been asked to taste chunks of raw liver instead of trays of sugary delights.

Sherry kept her eyes aimed at the floor, no doubt to avoid being spotted by the enemy. Meanwhile, Lara noticed another woman emerge into the gym from a different doorway. Her dark brown hair was encased in a hairnet, and she wore white vinyl gloves on her hands. Lara wanted to ask Sherry if she knew her, but her friend was busy making a spectacle of herself trying to be unobtrusive. Twice Sherry stepped on the heels of the woman in front of her. "Will you watch where you're going!" the woman finally snapped.

Lara breathed out a sigh of relief when they reached the hallway. "I'd better go relieve Aunt Fran," she told Sherry. "She's manning my table for me at the cookie sale. By the way, I saw your mom earlier. Did she leave already?"

"You couldn't have seen her," Sherry said. "She stayed at the coffee shop today. Said she didn't want to jinx her chances by coming anywhere near the school. I delivered her cookies here for her early this morning."

"But...I saw her, I'm pretty sure," Lara said.

"Well, you must have been seeing things," Sherry said.

Wouldn't be the first time, Lara thought wryly.

"Sorry, I didn't mean to snap." Sherry groaned. "I'm really on edge over this contest. If Mom doesn't win this year..." She shook her head. "Anyway, I think I'll head to the coffee shop. Lunch'll be starting soon. I'm sure Mom and Jill can use the help, even if it is my day off."

Jill was the new employee Daisy had hired right before Thanksgiving.

"So, Jill's working out pretty well, huh?" Lara said.

"Yeah. She's actually been a godsend, and she loves working weekends. It gives me a chance to spend a little more time with David." Sherry blushed to the roots of her black hair. "I just feel so guilty about Mom having to pay for extra help—"

"Stop it," Lara said. "You deserve the time off. Are you seeing David later?"

Sherry smiled, and her eyes lit up. "Yeah, we're going to the mall tonight. Just where I want to be three weeks before Christmas."

"You'll enjoy it," Lara said. "Catch up with me later, okay? When do the judges announce their decisions?"

Sherry looked at her watch. "Supposedly, they'll make their announcements by five o'clock. The school will be closed, but the contestants will be notified by email."

"Seems kind of anticlimactic," Lara said.

"Tell me about it."

"I'm sure you'll want to be with your mom when she gets the email."

"Uh...no," Sherry said. "I'd actually like to be on the North Pole with no internet connection when she gets it, but yes, I'll be with her."

"The North Pole?" a voice bleated.

Sherry jerked around and saw her mother standing directly behind her, hands on her hips, her navy pea coat spotted with melted snowflakes.

"Mom, what are you doing here? I thought you were staying away from the school today!"

"Hi, Lara." Daisy gave Lara a fast hug. "I was going to stay away, but I just couldn't. I'm too nervous about the competition. I knew I'd die from curiosity if I didn't see what the other entries looked like. Have you gals had a look-see yet?"

"We have, Mom, but unfortunately you're too late. They just hustled everyone out of the gym so the judges could get started."

Daisy groaned and made a face. "Darn it. I knew I should've left sooner. The roads were so slick I had to drive slow, and when I got here I had to park a mile away."

Lara slipped an arm around Daisy's shoulder. "Daisy, I can state with absolute certainty that no one else's cookies looked as scrumptious as yours. I can't believe the amount of detail you put into your Santas! Each one is a masterpiece. But...how did you change so fast? I just saw you in an olive-colored coat."

"Huh?" Daisy looked at her blankly. "I don't have an olive-colored coat."

It was Lara's turn to be stymied. "Oh. I...guess I saw someone else. I was sure it was you."

"Mom," Sherry said in a low voice, "I saw her, in the gym. The *you-know-what*."

Daisy's lip curled, then her gaze darkened. "The Plouffeinator?"

Sherry nodded soberly.

"Then I'm outta here," Daisy said. "If I never see that woman again it'll be too soon. I don't even want to risk running into her. Besides, I left Jill alone at the coffee shop. She's probably going nuts." She plopped a kiss on her daughter's cheek. "Get back as soon as you can, okay?" She turned on her boot heel in the direction of the gym.

"Wrong way, Mom." Sherry gripped her mother's shoulders and swiveled her around. "The exit's that way."

Daisy laughed. "With all these people standing around, I got mixed up. Bye, you two!" With a backhanded wave, she hurried off, weaving her way through the crowd until she disappeared.

"Oh, Lara," Sherry moaned. "I'll die if she doesn't win this year. She's been trying for so long."

"Don't think so negative. If her cookies taste as wonderful as they look, and we know they do, then she has to win, right?"

"I guess so," Sherry said, looking unconvinced.

"Oh, I forgot to tell you. Guess who I met a little while ago?"

"My brain's too fried for guessing."

"Todd Thryce, the CEO of The Bakers Thryce! He showed up this morning in a limo."

"Well, isn't that interesting," Sherry said slowly. "I heard he never left his New York lair. I wonder what brings him to town."

"Maybe he got sick of all the city noise and decided to visit his roots."

Sherry grabbed Lara's wrist. "Tell me. What's he like?"

"Pleasant. Polite." Lara cleared her throat. "Attractive."

Sherry's mouth opened in an O. "Look at you, blushing over another man. You, who has the cutest and nicest boyfriend in town."

Lara coughed. "I am not blushing. Something got stuck in my throat. And I'm only reporting what I saw. I have no interest in any man whose name isn't Gideon Halley."

Sherry mock-punched her. "I know. Just teasing ya. Hey, I gotta run. I'll text you later, okay?"

"Go," Lara ordered.

After they parted, Lara returned to the cafeteria. Aunt Fran was smiling like a kid in a candy shop. She held up a package of Lara's Cat Nips and mouthed, "Only one left."

By now people had jammed the room. If the crowd was any indication, the cookie sellers would turn in a nice profit for the food bank.

Lara wended her way over to her table. "You are amazing," she said to her aunt. "I had at least fifty packages of those cat cookies!"

"And now you have none," came a throaty voice from behind.

Lara swiveled on her heel. "Gid, you made it!" She reached up and hugged her significant other. Both his straight black hair and fleece-lined jacket were dotted with moisture. Gideon squeezed her around the waist and kissed her cheek.

"You bet I made it. Did you think I'd miss your entrepreneurial debut?" He waved at Lara's aunt. "Hi, Fran. How're things?" he asked.

"Oh, just peachy," Aunt Fran said with a wink.

Lara laughed. "Are you really buying the last package? In case you've forgotten, you don't have a cat."

"But my new neighbor does. You'd love her. She positively dotes on that spoiled feline of hers."

"Then I *would* love her."

"How's the cookie contest going?" Gideon asked. "Any word yet?"

"No. Sherry said the judges are going to email the contestants later in the day. In case you're wondering, it's too late to view the cookies. The judges are already sequestered with them behind the closed doors of the gym."

"Sequestered?" Gideon grinned and pulled Lara close. "I'll make a lawyer out of you yet. By the way, I forgot to ask you—"

"Help! Someone, please help!"

Everyone turned to see a woman rushing into the cafeteria, a hairnet dangling off her head. Her eyes wide with alarm, she cried out, "Please, someone, call an ambulance. Gladys Plouffe had a bad reaction to one of the cookies!"

Lara felt her legs wobble. She recognized the woman as the one who'd entered the gym shortly after Miss Plouffe had. Lara hesitated only for a moment, then squeezed through the crowd over to the panic-stricken woman. "Where?"

"The gym," the woman said in a shaky voice. "Hurry."

Gideon had already pulled out his cell phone and was calling 9-1-1. He followed behind Lara and the woman, all while giving instructions to the emergency operator.

The closer they got to the gym, the more light-headed Lara felt. She reminded herself to take deep, calming breaths. *Breathe in, breathe out. Breathe in—*

By the time they reached the gym, her head felt a bit clearer. Until she saw Gladys Plouffe, lying faceup on the gymnasium floor. A man huddled over her, one hand flattened over his fist as he pumped her chest. "Come on, Gladys, breathe!" he screamed.

Lara froze. Gladys's face was purple, her eyes wide open. In one outstretched hand she clutched the remains of a Christmas cookie. Lara recognized the cookie.

It was a Santa carrying a burlap sack stuffed with candy crunch gifts.

Chapter 4

By the time the paramedics wheeled Miss Plouffe into the ambulance, the snow had begun to accumulate. The sky had darkened to a dull ash-gray. Fortunately, Lara had been detained only for a short time. No one knew what had caused the deadly reaction in Gladys—only that it had been a fatal one.

All of the cookie sellers had been instructed to leave the building. Each was asked to give their contact info to the officer stationed at the exit. A few of the cookie sellers grumbled, but they packed up their belongings and shuffled out.

Two police cars were parked in front of the school. Lara suspected that by the time the police wrapped up things inside the school, they'd have a few inches of snow to brush off the cars.

Lara insisted that her aunt stay inside the Saturn while the car warmed up. Lara retrieved her windshield brush from the trunk and swiped the wet mixture off the windows. Hot tears stung her cheeks, blending into the cold flakes. When she was through, she flung the brush onto the back seat and slipped into the driver's seat.

They drove home in silence. Beneath her warm jacket, Lara shivered. She knew she and her aunt were thinking the same thing: *Was it Daisy's cookie that made Gladys violently ill?*

If Aunt Fran had any words of comfort to offer, she didn't voice them. The horror of the situation seemed to numb them both. Lara wondered if Daisy had been informed yet. Had the police contacted her? Or was she sitting at home biting her nails, waiting to receive the email announcing the winner of the cookie challenge?

Gideon, bless him, had gone ahead, following one of the police cars to the station. In case they decided to bring Daisy in for questioning, he wanted to be there for her.

Sherry was going to be devastated. Lara hated even thinking about it.

Lara pulled into the driveway and shut off the engine. She held her aunt's arm with an iron grip as they mounted the snow-coated porch steps. Once inside, Lara took her aunt's coat and scarf and hung them to dry in the utility room. She threw her own jacket over the back of a kitchen chair. "I'll do a little shoveling later," Lara said. "We're only supposed to get a few inches."

Her aunt nodded but said nothing.

At the sound of human activity, a posse of felines trailed into the kitchen. Snowball rubbed against Lara's leg, and Lara swept the cat into her arms. She plopped Snowball onto her shoulder, the cat's favorite perch, and held her gently in place.

"Some tea?" Lara asked her aunt and reached for the kettle.

"I think we could both use some, yes." Aunt Fran's face was white, and her eyes looked damp. She went over to the counter for a tissue and blew her nose.

Lara filled the kettle with water and set it down on the burner. She couldn't help smiling when Valenteena trotted into the kitchen. The assertive little feline with the valentine chin would not be ignored. She issued a loud mewl and grabbed at Lara's leg.

"Ow. Your claw is stuck again, Teena." Still clutching Snowball, she gently unhitched the claw and rubbed Valenteena's head. While the water heated, she removed a package of Cat Nips from the fridge and fed some to the cats.

A few minutes later, Lara and Aunt Fran were settled at the kitchen table, two mugs of steaming tea before them. Dolce had already found his way into Aunt Fran's lap, and Snowball had flipped into Lara's. If it hadn't been for Miss Plouffe's horrible death, it would have felt like a cozy scene.

"I want to talk about it, but I don't want to talk about it, you know?" Lara said.

Her aunt reached over and squeezed her hand. "I know. What started as a fun day turned into a nightmare."

Lara felt tears slide down her cheeks. She wanted to cry, really break down in sobs, but she didn't want to make Aunt Fran feel worse. "P-poor Miss Plouffe. I guess nobody liked her, but she didn't deserve to go like that. Her face, it was..."

Purple, Lara thought. *As if she'd fought for every last breath.*

"I know," Aunt Fran soothed. "But try not to think about that part of it. There's nothing you can do to help her now."

Lara squeezed her mug to warm her hands. "Okay, let's think about this. Daisy wouldn't have put anything bad in her cookies. That's a given. All she cared about was winning the contest. Ergo, it couldn't have been the cookie that killed Miss Plouffe, right? I mean, only a crazy person would poison someone openly!"

"I agree, Lara, but sometimes things aren't as simple as they seem."

Lara felt a sudden shard of guilt rip through her. She'd been thinking more about Daisy than about the victim.

"The sad part is," Aunt Fran went on, "that the poor woman didn't seem to have any friends. I wonder who they notified of her death."

"Maybe...you know, you could ask someone?" Snowball purred in Lara's lap as if to emphasize the point.

"Hint, hint?" Aunt Fran smiled weakly. "I'm sure I won't even get a chance to talk to Jerry until tomorrow. And you know how tight-lipped he is about official police business."

"Ohhh, yes. I've been lectured about it many times." Lara sagged in her chair. "Maybe I'm overthinking this. Once they do an autopsy and figure out how she died, they'll know Daisy had nothing to do with it, right?"

Lara's cell suddenly pinged with a text. She felt the blood drain from her face. "I'm afraid to look." Biting her lip, she dug the phone out of her pocket. "It's from Sherry." Lara read the text to herself:

Mom and me at police station. Cops think Miss Plouffe died from allergic reaction, something on the cookie. I'm sick.

Lara dropped the phone on the table and covered her face with her hands. "What is it?" Aunt Fran said.

Lara pushed the phone over to her. "This is bad, Aunt Fran. Really bad. We have to figure out how to help Daisy."

Chapter 5

Sitting cross-legged on her bed, Lara skimmed the mystery letter for the umpteenth time. In all the uproar after seeing Miss Plouffe's body, she'd forgotten all about it. Each time she reread it, she tried to glean something new, but the message only grew more baffling.

The part that bugged her most was the blue-eyed cat—the cat whose spirit supposedly "floated off to care for a new life."

Had that cat been Blue? If not, it was sure one crazy coincidence.

But then, the entire letter might be bogus. Who'd write something like that and shove it between the pages of a library book? Chances were good it wouldn't be found for years, if ever.

According to the letter, the murder was committed exactly one week before March 9, 1990. March 2, 1990 was the day Lara was born. Had Blue been her spirit cat from the beginning?

Valenteena leaped onto the bed and plopped herself between Lara's crossed legs. Lara smiled and stroked the cat, tickling the heart-shaped marking on her chin. "You don't like being ignored, do you, baby girl?"

Once more, she read the cryptic letter. Who wrote it? How did it end up in a recipe book for cat treats? Did someone snatch a random book from the shelf and tuck it in there? Or had the person who penned the note already had it in his or her possession?

Either way, it was almost thirty years old. No way would she dare show it to Chief Whitley now.

Tomorrow was Sunday, which was not an adoption day. Kayla, a vet tech student at a local college, was scheduled to begin work at eleven. Lara loved days when Kayla was there. The young woman adored cats, and in turn, the cats reveled in the attention she lavished on them. With Kayla

Lara poured carefully, shot him a forced smile, then refilled the mugs of at least five other customers. Her pot was nearly empty when she reached the last table. A man sat alone, his elbow propped on the table. His dull brown hair was mussed, and his pale gray eyes red-rimmed. "Coffee?" Lara asked him.

The man nodded. "Might as well. Can't get food in my stomach."

In that moment, Lara recognized him. He was the man who'd tried to save Miss Plouffe in the gymnasium the day before. If Lara had to guess, she'd say he was in his thirties, but he could have been as young as twenty. The remnants of acne made him appear more youthful.

"I saw you yesterday," Lara said. She refilled his mug, emptying her pot. "You tried to revive Miss Plouffe, didn't you?"

The man stared up at her. "Uh...yeah, I did. Was that you who came in with Rose?"

"I'm not sure who the woman was, but yes, that was me."

"Rose Stevens. She was judging the bar cookies. Supposed to, anyway. Everything went to the devil in a handbasket after Gladys bought it." He shook his head. "Sorry. That was crude of me."

"No problem," Lara said. "What were you doing at the school?"

The man sighed. "I work there, in the cafeteria. The principal asked if I'd help out with the cookie contest, so I went in early yesterday morning and set up all the displays." He shrugged. "It took me a while, but I liked getting the overtime. These days, every penny counts."

"It was a nice presentation," Lara said. "You did a great job."

He nodded glumly. "Thanks."

Lara felt bad for the man. He'd tried valiantly to pump life into Gladys Plouffe, with no luck. No doubt he felt distraught over his failure to save her. "May I ask your name?"

For the first time, he smiled feebly. "Jason Blakely," he said. "Yours?"

"I'm Lara Caphart. I live with my aunt at the High Cliff Shelter for Cats."

His smile brightened at the word *cats*. "Really? I love cats. Can't have one though. The apartment where I live doesn't allow them. Stupid, right?"

"Shortsighted," Lara said carefully. "And misguided." It was a known fact that having a pet was good for people's emotional well-being. This wasn't, however, an ideal time to hop onto her soapbox. Her own landlady from her Boston days hadn't allowed cats either. She'd been convinced that cat hairs would work their way through the air vents and contaminate her first-floor bakery. "Does Rose work at the school, too?"

"Yeah, she's the head cook. Super nice lady. Worked hard to get where she is. She worked at Pine Hollow for years before she started the job at the high school. She really loves supervising the kitchen, and she's a great cook, too."

Out of the corner of her eye, Lara saw Jill waving at her. "Hey, I have to run. Nice chatting with you, Jason. Sorry about...the circumstances."

"Yeah, me too. Thanks for the fill-up. Oh, hey, wait a minute. Can I ask you something?"

Lara paused. She had zero time for small talk. "Sure. What is it?"

"There's this cat that's been hanging around the school for almost a week now. I've been sneaking her food from the kitchen, but it's getting way too cold for her to live outside."

"She doesn't have a collar?"

"No. I'm ninety-nine percent sure she's a stray. I don't think she's feral, though. Every time I feed her, she lets me scratch her under the chin. She knows, now, to go to the back door of the kitchen around lunchtime." He smiled. "She waits for me. She's fussy, too. Quite the picky eater."

Lara fumed. Some idiot probably dumped the cat in the woods behind the school.

"I'd like to catch her and get her to a shelter," Jason went on. "If I could trap her somehow, would you guys take her in?"

"We would," Lara said without hesitation. "But first I'd take her to our vet and have her checked out. The vet will also see if she's microchipped. Are you sure it's a female?"

"Not really. I call her a 'she' because she has a feminine looking face, you know? Plus, she's a tortie, and they're usually female. My problem is, I don't have a pet carrier."

A crash from the kitchen made Lara jump. "Jason, I have to run. Will you call the shelter later and leave me your number? We're on Facebook, so we're easy to find."

"You bet I will," he said. "And thanks for listening to me."

She rushed off and slipped behind the counter, setting down the empty coffeepot.

"Everything's gone haywire," Jill said frantically. "Will you see if you can help?"

Lara nodded, then scooted through the swinging door and into the kitchen. Sherry stood between the oven and the stainless-steel worktable, tears streaming down her cheeks. Her face was red, and her raven-black hair looked as if birds were nesting in it.

Pulling in a calming breath, Lara glanced all around. The worktable was splattered with batter of some sort, along with scattered eggshell remains. A generous blob of something oily—melted butter?—graced the front of the oven. Grimy, unscraped dishes sat in a precarious pile next to the commercial dishwasher. If Lara didn't know better, she'd have thought a horde of kindergartners had been doing the baking and the cooking. Three overcooked eggs were stuck to the grill; they looked about as appealing as concrete. A pan of fresh-baked muffins rested upside down on the floor, sending the scent of warm chocolate wafting through the kitchen.

"I can't do this anymore!" Sherry cried, stamping one sneakered foot. "I am not a cook!"

Lara quickly went over, snagged a potholder off the worktable, and turned the chocolate-chip muffins right side up on the counter. "What happened?" she said. "Where's Daisy?"

"She's in the bathroom," Sherry groused. "She's been in there for fifteen minutes. Meanwhile, I'm supposed to be doing all the baking and cooking around here, and you know how crappy I am at it!"

"You're not crappy, you're overwhelmed," Lara said in a soothing voice. "How did you drop the muffins?"

Sherry sniffled. "I tried taking them out of the oven with a dish towel instead of a potholder—something Mom told me *never* to do because I could set myself on fire—and of course I burned myself. When I pulled my hand away, the muffins went flying. Oh, Lara, what are we going to do? I can't cook, I can't bake, I can't sew. How can I possibly get mar—" She stopped abruptly, her eyes wide, her face like a ripe tomato. She whirled around toward the sink so Lara couldn't see her.

"Sherry, did you say what I think you said?"

Sherry shook her head. "No. Yes. I mean, no, I don't know. At this point I don't know anything."

Lara went over and turned Sherry around by her arm. She gave her friend a fierce hug, then looked her straight in the eye. "Did David ask you to marry him?"

Sherry nodded, her dark lashes wet with tears. "Yeah, he wants to get engaged for Christmas. And I already know what you're thinking. It's too soon. We don't know each other well enough. Blah blah blah."

Lara smiled. "Sherry, I'm not thinking anything of the sort. I'm not thinking anything, really. I haven't had time to process it. The main thing is, what do *you* want to do?"

Her friend shrugged. "I don't know, but we can't talk about it now. If I don't get moving on these orders"—she waved a hand at the line of slips hanging above the grill—"Mom and I will be out of business for good. And who knows where Mom will be living if—"

The swinging door opened with a snap, and Jill stuck her head in. "The locals are getting restless out there. Should I tell them all to go home? Honestly, Sher, there's no shame in closing up early."

Sherry stood stock still, then nodded. "You're right. Tell them all to go home. In fact, for all I care, you can tell them all to taking a flipping—"

"Wait a minute," Lara said. She made a time-out sign with her hands. "Sher, is Daisy definitely out of commission for today?"

Her friend nodded. "She's so afraid the police are going to arrest her that she doesn't want anyone to know she's even here. I think she's going to go home and try to get some rest. She didn't sleep a wink last night."

Lara's heart ached for Daisy. She didn't deserve this. Neither did Sherry.

"Listen, Kayla's coming in today to help with the cats. I can take a day off from the shelter to help out here today. I'm not that much of a cook, but I can handle the basics."

"You know, that's actually not a bad idea," Jill piped in. "We can choose three or four favorites, and I'll print out a specials menu for the day. Daisy already made tuna salad this morning. She didn't get to the chicken salad, but that's okay. We can do grilled cheese, tuna melts, hot dogs, and maybe one other lunch item."

"But breakfast won't be over till eleven," Sherry whined. She ripped a paper towel off the roll above the sink and blotted her eyes. "What'll we do till then?"

Jill bit down on her lip. "Lara, can you handle scrambled eggs?"

"That I can do," Lara said.

"Then let's offer a breakfast special of scrambled eggs, bacon or sausage, and toast," Jill suggested. "Our customers won't perish if they have to do without pancakes and waffles for a day."

"I like the way you think, Jill," Lara said. "I'll keep the coffeepots going so we won't run out."

"If it's okay with you, Sher, I'll lower the price—just for today, of course."

Sherry threw up her arms. "Go for it. And...you guys, you're, like, the best," she said, then broke into a sob.

"If you cry in my scrambled eggs..." Lara threatened, wielding a spatula at her friend.

"Yeah, yeah, you're real scary," Sherry quipped. "Come on, let's get to work."

For the rest of the morning, they operated in tandem. Jill whipped up a "specials" menu on Daisy's aging printer and distributed copies to all the tables. A few patrons grumbled about the lack of pancakes, but no one walked out. By quarter to twelve, they'd successfully served eggs, toast, and bacon to half of Whisker Jog. Every chance she got, Lara scraped and rinsed the dirty dishes and plunked them into the dishwasher. Her feet were getting hot inside her winter boots. She'd be grateful once she could head home and kick them off.

A tap at the swinging door made Lara look up. Jill walked in, her face pale. Chief Jerry Whitley strode in behind her. He looked distinctly uncomfortable when he held up a sheet of paper. "Uh, Sherry, I'm sorry, but I'm afraid we have to execute a search warrant."

Sherry's face darkened. "A search warrant? What are you talking about? You are not going to search *anything* in this kitchen!"

Jerry stepped toward Sherry. It was then that Lara noticed another man standing in the doorway. His expression like granite, the man glanced all around as if trying to figure out where to start.

"I'm afraid we are, Ms. Bowker." The chief held up the warrant. "We'll be as tidy and as quick as possible, but we do need access. And we need it now."

"But how are we supposed to serve lunch?" Sherry squeaked at him.

"Chief, how long do you think you'll be?" Lara said, hardening her jaw. "We're already up to our elbows. This is a huge imposition."

Looking mildly amused, Whitley stared at her. "Do you work here now, Lara?"

"Um, well, no. Not exactly. But I'm working here today to help out in a pinch."

"Well then, you can help out after we complete our search."

Sherry staggered slightly. "Lara, this is too much. I can't take much more."

Lara moved to stand in front of her friend. "Chief, what is it, exactly, that you're looking for? Sherry has a right to know."

Whitley nodded and gave Lara the warrant. "She does. We're looking for anything that could or did contain shellfish."

Sherry jerked her head up. "Shellfish?"

Lara saw her friend swallow, and something inside her went icy cold.

"That's right, Ms. Bowker. Miss Plouffe died from a severe allergic reaction to some form of shellfish. Unfortunately, it appears it was on the cookie she was eating when she expired."

Chapter 7

"I guess we missed the noon church service today," Aunt Fran said. She stirred her tea absently, her other hand resting on the black cat snoozing in her lap.

Lara squeezed her aunt's shoulder and sat down at the kitchen table with her own steaming mug. "With everything that's been going on, I think we're allowed one transgression." She'd hoped to elicit a smile from her aunt, but Aunt Fran only frowned and stared into her teacup.

"So, the coffee shop's closed for the day?"

"Yup. No way we could keep things going with the police there pawing through everything. At least they wore vinyl gloves," Lara said soberly. "Anyway, Jill made an announcement to the customers that the coffee shop was closing early."

"I'm sure that went over big," her aunt said dryly. Dolce looked up from her lap and blinked, as if to second her pronouncement.

"Believe it or not, most of them were pretty understanding. There were a few grumblings, but everyone left peaceably. We didn't even have to call out the flying monkeys."

Aunt Fran didn't smile. "I still don't understand. Do the police think the shellfish was on Daisy's cookie?"

"I'm not sure, Aunt Fran. It sounded that way, but the chief didn't exactly give us much of an explanation. Miss Plouffe must have been allergic to shellfish, but who would've known that?"

"Certainly not Daisy. How ridiculous."

Munster leaped onto the chair next to Lara's and rested his chin on the table. He looked sideways at her as if to say, *I haven't eaten in years!*

Despite her glum mood, Lara couldn't help grinning at him. "You looking for more Cat Nips? You've already had about twelve today." She hopped off her chair and fetched some treats for Munster. With her supersonic hearing, Teena heard the crinkling of the cellophane and bounded into the kitchen. She pushed ahead of Munster and clambered halfway up Lara's leg. "Arggh." Lara winced. "Claws, Teena, remember? Those sharp things attached to your paws?" She lifted Teena with one hand and gently set her down. Then she fed the cats each two fish-shaped snacks and stuck the bag back in the fridge.

"Hey." Kayla Ramirez came into the kitchen, Snowball balanced on her shoulder.

"Hi, Kayla," Lara said, smiling at their shelter assistant. "Thanks so much for taking over today. With everything that's been happening, Aunt Fran and I are both kind of frazzled."

"Don't mention it," Kayla said. "You know I'm always glad to help." She slid her gaze sideways. "Kind of a bummer, huh? What's happening with the Bowkers?"

Lara sat up straighter in her chair. "Yeah, it is. But—you already heard about it? How?"

With her free hand Kayla pulled her phone out of her pocket and held it up. "It's all over Facebook." She shoved the phone back in her pocket.

Aunt Fran pushed her chair back sharply. "I've had enough of this nonsense. I need to call Daisy again. This time she *has* to talk to me, whether she wants to or not. Lara, take Dolce." She scooped up the little cat and handed her over the table to Lara.

Lara tucked Dolce into her arms. "You mean, you tried calling her before and she wouldn't talk to you?"

"Exactly," Aunt Fran said. "If she refuses to talk to me this time, I'm marching right over to her house."

Kayla and Lara exchanged worried glances. Kayla removed Snowball from her shoulder and set her on the floor. "Mrs. Clarkson, if there's anything I can—"

A buzzer sounded at the door to the back porch, interrupting her. Kayla made a worried face. "Who could that be? It's not an adoption day."

Clutching Dolce to her chest, Lara got up and followed Kayla into the shelter's meet-and-greet room. The buzzer rang again. A woman's face was peeking through the window pane. When she spotted Kayla and Lara, she tapped on the window and waved.

Lara opened the door to see Alice Gentry standing on the top step. Outside, in the shelter's small parking area, a black limo idled next to Kayla's car.

"Oh my gosh, Ms. Gentry," Lara said with concern. She set Dolce down, and the cat immediately scooted from the room. "I haven't had a chance to shovel out there yet. Be careful on the steps."

Clad in the same burgundy cape she'd worn the day before, Alice Gentry stepped into the meet-and-greet room and peeled off her leather gloves. Hatless today, she stamped her black leather boots on the bristled mat to dislodge any excess snow. Seeing her this close, Lara realized how lovely she was. As a young woman, she must have been a knockout.

"Please call me Alice," she said. "I hope I haven't come at a bad time."

"Not at all," Lara assured her. "We don't do adoptions on Sundays, but you're welcome here any time." She introduced Kayla, who looked entranced by the woman's fashionable ensemble.

Alice nodded at Kayla, then looked all around, her gaze coming to rest on the cat-themed runner draped across the wooden table Lara had refinished.

"Wow. I'm impressed. I'm not much of a cat person, but this room is quite adorable, isn't it?" She nodded at one of the chairs. "May I sit for a moment?"

"Of course. I'm sorry. Can I get you something warm to drink? Some tea or hot cocoa?"

"No, but thank you for the offer. I can't stay long." Alice sat on the nearest chair. She unhooked the top button of her cape and reached inside. From an apparent hidden pocket, she pulled out a legal-sized envelope and gave it to Lara. "Todd wanted to be sure you got this. We're not sure how long we're staying in town, so he asked me to deliver it this morning."

Curious, Lara took the envelope from her. It was unsealed, so she opened the flap and peeked. Inside was a check for a whopping amount, payable to the shelter. "Oh...my Lord, Ms. Gentry. This is so generous!"

"Todd was impressed with you, Lara," she said, a slight edge to her tone. She covered it quickly with a smile. "Your request to add pet cookies to the annual competition really touched him. He knew it would never fly with the directors, but he wanted to reward you for your ingenuity."

Ingenuity? There was nothing ingenious about making cookies for cats. It was really Lara's own personal crusade that inspired the idea.

"Well, please thank him for me," Lara said, "and I'll thank him as well." She was dying to show Kayla the check, but she didn't want to appear too mercenary. "And assure him that every penny will be spent on the cats, in one way or another."

"I'm sure it will. Todd actually loves cats, you know. He has two furballs of his own." She wrinkled her perfectly-shaped nose. "He calls them his little Siamese devils."

A sudden swirl of fur at Alice's ankles caught Lara's eye. It was Blue, and she looked extremely agitated. Lara tried to hide her surprise, but Alice Gentry was sharp. "Are you all right, Lara? You look as if you've seen a ghost."

Lara saw Kayla staring at her, probably wondering the same thing. Had her face paled that much?

"I'm fine. I thought I saw a spider, but it was only a shadow."

Liar.

Alice shuddered. "I hate spiders. If you see one, be sure to kill it. The fewer spiders in the world, the better."

Kayla frowned and pushed her glasses higher on her nose. "If you'll excuse me, I have litter boxes to attend to. Nice meeting you, Ms. Gentry." She went off without another word.

Blue had already vanished. Why had Alice Gentry's presence gotten the Ragdoll cat so riled? Had Blue sensed the woman's disdain for cats?

"So," Lara said, "how long will you both be staying in town?"

Alice huffed out a breath. "At this point, I'm not sure. The contest, as you know, got sidelined after what happened yesterday. I'm not even sure why Todd insisted on attending the competition this year. In past years, he's never shown much interest in it. Oh sure, it's sponsored by The Bakers Thryce. But so are several other baking contests all over the country. He rarely attends any of those." She stared at the wall, as if trying to recall something.

"Didn't he grow up around here?" Lara prodded. "Maybe he had friends he wanted to visit."

Alice looked hard at Lara, then rose from her chair. "We both grew up around here. Different sides of the track, as they say, but who cares? None of that matters anymore, does it?"

The abrupt change in mood startled Lara. Did Alice expect an answer? Lara opened her mouth, but nothing came out.

Alice refastened the top button of her cape. "Lara, let me explain something to you. In the event there's any doubt, Todd and I are a couple. We have been for a very long time, over a period of decades, in fact. It's been rocky at times, but we've endured."

"That's fine," Lara said. "I mean, I wasn't—"

"I sensed he was a bit taken with you when he met you yesterday," Alice barreled on. "Who wouldn't be? You're very fetching, and quite charming."

She inched toward the door and reached out a hand toward the doorknob. Her parting smile had all the charm of a barracuda's. "All I'm saying is, don't let it go to your head. Todd is spoken for. Are we clear on that?"

Lara couldn't believe her ears. Alice was warning her to stay away from Todd, a man she'd met only yesterday. A man old enough to be her dad!

Not that Lara had any interest in him—she didn't. She was grateful he'd wanted to support the shelter, but that was all. Lara was tempted to tell Alice about Gideon, but she refused to be baited. Lara's personal relationship was none of Alice's business.

"Well, thanks again for coming by," Lara said, ignoring Alice's question. She somehow managed to stretch her lips into a smile. "Have a great day, and stay warm."

Alice's own fake smile collapsed. She pulled open the door and clomped down the steps. Lara watched to be sure she made it to the limo without falling, then pushed the door shut, hard.

"Unbelievable! And since when am I fetching?"

"What are you fetching?"

Lara whirled to see Kayla standing directly behind her, Snowball perched on her shoulder. "I'm not fetching anything. Alice Gentry *called* me fetching."

Kayla shook her head. "I hate to be critical, but I did not care for that woman. Something tells me she is not a champion for animals."

"I think you're right." Lara reached over and rubbed Snowball's forehead. "The only one she's a champion for is Todd Thryce. She actually had the gall to warn me that he was spoken for. Spoken for! Like this was some nineteen eighties drama."

"You mean, she thought you had a thing for him?"

"Exactly. Oh, but wait till you see the donation we got from him!" She showed Kayla the check.

Kayla pumped a fist. "Yay! What a cool guy."

"Cool indeed," Lara said. "You and I have talked about so many projects. This will give us a nice boost, won't it?"

"Yes, it will." Kayla looked thoughtful. "Sometimes I get real down about stuff, especially around the holidays. I want to save every animal in the world, but I know I can't. No matter what we do here, it never seems like it's enough, does it?"

Lara got it. Mentally, she'd been down that road many times. "I know what you're saying, but look at everything we've done so far. Remember when you rescued that litter in July? Four of them now have permanent, loving homes. That's because of you, Kayla."

"Except no one wanted Snowball." She pulled the cat's face against her own.

"I know. But Snowball is safe here, and loved. That's also because of you." Kayla heaved a sigh. "I hear you, Lara. But doesn't it ever get to you? That we can't save them all?"

"It does get to me, but think of it this way: every cat we save is a victory. Which reminds me..." She told Kayla about the tortie at the school that Jason Blakely had been feeding.

Kayla dug out her phone and checked the time. "It's only a little after one. Maybe you and I should go over there and try to find her. Even if she doesn't show up, at least we can leave her some food."

"You know, that's not a bad plan."

* * * *

Kayla offered to drive to the school, so Lara hopped into the passenger seat of her little Honda Fit. Kayla had bought the used car during the summer and, so far, hadn't had an ounce of trouble with it. The car was reliable, if small—perfect for getting her to and from her vet tech classes.

On the ride over to the school, Lara grew tense. Alice Gentry's visit had temporarily distracted her. She needed to get back to the real problem— figuring out who killed Miss Plouffe. *If* it was even murder.

"Uh-oh," Kayla said, pulling into the school parking lot. "Cop cars. Two of them."

Kayla was right. Two unmarked Dodge Chargers sat facing one another at the far end of the lot. The crime scene van that had been there the day before was gone.

"Staties," Lara said. "Probably searching the kitchen again. Or maybe the entire school." She told Kayla what the chief had said about shellfish being on the cookie.

"I knew a guy once who was allergic to shellfish," Kayla said. "He couldn't go anywhere near the stuff, especially shrimp. This one time? He ordered a burger in a restaurant, but his girlfriend ordered a shrimp salad. All of a sudden, his throat closed up. I wasn't there, but I heard his face turned purple and he couldn't breathe at all."

Miss Plouffe's face had been purple. Lara shivered at the memory.

"What happened?"

"Like I said, I heard the story secondhand, but his girlfriend knew he carried injectable allergy medication with him. She dug one out of his pocket and jabbed him with it. Thank God she was a nursing student. She knew how to act fast in an emergency."

Did Miss Plouffe carry the same medication with her? Or had she been so sure she'd never come in contact with shellfish that she didn't bother taking precautions?

Kayla parked her car at the opposite end of the lot from where the police cars were. "Hopefully they won't try to stop us from approaching the school. Do you know where the back entrance to the kitchen is?"

"Nope. I went to high school in Massachusetts. I don't know the layout at all." She nodded toward the wooded area that lined the rear of the school property. "I'm wondering if the kitty hunkers down in the woods, assuming she's really homeless. I'm guessing there's a rear door to the kitchen in back of the school. Jason said that's where the cat comes to get food."

Kayla shut off her engine, and Lara pulled the cat carrier out of the back seat. Together they walked toward the school. They skirted the southern side, their boots crunching over the snow, and went around to the back.

"Hey!" a male voice called from behind them. "What are you two doing there?"

"Uh-oh," Kayla whispered.

Turning, Lara waved to the tall, heavyset man glaring at them from about twenty feet away. "Stay here," she said quietly, then smiled and strode toward him.

"Good morning, we're from the High Cliff Shelter for Cats. We're responding to a call about a stray cat that's been coming around the school. By any chance, have you seen a cat?"

The officer stood there, apparently unwilling to walk through the snow to meet her halfway. When she was a few feet from him, he opened his jacket and flashed his state police badge. "You have any ID?" he said sternly as Lara approached.

"I do, yes." She dug out her license and held it up.

He took it from her, then grumped, "This is a Massachusetts license."

"I know. I live in Whisker Jog now, but my Mass license is still in effect, so I haven't applied for a New Hampshire one yet."

The man gave it back to her and stared in Kayla's direction. As if to confirm their mission, Kayla held up the cat carrier and waved at him.

"I haven't seen a cat," he said, "but so long as you stay away from the building you can have a look-see. I suggest you make it fast. We've got enough to do without hanging around to babysit you two. Cat or no cat, you've got ten minutes."

Definitely not a cat person, Lara thought.

"Yes, sir. Thank you. We'll do our best."

Lara turned and headed back toward Kayla. "We've got ten minutes." They clumped around to the back of the school, then stopped to take stock of their surroundings. Behind the building, three separate doors greeted them. In front of the middle door, Lara spotted something jutting out of the snow. "Is that a paper plate?"

"I think so. Let's check it out."

They picked up the pace and trotted over to the thing sticking out of the snow. "Yup. Definitely a paper plate. This must be where Jason's been feeding the cat." Lara pulled the soggy plate out of the snow and shook it out. She held it up to her nose. "There was something fishy on it, for sure," she said and glanced toward the woods.

"Oh, Lara, look. There's fresh paw prints all around. That poor little cat must have come looking for food today."

Lara sighed with frustration. Sometimes trying to help a cat only ended in disappointment. Or heartbreak.

"Even if we don't spot her, we'll leave some food here for her," Lara said. "I sure wish she'd show her face, though. She's got to be hungry. If she smells the kibble we brought, we might be able to entice her into the carrier."

Lara reached into her jacket pocket and pulled out a plastic bag. She unzipped the top, set the paper plate down flat in the snow, and emptied the cat food onto it.

Kayla, meanwhile, was trudging through the snow, trying to follow the cat's prints. She returned several minutes later, looking dejected. "I got as far as the trees, but then her footprints, like, disappeared. Oh, Lara, what if a predator got her?"

"Think positive," Lara said. "She was here today for sure, because her prints are in the snow. Tomorrow's Monday, so I'll get in touch with Jason Blakely after school opens. Maybe we can work with him to trap her."

Kayla's gaze shifted. She stared over Lara's shoulder. "That trooper is back, and he's coming our way."

"That's okay. We left food out for her. She'll probably come looking for it after we leave."

"You girls done here?" the trooper said, breathing hard now as he approached them.

Lara pasted on her best smile. "Yes, and thank you for your patience, officer. Unfortunately, we didn't spot the cat, but we left some food out for her in case she comes back."

The trooper barely refrained from rolling his eyes.

Taking the hint, Lara hurried toward the parking area, Kayla trailing behind her. The officer turned and followed them. Arms crossed over his chest, he watched until Kayla started the little Honda and drove out of the lot. Lara buckled her seat belt. "Mission accomplished, partly," she said. "We'll try again tomorrow."

"I have classes tomorrow," Kayla said dolefully. "But I'd rather be here, trying to find that little tortie!"

"Kayla, don't stress over it. I'll contact Jason and try to work something out with him. He sounded as anxious as we are to get her into the shelter."

On the short drive back to Aunt Fran's, they stuck to safe topics, such as how to wisely use the donation from Todd Thryce. Cat food, kitty litter, and cleaning supplies ate up a sizeable portion of the shelter's funds. Veterinary bills used up another big chunk, and Kayla's salary, while not huge, was yet another expense.

Kayla swung into the shelter's parking area and killed her engine. "I wonder how things are going with the Bowkers," she said, pushing her glasses higher on her nose.

"I'll text Sherry as soon as we get in," Lara said. The search for the cat had temporarily distracted her, but now she really had to focus on helping Daisy and Sherry.

The other thing nagging at Lara was the letter, the one that had dropped out of the library book. No way could she show it to the chief. Not now, not with Gladys's death hanging over everyone. She didn't want to burden Aunt Fran with it. Her aunt was too worried about Daisy to add one more concern to her plate. And she certainly couldn't show it to Sherry.

Lara unbuckled her seat belt. "Kayla, something odd happened to me a few days ago. I've been wanting to share it with someone, but, well, the timing hasn't been right. I was going to wait till the cookie competition was over, but now, with Miss Plouffe..." She broke off and stared through the windshield into the snow-covered yard.

"Is it something bad?" Kayla asked, looking a bit frightened.

"Kind of," Lara said. "But it happened when I was born, close to thirty years ago."

"You're that old?" Kayla said. "I always thought you were only a few years older than me."

Lara couldn't help laughing. "I'll be twenty-nine next March."

"You've got to be kidding me. You look so young!"

"Well, thanks, I think. Anyway, I'm guessing this is something you'll be interested in." Lara had learned after they first hired Kayla that the young woman was an aficionado of true crime. Since she was a kid, she'd been collecting articles about real criminal cases in New Hampshire.

"Does it have anything to do with cats?" Kayla asked, trekking beside Lara toward the steps to the back porch.

"Be careful, I haven't shoveled out here yet," Lara cautioned. She unlocked the porch door. "It does, in a way, but it's bigger than that. It's about a possible murder...an old murder," she emphasized.

Kayla's eyes widened behind her glasses. "Then it sounds like it's right up my alley."

Chapter 8

Kayla pulled off her glasses and rubbed her eyes. "I don't know what to say, Lara. This letter kind of blows my mind, you know?" She stuck her glasses back on her face. "It's the timing that really slays me. This letter falls out of a book only a few days before the police start investigating a *real* murder." She pushed the sheet of paper across the table toward Lara.

"A *possible* real murder," Lara countered. She still wasn't convinced that Miss Plouffe's death had been the result of foul play.

Valenteena strutted into the meet-and-greet room, eliciting smiles from both women. The kitty issued a plaintive meow and leaped onto Kayla's lap. "Hey there, cutie-pie," Kayla said, pulling the kitty's face close to her own. "You looking for treats again?"

The cat responded by climbing onto the table and placing her forepaws on the window.

"She wants to go out, doesn't she?" Kayla asked.

"Oh boy, does she ever. I have to watch her like a hawk any time someone comes in. She's ready to make a dash for freedom at the slightest chance."

"I've actually thought a lot about her," Kayla said. "I think she'd do well in a large home that has lots of room to explore. Maybe that way she'd be less likely to want to escape."

"You might be right." Lara sipped her cooling cocoa.

Kayla stroked Teena's furry back. "Back to this letter. Today's Sunday, so the library's closed. I have classes most of the day tomorrow. My last class ends at three, though. Maybe I'll pop over there tomorrow afternoon and do some digging. I'm very familiar with their microfiche room."

Lara smiled. She'd learned from Kayla several months earlier that the Whisker Jog Public Library kept copies of newspapers from all over the state stored on microfiche. The library's records apparently dated pretty far back. "That would be terrific, if you could squeeze it into your schedule. I'd start with obituaries at the beginning of March 1990." "Maybe I'll even find your birth notice. That would be a trip, wouldn't it?" Kayla grinned at Lara.

"Yeah, that would be a hoot," Lara said dryly. "The victim—if there really was one—was an elderly woman. No way of knowing where she died, but it had to be someplace local for that letter to have ended up in the library book."

"Can you make a copy of the letter for me?"

"Sure can. Remind me before you leave, okay?"

They spent the remainder of the afternoon grooming the cats and freshening the litter boxes. Kayla left a little after four, a copy of the mysterious letter tucked inside her purse. She looked worried, and Lara knew she was thinking of the little tortie behind the school.

Lara checked the shelter's Facebook page again. So far, she hadn't gotten a call or a message from Jason Blakely.

"You look wiped out," Aunt Fran said from the doorway of the back porch. Snowball, the lovable shoulder cat, gazed at Lara from his favorite perch.

Lara gave her a wan smile. "I am. Funny how mental fatigue morphs into the physical. Right now, I feel as if I couldn't hold a paintbrush." She told her aunt about her and Kayla's jaunt to the school to search for the stray tortie.

"You'll get her," Aunt Fran said. "You said there were police cars at the school?"

"Yeah. Kind of depressing, isn't it? Did you ever reach Daisy?"

Aunt Fran shook her head. "She apparently doesn't want to talk to anyone. After giving it some thought, I decided not to go over to her house. If she wants to talk to me, she knows where I am."

"I'll try to reach Sherry," Lara said. "By now the police should have finished their search of the coffee shop."

Aunt Fran came farther into the room and sat down next to Lara. She snugged Snowball against her chest. "I went to the Shop-Along for a few things while you and Kayla were gone. I'd have sworn I saw Daisy in the market. I called to her, but she didn't seem to hear me. But when she turned the corner, I realized it wasn't her."

"Huh. That's interesting. I thought I saw Daisy yesterday, but Sherry insisted she hadn't gone to the school. She showed up after the judging had already started, but I was sure I'd seen her earlier in the school lobby, and wearing a different coat."

"Well, they say everyone has a doppelgänger."

"Yeah, somewhere on the planet," Lara said. "Not living right next door."

Lara's phone pinged. It was a text from Sherry that said: Call me!

"Bad news?" Aunt Fran's face went ash-gray.

"I'm not sure." Lara called Sherry's number. Her friend answered instantly.

"Oh, Lara, this is awful, just awful."

"What happened?"

Sherry sniffled loudly. "The cops found an empty foil bag in the Dumpster behind the coffee shop."

"An empty bag of what?"

"Of...of lobster meat!"

"Lobster? Is that what Miss Plouffe was allergic to?"

"She was allergic to all shellfish. When I was in high school, everyone knew it. And believe me, plenty of jokes went around about it. I remember this one kid drawing a cartoon of a lobster with Miss Plouffe's face choking on a ham sandwich. It got passed around for about a week before he finally got detention for it. Secretly, though, everyone was cheering him on."

A sick feeling settled like a stone in Lara's stomach. She looked at her aunt and shook her head. "Sher, I still don't get it. Why is it so strange that they found an empty bag of lobster meat? You guys run a coffee shop. Lobster is food. Period."

"Because we don't have anything with lobster on the menu." Sherry's voice shook. "I tried to explain to them that Mom runs specials sometimes. Especially around the holidays, she likes to do lobster salad rolls. Everyone loves them! The fresh lobster is too expensive during the colder months, so she uses the frozen kind."

"Okay, that makes perfect sense. Didn't they believe you?"

"Oh sure, they believed me. Here's the problem. They said the back of the cookie Miss Plouffe tasted had traces of lobster on it. How dopey is that? Like Mom would put lobster juice on...on her cookies!"

A low throb, like the beat of a tiny hammer, pulsed in Lara's head. She didn't believe for a minute that Daisy had tainted her cookies with traces of lobster.

"Sher, this is making me crazy. Your mom didn't have any reason to want to harm Miss Plouffe, right?"

A long silence followed. Then, in a quiet voice Sherry said, "Remember I told you that Mom had her share of run-ins with the—with Miss Plouffe when I was in high school?"

"You mentioned she'd had a few screaming matches with her, but that was ages ago."

Something crashed in Lara's ear. "Sorry," Sherry said. "I dropped the phone. Anyway, about a month ago, Miss Plouffe came into the coffee shop and sat at the counter. Which was weird, because she'd never done that before."

"Okaaay," Lara said, dreading the rest of the story.

"Mom, of course, knew her instantly. She's never forgotten that D in home ec on my report card, all because I couldn't thread that blasted sewing machine. I'm not saying I was a scholar, Lara, but I'd never gotten Ds. Not until that one."

A D in home ec wasn't exactly earth-shattering. Was it possible Daisy had held a grudge over it for this long?

"Anyway, Mom, being Mom, couldn't resist a wisecrack. Miss Plouffe ordered a grilled ham and cheese, and Mom made her a nice drippy gooey cheesy one. When she brought it over to Miss Plouffe and set it down, she put on this maniacal grin and said, 'Sorry it took so long. I had trouble threading the cheese through the slicer. You know how it is.' Then she winked at her and walked away."

Lara winced. She'd forgotten how overprotective Daisy had always been of Sherry. Being forced into the role of single mom had turned her into a mama lion.

"That was only about a month ago?"

"Yeah. I *literally* had to run into the kitchen so I wouldn't laugh in the woman's face. Oh, Lara, I know it sounds mean, but it's nothing compared to the nasty stuff she used to do to kids."

"She was that bad, huh?"

"She was. Anyway, two customers heard Mom say that. How could they help it? She practically announced it to the entire restaurant."

Lara's head spun. In a single rebellious moment, Daisy had acted like a high school kid herself. Now it was coming back like a boomerang to smack her on the head.

Nonetheless, it was still petty stuff. Not exactly a motive for murder.

"What did Miss Plouffe do when Daisy said that?"

"Oh, she sputtered like a steam engine. Acted like she didn't know what Mom was talking about, but I know she knew. I saw it on her face before I fled into the kitchen. When I finally went back out to the counter, Miss Plouffe had left all but one bite of the sandwich and taken off. She never even paid for it."

Lara had a bad feeling she knew what was coming next. "Did anyone tell the police about it?"

"Of course they did," Sherry said bitterly. "Old Mr. Patello couldn't wait to trot down to the police station this morning and spill the whole incident to Chief Whitley. I'm not sure if I can ever look at him the same again. It really turned my stomach."

Mr. Patello was a cranky, elderly gent who parked his hat on a stool in the coffee shop every morning to save it for his deceased friend Herbie. And heaven forbid anyone should try to sit there. Even if the place was jam-packed with customers, he'd insist that it was Herbie's seat.

"None of that is a motive for murder," Lara said. "No reasonable person could possibly interpret it that way."

"I know," Sherry said in a choked voice. "But what if they do, Lara? What if they do?"

Chapter 9

A light coating of snow had fallen overnight. By Monday morning, it was just enough to cause multiple fender-benders as people headed off to work. The plows did a valiant job of clearing the snow, but the roads were deceiving. What looked like bare pavement was actually an invisible layer of ice.

After performing her morning feline duties, Lara made her daily trek to the coffee shop. She tucked her favorite green scarf—a recent gift from Gideon—around her neck and plopped fuzzy ear muffs over her ears. The walk was tricky, with treacherous patches of ice dotting the sidewalks. The town did its best to keep the sidewalks clean, but keeping up was a challenge.

Lara pulled open the door to the coffee shop, and a blast of warm air caressed her cold cheeks. She stepped inside and looked around. The dining area was nearly empty. Only a few tables were occupied. The counter stools were even more sparsely populated. The crabby Mr. Patello was glaringly absent. Lara slid onto a stool and pulled off her gloves.

Sherry's expression was bleak. She poured a cup of coffee for Lara and set it down in front of her.

"Quiet today, huh?" Lara said. "Typical for a Monday, though." She cringed at her own lie.

"No, it's not typical for a Monday." Sherry's eyes were puffy. She'd foregone her eyeliner, and her thick black hair rested flatter than usual on her head.

"Want a muffin?" Sherry said dully. "Mom made cranberry-orange ones. God only knows what they taste like. I had to remind her to add the cranberries."

Lara felt an invisible fist squeeze her heart. Sherry's and Daisy's lives were in ruins, yet they carried on. They had to.

"Sure, I'll have one. Is David coming in today?" Lara hoped a change of subject might distract her friend from her gloomy thoughts.

"I'm not sure. His boss gives him his schedule every Monday morning, so he never knows till he gets there. If he has to travel up north, mostly likely he won't make it in here."

David worked as a salesperson for a regional tractor chain. According to Sherry, he was particularly busy at this time of year. Snow removal equipment was a big part of their inventory.

"Hey, don't tell Mom what I told you yesterday about, you know..."

Lara nodded. "Say no more. My lips are sealed with Elmer's Glue. Is there, um, any news on that front?"

"No way," Sherry said. "With everything that's been going on, that's the last thing I want to discuss with David right now." Her shoulders drooped. "I'd probably make a rotten wife, anyway."

Before Lara could protest, Sherry went off through the swinging door to the kitchen. She returned with a warm muffin and set it in front of Lara.

"I don't want to hear you talk that way," Lara said softly but sternly, "because it's not true and you know it." She broke off a piece of her muffin and popped it into her mouth. "Tell Daisy her muffin is delicious."

"She's just going through the motions," Sherry said. "Which doesn't matter anyway, since it doesn't look like we're going to be flooded with customers today. I'm thinking of shutting down before lunch and putting a sign on the door saying we had to close unexpectedly for the day, or something like that."

An old Sonny and Cher song, "I Got You Babe," rang out from the pocket of Sherry's pants. She flushed deeply and pulled out her cell. "Hey," she said, turning her back on Lara.

The old love song was Sherry and David's chosen theme song, and they both used it as their ring tone for one another.

Lara pulled her own phone out of her tote and pretended to study her text messages. She didn't want Sherry to think she was eavesdropping, even if she was straining her ears a bit in that direction.

While she had her phone out, she figured it was a good time to check the shelter's Facebook page. She did a fist pump when she saw that Jason Blakely had left a private message. Supplying his phone number, he asked if Lara could come by the school about a half hour before noon to help him trap the stray kitty. He'd provide the goodies if she'd bring along the cat carrier. He gave her instructions for meeting him at the back of the school—instructions she didn't need, since she and Kayla had already been there.

Her first instinct was to return his message with a phone call. Since he was working at the school, however, she didn't want him to get in trouble for taking a call during work hours. She messaged him back with a promise to be there, waiting behind the school with a cat carrier.

Sherry turned back to Lara and stuck her phone in her pocket. "He's gotta drive up to Littleton today, so he won't be coming in. Just as well. I look like a troll."

Lara wanted to protest, but she knew her friend despised being patronized. "I think you're mostly tired, which is understandable. I'll bet you didn't sleep much last night."

"You got that right."

The door opened, and a pair of senior women bundled in puffy coats hustled in. "Whew! Nice to get out of the cold," one of them said, rubbing her gloved hands together.

Sherry smiled weakly and sat them at a table, a task usually handled by Daisy. She took their orders and delivered them to the kitchen. When she returned, her eyes were watery. "Lara, you were a super friend to help us out yesterday, but I honestly don't think Mom and I can get through the day today. We're both dead on our feet. Jill has her office job weekdays, so she can't fill in. Do you think it would be terrible if we closed early? I can make a sign that says, 'Closed for family emergency' or something like that."

"Not at all," Lara said. "You need to cut yourselves some slack. I know you feel bad because the police forced you to close early yesterday, but people will understand." She smiled and pulled her trusty set of colored pencils out of her tote. "I'll even make you a sign."

Tears filling her eyes, Sherry nodded. "That would be great. I don't have enough energy to even do that much. If anyone else comes in, I'll tell them we're closing."

"Grab me a sheet of paper from your mom's printer, and I'll whip something up."

Sherry fetched a sheet of paper, and within two minutes Lara had sketched a whimsical drawing of Sherry and Daisy, their heads touching, cheeks red, thermometers sticking out of their mouths. CLOSED FOR FAMILY EMERGENCY. PLEASE STOP BY TOMORROW!

"Tomorrow?" Sherry groaned. "What if we're not ready by then?"

"Take the entire day to rest," Lara said. "I know it's hard, but you need to try. Tomorrow, things will look a lot different." *I hope,* she added silently,

"Yeah, tomorrow Mom might be staring at us through prison bars."

"That's not going to happen. Your mom didn't do anything wrong." Lara leaned over the counter and hugged her friend. "We'll figure this out. I promise."

Sherry swiped away a tear. "You *are* good at catching murderers, I'll give you that. But if you figure this one out, you'll be a miracle worker."

Chapter 10

Unlike the day before, the parking lot at Whisker Jog High School was packed with cars. Lara managed to squeeze her car between a monster-sized pickup and an SUV with a massive wreath attached to its grille. The Saturn looked like a pathetic filling to an oversized vehicular sandwich.

She sent a quick text to Jason letting him know she was there.

When she rounded the corner at the back of the school, he was already waving to her. She waved back and trudged through the snow until she reached the rear door of the cafeteria.

"Hey, great to see you again," he greeted her.

"You, too," Lara said, her breath forming puffs in the air.

Jason dipped his head toward the cat carrier. "Leave that there for a minute and come on in. Get out of the cold for a few. You look frozen."

Lara's fingers felt icy, but the rest of her was warm. But she wasn't going to pass up an opportunity to get a peek at the school's kitchen. "You're sure it's okay?"

"Technically we're not supposed to have visitors in the kitchen, but don't worry about it. It's only for a few minutes."

Jason held the door, and Lara set her carrier against the side of the building. She stepped inside, and the scent of cafeteria food swirled around her. Memories of her school days skipped through her head. "Let me guess. I'm detecting tomato sauce and basil. With a hint of garlic."

Jason laughed. "You're exactly right. Vegetarian pizza buns are the main course of the day. The alternate is a chicken salad wrap. With a banana or a ginger cookie for dessert."

"No cake?" Lara grinned. When she was in high school, her favorite dessert had been the spice cake the head cook was known for.

"Not today. But tomorrow we're serving slices of plum pudding with sprigs of holly."

"Umm...you know holly berries are poisonous, right?"

Jason smiled and pulled a metal chair over for her, setting it next to the commercial oven. "Sit for a minute. The holly will be made from royal icing. Rose is going to a lot of trouble to make the desserts. They're gonna be awesome. She's a culinary rock star."

Rose. Wasn't she the person who'd been assigned to judge the bar cookies at the cookie competition? The woman who'd run for help after Miss Plouffe fell ill on Saturday?

"I hear you throwing my name around," said the woman coming up behind Jason. She had a slight, lilting accent that Lara hadn't noticed on Saturday. Her hair was encased in a brown hairnet, and her hands in vinyl gloves. From the lines around her eyes, Lara guessed her to be around fifty. "I'm Rose Stevens," she said, offering a faint smile. She wiggled her gloved hands. "For obvious reasons, I won't shake your hand. I recognize you. You're the woman who tried to help us the other day. When Miss Plouffe..." She shook her head, and her dark eyes grew moist.

"I'm so sorry I couldn't have done anything," Lara said.

"You called for the ambulance, and that was a biggie, as my kids would say. Jason and I were so upset we couldn't even think straight."

It was actually Gideon who'd called, but Lara didn't contradict her.

Jason's face fell. "I thought she was having a heart attack. That's why I kept pounding on her chest. If I'd known it was an allergic reaction, I'd have tried to find that allergy thing she always carried."

"Wait a minute. You knew she was allergic to shellfish?"

"Everybody did," Rose said. "She always made a big deal out of eating alone so she wouldn't accidentally get near someone's lunch that might have the tiniest bit of shellfish."

"Which was totally weird," Jason offered. "No one brings that type of stuff for lunch anyway. Even the teachers only bring ham or turkey or cheese sandwiches."

Rose nodded grimly. "It gave her a good excuse for why she had to eat alone. The real reason was that no one wanted to be around her." The woman crossed herself, then winced. "I'm sorry. I know I should not speak ill of the dead, but that's the God's honest truth. The poor soul didn't have a friend in the world."

Lara didn't know what to say. Had Miss Plouffe been that awful, even to her coworkers? If so, it begged the question: How had she kept her job for so long?

A buzzer went off. "Those would be my pizza buns," Rose said. "Excuse me. I have to go feed a horde of hungry students." She paused. "I'm sorry, but I never got your name."

"My fault, I didn't introduce myself. I'm Lara Caphart. I live with my aunt at the High Cliff Shelter for Cats."

Rose smiled, and her dark brown eyes sparkled. "Ah, you must be the one everyone calls the cat lady." She slid a teasing glance over at Jason. "Now I know why he invited you here. He wants you to help him get that stray."

"Can you cover for me, Rose?" Jason said, looking a bit guilty.

"Yes, but don't be long. It's almost lunchtime."

They said their goodbyes, and Jason threw on a ski jacket. "I've got some food all ready for her. For a stray she sure is a fussy little thing, but she'll have to get by with canned chicken today. It was on sale at the market." He pulled a plastic food bag from the fridge and shoved it into his pocket.

Outside, the sky was still overcast. Lara glanced toward the wooded area beyond the school property. "My friend Kayla and I were here yesterday. We didn't spot her, but Kayla followed her prints into that section of the woods. They kind of disappeared after that."

"Yeah, not surprising," Jason said. "I think she must have found a safe spot to hunker down in the hollow of a tree, or something like that. I'm worried that she's going to freeze. She's not very big, poor little gal. I—oh, wait." He grabbed Lara's forearm. "Look, that's her. She knows my voice now. I think she associates it with food."

Sure enough, a tortoiseshell cat was coming toward them, her paws sinking into the snow with every step. Wary of her surroundings, the cat paused and looked around. Lara was grateful the snowfall hadn't left more than a few inches. Otherwise the whole kitty would have sunk into the snow.

Jason knelt down slowly and pulled the plastic bag from his pocket. "Come on, sweetie," he cooed. To Lara, "See, she knows I have food."

When the tortie was about ten feet away, she picked up her pace and darted toward Jason. She had a darling face, half gold and half black, with adorable, big green eyes. Jason dumped some chicken pieces into his cupped hand. When he held it out to her, she sniffed his fingers for a few seconds. Then, with her delicate little teeth, she gobbled a chunk of chicken.

Remaining very still, Lara watched Jason. She was impressed with the way he'd been able to lure the cat into eating from his hand. Hadn't he said she'd only been coming around for less than a week? The kitty didn't appear to be feral. Her demeanor supported Lara's suspicion that she'd been dumped by someone who didn't want her.

In a soft voice, Lara said to the cat, "What a pretty girl you are."

The tortie sniffed the tips of Jason's fingers again, then sharply pulled her head back. He laughed. "I bet she smells the nutmeg. I was rolling out dough for Rose and got some on my hands. I love the scent, but it's strong. Cats have sensitive noses, right?"

"Right," Lara said. "Jason, I think you just named this cat. Do you mind if I call her Nutmeg?"

"That would be awesome!"

They stood in the cold for another two or three minutes, until Nutmeg had devoured every last shred of chicken. The tips of Jason's ears were red. Lara saw that he was freezing.

"Jason, I'm going to slowly unzip the carrier. Can you scooch your hands around her and lift her into it?"

"Yeah, it's time we nabbed her. I really gotta get back inside before my you-know-what is grass."

"Yup. I hear you. She seems to trust you. I think she'll let you pick her up."

Using careful motions, Lara unzipped the carrier. Jason distracted the cat by circling both hands around her torso. He lifted her into the carrier, and Lara quickly zipped it closed.

The two did a high-five. "Yesss!" Jason said. "That was easier than I thought. What a relief that she won't be out in the cold anymore."

Lara smiled at Nutmeg's rescuer. "She's in good hands now, Jason. Thank you for letting me know about her. I wish more people cared as much as you do."

Jason's face flushed as he peered into the carrier. Nutmeg was huddled at the back, looking confused at her sudden prisoner status.

"Don't worry, little girl, we're going to take good care of you," Lara told her. "You'll have a good home before you know it."

"Lara, thanks for doing this. I'll try to donate some money to the shelter before Christmas. I have a second job at the Shop-Along. I'm trying to save enough to move into some better digs."

"Donations are always appreciated, but don't strain your budget." Lara hesitated, then plunged ahead. "Actually, before you go, can I ask you something real quick? How did you know Miss Plouffe carried one of those injectable thingies with her?"

He looked perplexed by the question. "Gosh, let me think. Okay, yeah, I remember now. That last year she worked here, I had to go up to her classroom to ask a question about one of the ingredients we were using in the kitchen. Snippy as she was, I figured she'd have the right answer. Anyway, that gaudy flowered purse of hers was sitting on her desk and the top was unzipped. I saw the injector thing sticking out of a pocket."

"Thanks, I just wondered. Didn't mean to put you on the spot."

"No problem."

Jason waved goodbye and headed back inside. Lara lifted the carrier and hurried off to her car with Nutmeg.

Chapter 11

Glancing over at the school's snow-covered athletic fields, Lara steered the Saturn along the frozen driveway leading away from the school property. The wind had picked up, sending drifts of frozen particles dancing across the football field.

Lara peeked into the rearview mirror. Nutmeg was huddled at the back of the pet carrier, which Lara had secured on the back seat. "You're being quiet, little girl. But don't worry, you don't have to live in the woods anymore. You'll be warm and well fed. Soon you'll have a permanent home with someone who loves you."

Lara was grateful for Jason's persistence in feeding the little tortie. He'd done the right thing, contacting the shelter—although it was her accidental meeting with him at the coffee shop that had been the *cat*alyst, so to speak. She smiled at her own pun. "Doesn't it feel better to be in a warm car?" she asked Nutmeg.

The cat remained still, but Lara saw through the carrier's zippered screen that the tortie's eyes were watchful.

The receptionist at Amy Glindell's veterinary clinic beamed when she saw Lara striding through the door. The carrier clutched in one hand, Lara loosened her scarf with the other. "Hi, Gail. This is the little stray I called about. We've already named her Nutmeg."

Gail Grimaldi slid aside the Plexiglas window separating the office from the waiting room. She peeked into the carrier, a grin splitting her thin, freckled face. "Oh, look at her. Isn't she a sweetheart?"

All cats were sweethearts to Gail, who had four felines of her own in the home she shared with her husband and two aging Doxies.

"Here's the prob. I got two other patients waiting, and Amy got called into emergency surgery. A little pup with an intestinal blockage. His owner thinks he might've eaten one of her earrings."

"Oh, poor little guy," Lara said. "I hope he'll be okay."

"He's in good hands, that's for sure." Gail waved a hand toward the waiting room. "Why don't you have a seat? I'll see if I can get an idea of how long she'll be." She went off through a rear door.

Unhooking the top button on her jacket, Lara went over to the row of molded plastic chairs along the front window. She set Nutmeg's carrier on the vacant chair beside her, next to a woman who was tapping away at her cell phone. Something about the woman looked familiar.

Lara looked all around the waiting room. The floors were tiled in speckled gray, the walls painted a pale, textured green. A sizeable watercolor graced the main wall. The painting depicted two cats—one pure black and one solid white—curled lovingly around one another as they snoozed in a flower-patterned chair. They were Amy's cats, Sleepy and Bianca.

When the High Cliff Shelter was in its infancy, Lara had learned that one of Amy's clients, a Doberman with a congenital heart defect, was in dire need of surgery. Without it the dog wasn't likely to survive. Lara had overheard the dog's distraught owner talking about it one day in the waiting room. The owner, who couldn't afford the dog's surgery, was terrified she'd be forced to euthanize the Dobie.

That day, after taking the veterinarian aside, Lara made a secret deal with her—she'd paint a watercolor of Amy's cats in exchange for the dog's urgently needed procedure. The owner was told only that a local sponsor had covered the cost.

The surgery was a success, but it was a revelation for Lara—a heartbreaking one. How many other loving owners couldn't afford lifesaving procedures for their pets?

That single incident ignited an idea in Lara's mind. Using the fee collected from the sale of one of her commissioned paintings, she started a fund for animals in need of lifesaving surgery. The account had started small but was steadily growing. A few local business owners had also made contributions, which helped tremendously.

Nutmeg issued a tiny meow, reminding Lara that she was there. "I know, it's hard to wait," Lara told the cat. "But it shouldn't be too much longer."

A man sitting at the opposite end of the row of chairs shot her a look. Fifty or so, his roughened hand was wrapped loosely around the leash of a lethargic black dog. He nodded at Lara, and she smiled in return.

Lara's charge looked more at ease now, her black nose lifting to take in the various scents around her. Nutmeg leaned her head against the screen, and Lara pressed her hand to it. When Lara looked up, the woman sitting beside Nutmeg's carrier was gawking at her. Lara's heartbeat spiked. The woman's haircut was the mirror image of Daisy's, the color nearly identical. Could this be the woman Lara saw at the cookie competition, the one she'd thought was Daisy? The same one Aunt Fran was sure she'd spotted at the supermarket?

The woman reddened when she realized she'd been caught staring.

Lara disarmed her obvious embarrassment with a smile. "Are you here to pick up your pet?"

"Yes, I'm Loretta. I didn't mean to stare, but your hair... It's such a stunning color."

Loretta.

Was she David's mom?

"Well, thanks," Lara said. She looped a finger through one coppery curl. "I could do with fewer curls, though. Sometimes they're a nightmare to work with, especially when I'm in a rush."

"Oh, never complain about your curls. I would simply kill to have curls like yours."

Would you kill to knock Daisy out of the cookie competition?

The thought had popped, unbidden, into Lara's head. She realized that in a back corner of her mind, she'd been suspecting Loretta all along of some devious action. Murder? Or simply sabotage of the woman whose daughter was dating her son?

Maybe Loretta was one of those moms who doted on their sons, who thought no woman was good enough for them.

"I never answered your question," Loretta said. "I'm here to pick up my Cookie. Dr. Glindell spayed her on Friday. I had to leave her here until today because I had some events going on over the weekend. I've missed her awfully."

Spayed her cookie? Lara giggled inwardly at the image. "Is Cookie your cat?"

"Cat?" Loretta looked aghast. "Heavens, no. I'd never have a cat." She wrinkled her nose, which, strangely enough, resembled Daisy's. "All that litter to fuss with? That's not for me, thank you very much. No, Cookie is my Maltipoo. She was a rescue from one of those hoarding situations a few months ago in Rhode Island. Poor angel, she was a mess when she was rescued. Now she's happy and loved."

"I'm pleased, for both of you," Lara said. "Cookie clearly lucked into a wonderful home."

"Thank you." Loretta squinted at Lara's pet carrier, then her face flushed. "Oh dear, you have a cat in there. I'm awfully sorry. I didn't mean to imply that cats were bad or anything. I just meant that, you know, they're not for me."

"No worries," Lara said. "Different pets for different folks, right? I'm Lara, by the way. My aunt and I run the High Cliff Shelter for Cats."

Loretta's jaw lowered slowly. "Oh. Then you must be Sherry's friend?"

"I am," Lara said. "Such a shame, wasn't it, about what happened on Saturday? Sherry told me you were one of the final contestants."

Lara felt like the worst kind of gossip, but she wanted to gauge Loretta's reaction. She also wanted to find out if Loretta had been at the school on Saturday.

"Yes, it was awful," Loretta said, her eyes glittering. "You know"—she leaned toward Lara—"lots of people are saying that Miss Plouffe was a very unlikeable person. I didn't know her, of course. But I heard someone say that she might have eaten a poisoned cookie right before she..."

Lara nodded. She needed to prod Loretta a bit more. "I heard something about a cookie, too. I wonder if the police have any more news about that."

A worried look creased Loretta's face. "Do you think, I mean...will the police check into her background? To see if she might have had a run-in with anyone lately?"

"An argument, you mean?" Lara tried to adopt a naïve expression. "I'm not sure, but you have a good point. Especially if Miss Plouffe really did have enemies. Maybe someone threatened her and followed through by poisoning her?"

Loretta was clearly disturbed by Lara's response. Her lips puckered, and her nostrils flared. "The police don't always get it right," she said sourly. "I had to go to court once over a ticket I definitely didn't deserve."

Interesting, Lara thought. Was Loretta one of those people who believed nothing was ever their fault? Even if it was their fault? It made her wonder about Sherry's future as Loretta's potential daughter-in-law.

"It's funny," Lara said in a casual tone, "now that I think about Saturday, I remember seeing you at the school. You were waiting with a crowd of people, right? Someone had arrived in a limo, and everyone wanted to see who it was."

Loretta's hands fluttered in her lap. She looked as if she didn't know whether to lie about it or admit that she had, indeed, been at the school that day.

"I...only stayed a short while. I entered my butterscotch brownies with snowflake patterns on them. I knew if I looked at the other entries it would only make me more nervous."

So that's why Sherry was so bummed about those brownies, Lara thought. *They were Loretta's!*

Gail emerged from a side door. Clasped in her right hand was a bright pink pet carrier. "Here we are," the receptionist chirped, walking toward Loretta. "Cookie did just great. I've printed out post-surgery instructions, but be sure to call if you have any questions."

Loretta's face melted at the sight of her dog. She took the carrier from Gail, and they chatted for a few moments. Then she thanked Gail profusely and turned to Lara. "Hey, it was so nice meeting you. Maybe we'll see each other soon."

"Maybe we will," Lara said and bent toward the carrier. "Bye, Cookie."

After Loretta was gone, Gail said, "Amy's going to be a while. Why don't you leave Nutmeg here? She'll get a thorough exam, and we'll see if she's chipped. Most likely she'll need to be spayed, and possibly wormed."

"Thanks, Gail." Lara gave her the carrier with Nutmeg inside.

"Hang loose. I'll get her settled in a clean cage and bring your carrier back in a jiffy."

Lara sat down, relieved that Nutmeg was in caring hands. She was checking her phone for messages when the man with the dog mumbled something to her.

"Excuse me?" Lara said politely. "I didn't catch that."

"I *said,*" he answered testily, "that Plouffe woman you guys were talking about was a real piece of work. She harassed my kid to no end when he was in school. Believe me, there won't be a lot of mourners at her funeral."

"Is that so?" Lara rose and went over to sit beside him. "Why do you say she was...a piece of work?"

The man huffed out a sigh. "My kid, Trey, insisted on taking home ec when he was a sophomore. Lots of schools don't even teach it anymore. I think it's weird myself, but Trey wants to be a pastry chef. What was he supposed to do, take woodworking? The kid can't even hang a picture on a wall without bashing his thumb."

"He should be able to take whatever classes are offered," Lara said. "Did Miss Plouffe object?"

The man's lip curled in disgust. "Yeah, big-time. She gave him all sorts of crap over it, the flippin' witch. Everyone at the school knew she didn't want boys in her classes. A while back I heard there was another kid—a boy, of course—who was so traumatized by the way she treated him that he transferred to another school. No way that should be allowed to happen. *No way.*" His eyes flared with anger. "But my Trey, he's a rebel. He was determined to take that class, no matter what he had to put up with. He was so sure he could win her over with his baking skills."

"What happened?" Lara asked him.

"Turned out he was wrong. She made his life a misery."

Lara sat back, her mind racing. How had Miss Plouffe gotten away with it? Why had she been allowed to bully kids for so long?

"I'm sorry about your son. I hope she didn't discourage him from pursuing what he wants to do."

"Nah. My kid's pretty tough. Doesn't look it, but he's strong inside. Mark my words, one of these days he'll be opening his own bakery. People will be lining up out the door." He patted his protruding stomach and grinned. "How do you think I got this gut?"

Lara smiled. "Wish him luck for me. Don't you think it's odd, though, that Miss Plouffe was never called out for her behavior?"

"Odd? More like freakin' suspicious, if you ask me. Oh sure, she got the occasional slap on the wrist, as they say. And believe me, Principal Casteel had enough complaints about her to fill a book. But she always sleazed her way out of it, you know? The b—witch still kept her job. The best thing she ever did was retire. Makes me wonder if someone pressured her to quit."

Maybe someone *had* pressured her to quit. Had Principal Casteel issued her a final warning—quit or be forced out?

Or had something more sinister been at play?

And why had Principal Casteel—whoever that was—been protecting her?

Chapter 12

Late Monday afternoon, Kayla rang Lara's cell phone. "Hey, I just left the library, and I found out a few things. Can I pop over for a minute?"

"You bet. I'll put on some water for hot chocolate."

"It's a date."

Minutes later, Kayla plunked copies of two obituaries on the table in front of Lara. Snowball trotted into the kitchen the moment she heard Kayla's voice. The cat climbed into her lap and curled into a furry white ball.

"Aunt Fran's going to join us in a minute," Lara said. "I wanted to get her thoughts on all this."

After she'd returned from her trip to the vet, Lara had decided it was time to fill in her aunt on the mystery letter. She'd shown her the copy she'd made. She kept the original safely ensconced in the plastic bag, just in case the police ever needed to get prints from it.

Aunt Fran came into the kitchen and went over to the stove. She looked cozy and warm in her forest-green sweats, her hair coaxed away from her face by a wide red hairband. She ran the water and put the kettle on.

Lara prepared hot chocolate with marshmallows for her and Kayla, while her aunt opted for tea.

"Okay, I found two possibilities," Kayla said, opening her oversized purse. She gave each of the women a copy of a different obituary.

"Sarah Nally," Lara read aloud from hers. "She was seventy-nine. Died from a heart attack after shoveling snow." She skimmed and read down further. "This is interesting. She didn't die right away. They treated her in the hospital, after which she was released and sent home. Three days later she suffered a more severe attack. She passed at home on March 2, 1990." Lara's heart thumped, and she looked at her aunt.

"That was the day you were born," Aunt Fran said. She took a small sip from her mug. "I remember it like it was yesterday. You weighed six pounds, seven ounces. And had very little hair," she added dryly.

"I can't believe you remember what I weighed." Lara read through the rest of Sarah's obituary. "Sarah was survived by three kids and a gaggle of grands. None of the names rings a bell. There's no mention of a cat. Her hobbies were knitting, reading historical romances, and playing Monopoly with her grandkids."

"You know," Aunt Fran said, "the part about the cat in that mystery letter makes me wonder. It was a touch too dramatic, in my opinion. I think there's a strong possibility that the letter was nothing more than a gag. Someone got bored and thought it would be fun to make up a murder and pretend he, or she, had been a witness."

It was a scenario Lara hadn't even considered. She had to admit—it was possible. Were they sitting here spinning their mental wheels over a fake murder?

Somehow, Lara didn't think so. Something about the letter told her it was real. The tone was somber, but also apologetic. The part about the cat's spirit floating off to bond with another soul had gripped her on a deeply personal level. Unfortunately, she couldn't tell either Kayla or her aunt the reason. For now, Blue was her secret. And hers alone.

Aunt Fran glanced at the obit Kayla had given her. "Let's see. This one is Irma Hansen Tisley, eighty-two, late of Whisker Jog."

"Local," Kayla noted, rubbing Snowball's head absently.

Aunt Fran read to herself for a moment. "I don't think this one fits," she said finally. "Irma died in the nursing home, so there couldn't have been a cat with her. According to this, she'd been married to Robert Tisley, who predeceased her. She had three kids by him and two by her first husband, Elvin Hansen."

Lara took a sip of her hot chocolate, then licked marshmallow off her lips. "Does it mention the cause of death?"

"It only says that she died in the nursing home. I guess we can presume it was natural causes."

Kayla sagged in her chair. Her glasses slid down her nose, and she pushed them back in place. "I think we can all agree, then. These obits are both dead ends. So to speak," she added.

"Yeah, I think you're right, but I'll hang on to them anyway. I'll keep them with the letter." Lara reached over to collect the obit her aunt had read, but it fluttered to the floor before she could grasp it. She picked it up and tucked it behind Sarah Nally's obit.

Aunt Fran looked troubled. Her gaze was fixed on the tea cooling in her mug.

"You okay, Aunt Fran?" Lara reached over and touched her aunt's arm.

"I can't stop stressing over Daisy. I've texted Jerry several times, but he's clearly ignoring me. I called him twice, but only got his voice mail. I'm not very pleased with him at the moment."

"And Daisy hasn't called you back either?"

"No, she hasn't. Right now, they are both on my you-know-what list."

Aunt Fran's best friend was under suspicion of murder, and her police chief boyfriend was incommunicado. *Double whammy,* Lara thought soberly.

* * * *

"I'm so glad we decided to eat out," Lara said, smiling across the table at Gideon. "It gives me a chance to clear the cobwebs out of my head."

The Irish Stew had been a staple in Whisker Jog for as long as Lara could remember. Even when she was living in Boston, she'd seen the pub featured numerous times on shows highlighting area restaurants. Photos of celebrities—mostly ball players from earlier eras—graced the dark paneled walls. The scent of onions and herbs filled every nook and cranny, wafting up to the tin ceiling in an aromatic potpourri. Nat King Cole's smooth voice sifted through the hidden speakers, the silky notes of "The Christmas Song" barely audible over the din.

They'd arrived too late to claim one of the coveted booths, with their high wooden backs and comfy benches padded in soft green leather. The table where they were seated was fine, except for the occasional bump of her chair as customers continually streamed in.

While the pub was famous for its hearty Irish stew, Gideon always opted for a cheeseburger, made from Kobe beef and oozing with cheddar. Lara's fave was the BLT, packed with crispy bacon and juicy tomatoes, and enhanced with melted Swiss.

Gideon swallowed a mouthful of his burger, then washed it down with a swig of ale. He dabbed his lips with his napkin. "I knew you'd be worried sick about Daisy, honey. If you want to talk about it, I'm all ears. I'm not sure I can add much to what you already know, though. Right now, Daisy's status is in limbo."

"Aunt Fran's been trying to reach her, but Daisy won't call her back."

"I know. I think Daisy's both horrified and embarrassed by all the publicity."

Lara wiped her fingers on her napkin. "Have you talked to her?"

"Yes, but only on the phone. She's worried she might need a criminal attorney. She called me late yesterday and asked for a referral."

"You gave her one, right?"

"I did." He stabbed his fork into a fat fry. "A woman in Manchester. She's a powerhouse. She'll do right by Daisy, if it comes to that. Let's pray it doesn't."

Lara groaned. "But it's not just Daisy, Gid. This is killing Sherry, too." She picked at a crisp bacon slice sticking out from the edge of her sandwich.

Gideon took another sip of his ale. "Maybe they should close the restaurant for a few more days? It would give them both time to regroup."

"Yeah, but it would be really bad for business if they did that. Plus, I'm not sure they can afford to shut down for that long. And why should they? Wouldn't that be like an admission of guilt?"

"You're preaching to the choir, Lara. I don't know how to answer that."

Lara reached over and squeezed his wrist. She caught a glimpse of his Superman watch, which always gave her a chuckle. Gideon entwined his fingers with hers for a moment, then they finished their meal in silence.

It gave her comfort simply to be here with him. Somehow, he managed to add joy to her day, even when she was feeling low.

The decibel level in the pub had risen. A basketball game was broadcasting on the TV above the bar. Patrons sitting at the polished bar cheered one moment and jeered the next. It was making Lara's head throb.

"Sorry. I didn't know it would be so noisy in here tonight," Gideon said.

"It's fine, honestly." Lara pushed aside her plate, hoping they could leave soon.

"Forgot to tell you," Gideon said. "I had a nice chat with Uncle Amico today. Naturally he asked for you. Ever since he met you, you've been the light of his life."

Gideon's uncle Amico lived in a nearby assisted living facility. Lara had met him during the summer. He was a charming, delightful gent who was inching into his nineties. She'd known him only a short time when he'd given her a vital clue in the murder of a local car salesman.

"I hope we can pay him a visit before Christmas," Lara said. "I love that sweet old guy."

Gideon looked up from his empty plate, which he'd pushed aside. His brown eyes twinkled at her. "There's popcorn at my place," he said teasingly. "We can settle in with a big bowl and watch one of the old holiday classics. I think *A Christmas Carol* is on at nine. It's the 1951 version, your favorite."

Lara was impressed that he remembered that. She'd mentioned only once that Alastair Sim was her favorite Scrooge.

"Hmm," she said. "I do have a bit of a crush on old Ebenezer. But popcorn? After all this food?"

Gideon shrugged. His smile faded a bit. "Okay, then. Just the movie. And if my company gets too boring, we can always go next door and borrow Mrs. Appleton's cat. I'm sure Muffin would love to spend an evening lounging in your lap."

Something about his tone sent a shard of alarm through Lara. After all the months they'd been dating, why did he think she'd find him boring? Had something gotten under his skin that she wasn't aware of?

Adopting a cheery voice, she said, "Okay, Gid, now you're just being—"

"Counselor Halley."

A heavyset man with thick white hair had come up behind Gideon. Clad in a black wool coat, a tartan scarf draped around his neck, he clamped a hand on Gideon's shoulder.

Gideon turned and looked up, a smile creasing his handsome features. "Andrew Casteel, as I live and breathe. How are you, buddy?" He rose from his chair and shook the man's outstretched hand.

"Oh, not bad for an old teacher." Casteel's gaze drifted over to Lara.

"Andy, this is Lara Caphart," Gideon said, beaming at her. "Lara, this is Andy Casteel, principal extraordinaire at Whisker Jog High. Also, a favorite client of mine."

Lara took the man's proffered hand. It was smooth to the touch and well-groomed. "Pleased to meet you, Andy."

"The pleasure is mine, I assure you. Gideon, I'll be making an appointment with you after the holidays. It's time to update my estate plan. I lost my younger brother last year, and I'm starting to rethink how I want to do things."

"Oh gosh, sorry to hear that, Andy," Gideon said quietly. "Call me any time, and we'll set up a date."

Casteel apologized for interrupting their meal, wished them both a happy holiday, and then wove his way through a throng of patrons and headed toward the entryway.

"Nice guy," Gideon said, signaling their server for the check. "I'm guessing he's getting ready to retire and wants to put things in order."

"How long has he been the principal at Whisker Jog High?" Lara asked.

"Let's see, eighteen or nineteen years?"

"I noticed he was dining alone," Lara said. "Is he married?"

"He was, but he and his wife had kind of a sad breakup. It was recent, too. They separated after decades of marriage. Andy doesn't talk about it, and I don't ask."

"Oh wow, that *is* sad." Lara shoved her arms into the sleeves of her jacket. Gideon went over and helped her pull it up over her shoulders. "Isn't it odd that he didn't mention what happened at the school on Saturday?"

"No, not really. I'm sure the police have been in touch with him, though. He's probably been cautioned not to talk about it."

Lara told him what the man in the veterinarian's office had related to her, about the principal protecting Miss Plouffe even after all the complaints the school had received about her.

Gideon pulled his wallet from his pocket. "I'm treating tonight. You treated last time."

"Got it. Thank you." She tucked her scarf around her neck. "So, what do you think about Miss Plouffe and the principal?"

Gideon paused and looked at her. "Well, I certainly don't think they were an item, if that's what you're implying. I had a private chat with Chief Whitley this morning. According to him, Gladys Plouffe was a known loner. She lived alone, had no pets that anyone knew of, no family left. If you're thinking she was blackmailing him over something, I can't imagine what it could've been. I've never heard anyone utter a word against Andy."

But there had to be something, Lara thought. She didn't want to press Gideon on it. Casteel was his friend, as well as his client. Even if Gideon knew something, he'd be bound by confidentiality not to disclose it.

Truth be told, she was a little annoyed at the way Gideon had introduced her to the man. She'd expected him to add "my significant other" or "my girlfriend" to the introduction, but he'd said neither. Not that Lara was crazy about either term. *Significant other* sounded clichéd, and *girlfriend* seemed juvenile. Still, it bothered her. Just a tiny bit.

"Gideon," she said suddenly, "what do you want for Christmas?"

Gideon's eyes widened, and in their depths Lara saw a thousand twinkling stars. He reached over and took her left hand in his. "Do you really want to know?"

Chapter 13

Lara had lain awake for a long time before drifting into a troubled sleep Monday night. Everything seemed to be happening at once—Miss Plouffe's demise, the letter in the library book, her relationship with Gideon reaching critical mass.

Or had it?

Over the summer their romance had cruised along steadily. Despite their busy schedules, they'd squeezed in bike rides, picnics at Squam Lake, and lazy nights curled in front of Gideon's TV with his vintage air conditioner blasting so loud they could barely hear each other speak. The memories made Lara's heart curl into a protective ball.

Lately, she'd sensed a change. It was almost imperceptible, but it was there—Gideon seemed restless, less sure of himself. Not because he was pulling away, but because he wanted to move closer. Lara felt the same, but she wanted it to happen at a slower pace. Gideon seemed to be revving up, while she'd been tapping her foot on the brake.

She couldn't think about it now. Sherry had texted her late the night before. She and Daisy intended to open the coffee shop this morning, regardless of the consequences.

After performing her usual cat duties—which included peeling Valenteena off her thigh about twelve times as she prepared the food bowls—she dressed and headed outside into the brisk morning.

By the time she pushed open the door to the coffee shop, her cheeks stung from the cold and her fingertips felt like icicles.

"You look frozen," Sherry said without a smile. She poured a mug of coffee for Lara and set it down in front of her usual counter seat.

"What the heck happened? It's close to zero today!" Lara loosened her scarf.

"We're in the deep freeze now," Sherry said. "Weather guy on TV said it's going to be like this through the week. You want a cinnamon-chip muffin?"

"You bet I do. I can smell them already." Lara leaned forward and spoke quietly. "How's your mom today?"

"The same. We both decided we couldn't afford to stay closed any longer. We don't need bankruptcy on top of everything else," she added on a bitter note.

"Any word from the police?" Lara asked, glancing around. Three tables in the dining area were occupied, and two workers from the power company were hunkered over their bacon and eggs at the opposite end of the counter.

"Far as we know, they're still doing tests on that blasted cookie. I'm, like, ready to run away from home like I did when I was nine."

Lara smiled. "I remember that. All over a CD your mom refused to buy you because of its objectionable lyrics."

"Yeah, those were the days, right?" Her face darkened. One of the men sitting at the counter raised his mug at her. "Coming," she said, grabbing the coffeepot.

Lara waited for a lull, then told Sherry about running into Loretta at the veterinarian's office the day before.

"So, she admitted being at the school Saturday?" Sherry's face twisted into a scowl. "What's her gig, Lara? Why is she trying to look like Mom?"

Lara took a long sip of her coffee. "Honestly, I don't know. But don't read too much into it. It could be simple admiration for Daisy's style."

A pained looked pinched Sherry's features. "Should I talk to David about it? I mean, I know he's noticed it. No one could be that oblivious."

Inwardly, Lara groaned. "Sher, I really hate to advise you on that. I don't know either Loretta or David well enough."

Sherry held up a finger. She popped through the swinging door into the kitchen and returned with Lara's muffin. She plunked it down in front of her with a clang.

Lara broke off a piece and slid it into her mouth. The cinnamon lingered there, spicy and warm and fragrant.

Sherry looked around the coffee shop, then bent over the counter closer to Lara. "Okay, I'm going to hit you up for a favor. If I approach Loretta and ask her if we can have a chat about it, would you be willing to go with me? Maybe we could ask her to meet us somewhere. Or we could ask her to come here some day after the coffee shop closes?"

Neither prospect thrilled Lara. In fact, she'd rather shampoo her hair with an army of fire ants than confront Loretta. Still, she'd do it for Sherry. It was the least her friend deserved. "If you can set something up, I'll be glad to go with you. Remember, though, our classics book club meets here tomorrow, so maybe not until Thursday?"

Sherry's face sagged in relief. "Thank you, Lara. You're the best. Are you guys still on *Little Women?*"

Lara and Aunt Fran belonged to a book club that read the classics. Since one of the members, Brooke Weston, was a high school student, they met weekly at the coffee shop after the school bus dropped her off. The fourth member was Mary Newman, who owned the gift shop adjacent to Bowker's Coffee Stop.

"We're just finishing it up. Gosh, I love that book! It'll be Mary's turn to choose the next classic. I sense she's leaning toward *Rebecca,* which I've read twice. I don't mind reading it again, though. Brooke's only seen the movie, so she's anxious to read the real thing."

"All right," Sherry said, getting back on track. "I'll see if Loretta can have coffee with us Thursday or Friday. In fact, maybe we should meet her at the bagel place on Elm Street. Neutral territory," she added meaningfully.

"Sounds good to me," Lara said. "Keep me posted on the other stuff, okay? And give Daisy a hug for me."

* * * *

Later that morning, Lara was working on a watercolor for a client in Boston when Gail from the veterinary office called. "Your girl is all set to rock and roll," she said, a smile evident in her tone. "She wasn't chipped, but here's the odd thing. Amy discovered she'd already been spayed. She thinks this cat might be lost, not abandoned."

"Really?" Lara said.

"Yup. Amy guesses she's about a year old, give or take. Anyway, she's gotten a lot friendlier since you brought her in. I think she knows she's in good hands now. She's gonna make somebody a great little companion."

"I'll be right over."

Half an hour later, Aunt Fran was cooing over the newcomer. "Oh, look at her. She has the sweetest face." Aunt Fran pulled Nutmeg into her arms. Lara was shocked when the kitty nuzzled right up and sniffed her hair.

"My gosh, she's an absolute love," her aunt said.

Lara offered the tortie some kibble, but Nutmeg sniffed at it and strode away. Either she wasn't hungry or she wanted something different, Lara surmised. She recalled Jason telling her that the cat was fussy. She wondered how he'd figured that out in the short time he'd been feeding her. Lara scooped her up. Normally, she'd arrange a cozy spot for a newcomer in the isolation room upstairs. After a day or so, she'd gradually introduce the cat to the rest of the household. But Nutmeg was such a sociable kitty that she decided to bring her into her own bedroom, where a carpeted kitty tree had been installed with a view of the backyard.

She carried the tortie upstairs, earning a hiss or two from Valenteena, who watched from the top of one of the chairs in the large parlor. Lara gave Nutmeg a tour of where the litter boxes were located, then brought her into her own bedroom. She set her down on her braided carpet. Nutmeg sniffed the rug, looked around, and promptly jumped onto the cat tree.

Lara sat on her bed and observed the tortie settling into her new digs. Someone had taken good care of this cat. So, who dumped her? Why had someone tossed her away? Or, as Amy had opined, was she simply lost?

Today was an adoption day, but Nutmeg needed to remain in the shelter for seven days before she could be adopted. Besides, Lara wanted her to adjust to her new surroundings first. That way she and her aunt could evaluate her personality, as well as her individual needs.

Lara smiled when Purrcival poked his head around the corner. He'd spent the night nestled under Lara's chin. Valenteena had tried to inject herself between them, but he'd stubbornly refused to move. Lara almost had to pry him off her shoulder in the morning so she could get out of bed and perform her cat duties.

A sudden feeling of discomfort gripped Lara's abdomen. She couldn't put her finger on the reason. What was it that bugged her?

Taking advantage of Valenteena's absence, Purrcy strolled into the bedroom to investigate. Lara patted her knee, and he went over and wrapped his swirly form around her legs.

"Hey, Purrcy, you have a new friend," Lara told him, lifting him onto her lap. A deep rumble issued from his throat. Nutmeg studied him from her perch, tail twitching. After a minute or so, she grew bored and turned her gaze back to the window.

Lara set Purrcy down. She needed to get ready for visitors, assuming anyone showed up today. Adoption days were Tuesday, Friday, and Saturday afternoons, but Tuesdays were typically slow.

Aunt Fran peeked her head inside Lara's room. "Everything okay in here?" She grinned at the tortie nestled on the cat tree. "Look at her. She's already made this her home."

"She won't have any trouble getting adopted, that's for sure," Lara said, and bit her lip. "Poor Kayla. She's really worried about Snowball. She thinks no one will ever adopt her because of her eye color."

Aunt Fran sat down on the bed next to Lara. "I don't think the eye color has much to do with it. She'll find her forever home, I'm sure of it. But in the unlikely event she doesn't, she stays with us. I've just cut up some tiny bits of cheese for her. I'm saving them for her snack later."

"Oh, you'll be her hero." Lara grinned.

"By the way, I had a thought. With Sherry and Daisy having such... troubles lately, why don't we move book club here tomorrow afternoon. I'll make us some mini-sandwiches, and we can have hot chocolate or hot mulled cider. I'll make it look all festive for the season. How about it?"

Lara slid her arm around her aunt's shoulder. "As always, I love the way you think."

Chapter 14

Kayla stopped by after her last class late on Tuesday. "No visitors today?" she said gloomily, taking a seat at the kitchen table. She hooked the strap of her book bag around the back of her chair.

"Not a one," Lara said. "Honestly, though, it doesn't surprise me. People get so frazzled this time of year with all their seasonal chores. Although we did get a call from a woman who wanted to stop by and reserve a kitten, as she put it, as a surprise Christmas gift for her grandson."

Kayla shook her head. "Unbelievable."

"I know. I had to patiently explain why surprising a child with a pet on Christmas morning was not a good idea, especially when no one's prepared for it. I started to give her my spiel about a pet not being a toy, but she hung up on me before I could finish. Hey, I was just putting the kettle on. Want to have some cranberry tea with me?"

"Thanks. Cranberry tea would definitely hit the spot."

At the sound of Kayla's voice, Snowball padded into the kitchen. Kayla lifted the kitty onto her lap and scratched her under the chin. "Any word yet on Nutmeg?"

Lara had texted Kayla the day before to let her know that the tortie had been rescued.

"Believe it or not, she's here. She's been hanging out on the cat tree in my bedroom. Amy discovered she's been already spayed. I don't think she'd been living outside too long. Someone was taking good care of her."

"Before they dumped her," Kayla said sourly. She bent and kissed Snowball's head.

"Amy's not convinced she was dumped, Kayla, and I'm beginning to agree. She's pretty sociable, so she might just be lost. I'm going to post her pic on our Facebook page. For all we know, her owner is out there frantic with worry."

"You're right. We shouldn't make assumptions." Kayla opened her book bag and pulled out a handful of papers. "Can I see her before I leave?"

"You sure can. I'll take you upstairs before you go. So, what's all this stuff?"

"Something was bugging the heck out of me, so I went back to the library."

Lara prepared two mugs of cranberry tea and set them on the table. Kayla stirred sugar into hers.

"I got thinking about the first obit we read," Kayla went on. "The one about the old woman who had a heart attack shoveling snow. I thought— Wait a minute. Maybe we should bring your aunt in on this, too. Is she home?"

"Nope. She's out doing a little shopping. We're going to have book club here tomorrow, so she wants to serve some light snacks."

Kayla made a face. "Wish I had time to join your book club. As it is, my classes are keeping me buried. This shelter—and you guys—are my social life."

"I hope that's a good thing," Lara said, and Kayla smiled. "Anyway, why did you go back to the library? Something about that first obit?"

"Yeah. Sarah Nally. She died at home after a *second* heart attack, remember? I got thinking, what if someone in her family decided to end her misery?"

Lara frowned. "You mean, they thought she'd never be her old self again and wouldn't want to...hang around?"

"It's possible, right?" Kayla pushed up her glasses. "Or maybe they just wanted to be rid of her. Remember, the mystery letter said she'd gotten nasty and mean. Whoever *she* was."

"I don't know, Kayla. I think that's a stretch." Lara took a sip from her mug. "Anyway, did you find out anything new?"

Kayla grinned. "Yeah, I did. I did some Googling last night—should have thought of that first—and discovered that Sarah Nally had been, like, this major cat lover. She even fostered kittens in her home!"

"Hmm." Lara sat up straighter. "Her obit didn't mention that."

"No, it didn't. Isn't that odd?"

"Not really. Someone in her family wrote that obituary. If that person didn't like cats, I can picture them omitting it altogether."

Kayla pushed a sheet of paper over to Lara. "Look at this. She was mentioned in a feature article in 1983. She belonged to a group that knitted catnip toys for one of the local cat rescue operations. Evidently, these ladies raised so much money that they got a mention in the local paper." Lara skimmed the article. A smiling Sarah Nally, her head covered with tight curls, was pictured holding a basketful of knitted cat toys. "Okay, she loved cats. But I'm still not making the connection to murder."

"There is no connection. Just my theory," Kayla said, a bit defensively. "I'm only pointing out that there could've been a cat with her when she died. And if her death was hurried along by someone..."

"Then someone in the household could have witnessed her death and written the letter."

Kayla's shoulders drooped. She sank her fingers into Snowball's soft white fur. "You think I'm imagining things."

I'd be the last person to accuse anyone of that, Lara thought wryly.

"No, I think you've given this a lot of thought, and I appreciate it. Honestly, I do. I'm only saying that it's a big leap from her being a cat lover to her being murdered in her bed." Kayla started to protest, but Lara held up a hand. "But you've made a good point, so I think it's worth looking into. Maybe we can make some quiet inquiries."

Kayla looked somewhat appeased. "Okay. But we need to come up with a game plan."

Squirming in her chair, Lara softened her voice. "Kayla, I have to ask you something. The letter also talked about the spirit of the cat leaving to care for a new life. What did you make of that?"

For a long time, Kayla said nothing. Then, shaking her head, she said, "I don't know what to make of it. But I do believe that our souls leave our bodies after we die and go on to a different...realm, I guess. Why shouldn't animal souls do the same? Why should humans—" Her eyes brightened, and a smile lit up her face. "Lara," she whispered, "look behind you."

Lara turned in her chair. Nutmeg was padding into the kitchen, her nose lifting to assess the various sights and scents around her. "You came down to visit us," Lara said softly. She swiveled on her chair and patted her lap. "Do you want to sit with me?"

The tortie gazed at her, then sat down on the linoleum floor. She seemed to be deciding which route to follow.

In the next instant she leaped onto Lara's lap. She purred softly, then more loudly as Lara stroked her head. "Oh, you are such a darling, aren't you, sweetie?"

Nutmeg leaned into her hand, as if to say, *You bet I'm a darling.*

The cat parade began. Munster, not one to be left out of a party, strutted in to check out the newcomer. He leaned both paws on Lara's knees and sniffed Nutmeg's tail. Apparently, she met with his approval. He dropped down and curled up with his head on Lara's shoe.

"Shall I add some kibble to their bowls?" Kayla asked.

"It's not their suppertime, but that's a good idea," Lara said. "I want Nutmeg to feel comfortable eating with the other cats."

Within a few minutes, Purrcival and Valenteena had joined the party. Teena hissed a warning at Nutmeg, then went over to the food bowls and tried to shove Purrcival aside. This time Purrcy didn't budge—he stayed right where he'd planted his paws.

Kayla grinned. "Purrcy's getting better at holding his ground. Good for him."

Lara agreed, but a part of her ached for Valenteena. The little female, so malnourished as a kitten, still ate like every meal was her last.

"Butterscotch still doesn't eat if anyone's in the room, does he?" Kayla asked.

"'Fraid not. All humans need to be absent before he feels comfortable at the food bowls. I really want to work with him over the winter. Right now, he's not social enough to be adopted."

Kayla frowned. "I wish I could be here more. My classes are brutal this semester."

"Your studies come first," Lara said. "Once you get your vet tech degree, you'll see it was all worth it."

"Yeah, I guess. Hey, I better go. I've got a load of studying to do tonight."

Lara thanked Kayla for the additional research and gave her a hug. "You've been doing all the legwork on the mystery letter investigation. I'll try to dig around on the internet and see if I can find out anything else. I might even pop over to the library tomorrow. I have that book to return."

* * * *

Neither Aunt Fran nor Lara had felt like cooking dinner, so Lara picked up a pepperoni and mushroom pizza from Whisker Jog's sole pizza parlor—Paddy's Pizza. After they'd finished, she wrapped up the three uneaten slices and stashed them in the fridge. Aunt Fran headed into the large parlor with her latest historical novel, Dolce nestled in her lap like a furry hand rest.

Leaving her aunt to read, Lara went to the fridge for a few Cat Nips. She offered one to Nutmeg, but the tortie turned up her nose at it. Lara stuck them in her pocket, scooped up Nutmeg, and went upstairs to her room. After setting the kitty on her bed, she plopped onto it herself and turned on her tablet. She brought up Google and entered Loretta Gregson's name in the search box. A list of links popped up.

The first Loretta Gregson was a state rep in one of the Midwestern states. Another was a realtor in Arkansas. A third one lived in the UK. The fourth link made Lara's breath catch in her throat. It was an article in one of the local papers about an altercation at the Shop-Along back in June.

The incident involved a woman, Loretta Gregson, who'd parked her car in a handicapped slot in the supermarket's parking lot. A patron who'd just left the market noticed it, took a pic of the license plate, and reported it to the police.

Loretta might have gotten away with a fine notification in the mail, except that a squad car happened to be close by. It arrived just as Loretta was wheeling her car out of the parking space. The patron who'd called the police was none other than Gladys Plouffe.

Instead of admitting her guilt, Loretta had apparently railed at the officers, claiming she'd injured her leg in a fall and was forced to park in the space reserved for the handicapped. But Miss Plouffe told the police she'd seen Loretta in the store, zooming her cart along the aisles as if she were at NASCAR.

The situation escalated. Threats were made, and fists were raised, resulting in both women being escorted to the police station. A court date was scheduled for the following Monday.

Lara racked her brain. What was it Loretta had said to her at the veterinarian's office?

The police don't always get it right.

It explains why Loretta was so worried about the police delving into Miss Plouffe's background.

Lara saved the link to the article. Even if it was flimsy, she'd found the connection she'd been looking for between Loretta and Miss Plouffe. A big question loomed, though: Did Loretta know about Miss Plouffe's deadly allergy?

Nutmeg hopped up on the bed next to Lara. She sniffed at Lara's pocket, then pawed at it.

"Oh, so now you want the Cat Nip?" Lara laughed and gave her the last one. Nutmeg sniffed it again, deemed it edible, and swallowed it without much enthusiasm.

A sudden movement on the cat tree caught Lara's attention. Ballou, who normally sat like a sphinx on the top level, was poised at the edge of his perch, his gaze fastened on Nutmeg.

"Oh my glory," Lara whispered. "Look at the way he's watching you, Nutmeg. He looks like he's getting ready to hop up here on the bed with you." Nutmeg didn't so much as glance in his direction. She flopped against Lara's leg, licked a forepaw, and began taking a leisurely bath.

Very slowly, Lara scooped up her tablet and set it on her night table, then rose from the bed. She left the room quietly, leaving the door open about three inches. If Ballou had any designs on joining Nutmeg, he wouldn't do it with Lara still in the room.

Giggling, Lara started to head downstairs. Had she witnessed a possible breakthrough for Ballou? The thought made her feel elated.

When she reached the bottom step, she called out, "Aunt Fran, you should've seen Ballou—" Abruptly, she stopped.

A sleepy Munster curled in her lap, Sherry sat on the sofa, crying silently into the pink tissue crushed inside her fist.

Chapter 15

Feeling her heart drop like a stone, Lara hurried over to her friend. She put an arm around Sherry's shoulder. "What is it, Sher? Did something happen?"

Sherry shook her head and then sucked in a shaky breath. Her eyeliner was smudged, and her nose was red from crying. "I-I just couldn't take it anymore, staying in that house with Mom. She's...she's driving me crazy!"

"I already put the kettle on," Aunt Fran said, getting up from her chair. She set Dolce on the floor. "I'll go make us some tea."

"I'm serious, Lara. I want to run away. Someplace where no one can find me. *No one!*"

"You're not running away," Lara said. "We're going to figure this out. All of it."

"You said that before," Sherry sniped at her.

Ouch. The barb stung.

"I know I did," Lara said quietly. She squeezed her friend's shoulder. "Sher, tell me what happened."

Sherry blotted one eye with the tissue. Munster snuggled against her and yawned. "D-David called me a little while ago. He sounded weird, not like himself at all. I asked him if everything was okay, and he said it was, but—" She shook her head. "Lara, I was a fool to think this would work out. Nothing's ever worked out for me before. Why should it now?"

"Sherry, that's nonsense," Lara chided. She glanced toward the kitchen and then lowered her voice. "You told me that David wanted to get engaged for Christmas. Even if you're not ready, doesn't that tell you something about his feelings?"

Tears leaked from Sherry's eyes. "It tells me that he's impulsive. That he's not thinking it through." She stroked Munster's back.

Aunt Fran came in with a tray, and Lara fixed a mug of tea for Sherry.

"Thanks." Sherry blew a ripple of air over the steaming liquid. "I sent Loretta a text this afternoon. I asked her if she could meet us at the bagel place on Thursday."

"Okay, that's a start," Lara said, trying to sound chirpy. "Did she respond?"

Sherry nodded, her eyes glazing over. "She said yes. You'll still go with me, right?"

Aunt Fran shot Lara a silent question, but Lara only nodded. "You know I will. I won't let you go alone, okay?"

"Would someone fill me in, please?" Aunt Fran said, stirring the tea in her mug.

"Aunt Fran, remember when you saw Daisy in the market?"

"Certainly I do. I called to her, but she ignored me."

"No," Lara said. "She didn't ignore you. That wasn't Daisy. It was David's mom, Loretta Gregson."

Aunt Fran looked surprised. "I'd have sworn it was Daisy. From the back, anyway."

Sherry pulled in a loud sniffle. "She's been copying Mom's hairstyle, wearing more makeup," Sherry said. "It's like...she wants to be exactly like Mom!"

"I'm not sure what to say," Aunt Fran said after a pause. "But...honestly, Sherry, I don't see that as a bad thing. Maybe she admires Daisy's style and wants to be more like her. There are worse things. It's also possible she might not realize how she appears to other people."

Sherry brightened a little. "You think so?"

"Aunt Fran's right," Lara said, not entirely convinced. "She might be copying Daisy without even realizing it."

Sherry set down her tea, then reached over and hugged Lara. Munster meowed a tiny protest, then settled back into Sherry's lap. "What would I ever do without you two? I can't even imagine it anymore."

"Don't sound so glum," Lara said lightly. "We're here to stay."

Aunt Fran smiled in agreement. "Sherry, what about your mom?" she asked gently. "Is there anything we can do for her?"

While the two chatted about Daisy, Lara's thoughts veered off. Should she tell Sherry what she learned about Loretta and Miss Plouffe? Lara hated keeping a secret from her friend, especially one that involved Sherry's possible future mother-in-law.

Still, Sherry had a right to know. If Loretta was involved in any way in Miss Plouffe's death, everyone had the right to know—especially the police.

Lara waited for a lull in the conversation, then told Sherry and her aunt what she'd learned from Googling Loretta.

"Oh my God," Sherry said. "Then she *did* have a run-in with Miss Plouffe. That's why she tried to look like Mom that day, to throw the police off her trail. The woman is diabolical, Lara. She must be the killer!"

Aunt Fran held up one hand. "Hold on a moment. Let's all take a deep breath. It's a big leap from Loretta wearing her hair like Daisy to killing someone."

"Aunt Fran's right," Lara piped in. "Besides, Loretta had no way of knowing your mom had originally planned to stay away from the school that morning, did she?"

"I guess not," Sherry conceded. "I never mentioned anything to David about it."

"And there's something else—a big something else. We don't know if Loretta knew that Miss Plouffe was deathly allergic to shellfish. That's the missing link."

Sherry's face fell. "I forgot about that." She looked at Lara. "When we see her on Thursday, we have to find out. I don't think the police have revealed what the so-called poison was. Maybe we can trick Loretta into tripping herself up!"

Lara didn't like the idea. In fact, she hated it. If Loretta was the killer, Lara wanted no part of it. Let the police figure it out. Let the police take her into custody.

Lara looked at Sherry, at her best friend in the entire world. Even as kids, they'd stood up for one another. She reached over and squeezed Sherry's hand. "We'll give it a try. But we have to come up with a plan first. We can't just go bumbling into that bagel place and ask her if she killed Loretta."

Sherry jiggled her fists. "You're right. We need a plan." Her face dropped like a fallen cake. "Except...if we do prove that she killed Miss Plouffe, then David will never forgive me. Either way, our relationship is doomed."

Chapter 16

On Wednesday Lara performed her morning duties—dress, feed, scoop—and then bundled up and went off to the coffee shop.

"Hey, you," Sherry said, plunking a mug of steaming coffee in front of Lara.

Lara thought her friend looked a bit better today. Her eyes were brighter and her smile more natural. Given that Sherry had declared her relationship with David doomed, Lara wondered how long her friend's cheerful countenance would last.

The coffee shop was super busy. Nearly every table was filled. Lara spotted Daisy clearing dishes off one of the tables. She smiled and waved at her, but Daisy offered only a forced smile in return, along with a tiny wave.

Sherry rolled her eyes at Lara. "She finally ventured into the land of the living. That's what you're thinking, isn't it?"

"No, not at all," Lara scolded her friend. "She's been through a lot, Sher. We have to cut her some slack."

"I know." Sherry groaned. "Let's talk about something else. Have you thought about how we're going to approach Loretta?"

Lara loosened her scarf. "I've thought about it, but I haven't come up with anything." She took a slow sip of her coffee. If she were honest with herself, she'd confess that she didn't have a clue what they were going to say to Loretta.

Sherry's gaze drifted toward the glass front window. "Whoa. That's weird. There's a huge black limo idling out there."

Lara swiveled on her stool. She followed her friend's line of vision, a gasp snagging in her throat. A sleek black limo, which looked freshly washed, was double-parked in front of the coffee shop.

Lara swung back around, her heart pounding. "Sher, I think that's Todd Thryce's limo."

Poker-faced, Sherry nodded and lowered her voice. "Then I'll bet that's him strolling through the door right now."

Lara felt a whoosh of cold air as the door opened. She turned again, and Todd Thryce stepped inside, rubbing the cold from his hands. He sported the same wool coat and Burberry scarf she'd seen him wearing on Saturday.

"Lara, I thought that was you!" Todd Thryce beamed a warm smile at her, displaying perfect white teeth. He pulled off his gold-rimmed spectacles and wiped them with a crisp white handkerchief. "I'd forgotten how cold the New Hampshire winters can get."

For a moment Lara was speechless. When she finally found her voice, she said, "Mr. Thryce, hello. I'm surprised to see you here."

"It's Todd, remember?" Smiling, he dipped his head toward the vacant stool beside her. "Is it okay if I join you for a minute?"

"Be my guest," she said, ignoring Sherry's questioning stare.

"Coffee, sir?" Sherry asked him.

"You bet," he said. "Smells wonderful."

"So, you're still in town," Lara said.

Todd's smile faded. "I delayed our trip back to New York. I'm hoping the police will figure out what really happened to Gladys Plouffe before we have to go back. We're both very distressed by all of this."

We, Lara thought. *As in...he and Alice?*

"I'm sure you are. It was a horrible thing."

Sherry set a mug of piping hot coffee in front of Todd. "Anything else I can get you?" she asked, pasting a fake smile on her face.

"I'd love a blueberry muffin, if you have one," he said. "And two more to go for my driver. Poor guy. I rousted him out of bed early this morning so I could come into town and chat with the police chief."

"You're not staying in town?" Lara asked as Sherry hustled off into the kitchen.

"No. Whisker Jog doesn't exactly abound with hotels. But we're not staying too far from here." He smiled, but his eyes were sad. He touched Lara's hand with his own manicured one. "Lara, I understand you were one of the first people to find Gladys."

"I was. I mean, my boyfriend and I were. A woman ran into the cafeteria screaming for help, so we followed her and called nine-one-one. I think it was just happenstance that we got there first."

"I see." Todd shook his head. "But it was already too late, wasn't it?" he added gravely.

Tears pushed at Lara's eyelids. She didn't want to rehash it. Once was bad enough.

"It was," she said. "A man who worked at the school was trying to revive her, but even he saw that it was hopeless."

"I'm sorry. I didn't mean to upset you by bringing it up again."

Lara blotted one eyelid with her finger. "It's okay." *I'm getting used to finding dead bodies.* "Um...I noticed that you called her Gladys. Did you know Miss Plouffe?"

For a moment, Todd appeared to study Lara's face. Then he turned away and stared into his mug. "Actually, I did know Gladys, a lifetime ago. She used to sew for my grandmother. Every time Gran lost weight, all her clothes had to be taken in. You'd think she'd have just bought new ones, but she couldn't shake that Yankee frugality. It was in her genes, I guess." He took a long sip from his mug. "Ah, that hits the spot."

"Was Gladys a good seamstress?" Lara asked him.

"Well, I was only a grade-schooler when she started sewing for Gran. But I can still remember my gran saying, 'What would I ever do without Gladys?' Sometimes I'd come home from school and see her in my grandmother's room. She'd always slam the door shut when she saw me, because Gran would be trying on clothes." He smiled wistfully. "Funny, how I remember that. After sixth grade I got shipped off to a private school. I don't think I ever saw Gladys again. Nonetheless, I'm grateful to her, for the way she treated my grandmother. If she was, in fact, poisoned, then I want to see her killer brought to justice."

Lara felt stunned. It was the first kind word she'd ever heard spoken about the home ec teacher. The utter sadness of it struck her like an arrow to the heart.

"Todd, I'm really glad you told me that story about Miss Plouffe. You're the first person who's had anything good to say about her."

Sherry burst out of the kitchen and set down a muffin oozing with blueberries in front of Todd. "I'll keep the other two warm until you're ready to leave," she told him. She gave Lara a meaningful glare.

"Hey, thanks. This looks great." He grinned at her.

Lara got the message. "Um, Todd, I'm sorry, I never introduced you. This is my best friend in the entire world, Sherry Bowker. She and her mom own the coffee shop. Sher, this is Todd Thryce."

Todd's grin wilted. He held out a hand. "Pleased to meet you, Ms. Bowker. I hope your mom is doing okay."

Sherry shook his hand briefly, then dropped it as if it were electrified. "She's managing, no thanks to that stupid cookie contest. I'm sorry she ever got involved."

Lara gawked at her friend. Sherry had always been blunt, but this time she was being downright rude.

Todd's jaw tightened, and his face flushed. "I'm...sorry you feel that way. I know it hasn't been easy—"

"You know nothing," Sherry sputtered, her words coming out in bitter tones. "You don't even live around here. This is a small town, Mr. Thryce. Everyone knows everyone else's business, and now all our customers look at Mom like she's some sort of demon!"

"Ms. Bowker," Todd said softly. "Please calm down."

"Don't tell me to calm down. I will *not* calm down. This whole mess has been a travesty, and Mom and I have taken the brunt. I'm sick to death of it. All of it!"

She spun on her heel and slammed through the swinging door into the kitchen.

Lara felt the eyes of everyone in the coffee shop swerving in their direction. "I need to talk to her," she said, rising from her stool.

Todd got up quickly. He pulled a twenty-dollar bill from his wallet and stuck it under his coffee mug. "Please give your friend my apologies. I certainly didn't mean to upset her."

Lara nodded. "I know. I'll tell her."

He gave Lara an earnest look. "Is it okay if I stop by your shelter before we head back to New York? Maybe Friday?"

"Sure. Great. Look forward to seeing you," Lara said, not caring if she ever saw him again. "Sorry, but I have to run."

She left him with his mouth hanging open.

With dread weighting her heart like a dense rock, she pushed through the swinging door into the kitchen.

* * * *

"Your day hasn't gotten off to a very good start, has it?" Aunt Fran said. She stood at the counter dicing an onion into tiny, even squares.

Lara pulled her hair into a tight swirl and secured it with a scrunchie at the back of her head. "No, it hasn't. If the cops don't find Miss Plouffe's killer soon, Sherry and Daisy are both going to go nuts. If they haven't already," she added dismally.

After she'd returned from the coffee shop, Lara had vacuumed and dusted the entire downstairs. With the exception of Valenteena, the cats had made themselves scarce. Teena, the rebel, had opted to wrestle with the vacuum cleaner hose as Lara commandeered it over the carpets.

"Shall I get the crabmeat out of the fridge?" Lara asked her aunt.

Aunt Fran swept the diced onion into a glass mixing bowl. "Not yet. I still need to chop the celery."

Lara went over and kissed her aunt's cheek. "This is so sweet of you to do. A lovely holiday treat for the book club."

"Not a problem. I enjoy it," Aunt Fran said. She repeated the dicing process with a slender stalk of celery, adding that to the mixture as well. "I hope you remembered that we're having a Yankee swap. Five-dollar limit," she added sternly.

"I'm all set for it," Lara said. The five-dollar limit had been a challenge, but she'd lucked out by landing on the perfect item. On the bargain table at Jepson's Crafts, she'd found a green velvet change purse embroidered with a darling cat. Inside, she'd stuck a one-dollar lottery scratch ticket.

Her aunt had suggested the spending limit, Lara knew, because of Brooke Weston. Since Brooke's income consisted mostly of her babysitting earnings, five dollars was a lot for her.

"I'm ready for the crabmeat," Aunt Fran said, sprinkling coarsely ground pepper into the bowl. "And the mayo."

Lara removed a plastic container of Louisiana crabmeat from the fridge and pulled off the cover. The slightly fishy scent made her nose wrinkle. She grabbed the jar of mayo and set it on the counter next to her aunt's bowl.

"Thanks," her aunt said. Using a fork, she flaked the crabmeat into the diced celery and onion, then gradually added spoonfuls of mayo until the texture was perfect.

"That looks great," Lara said. "Flaky and not too dense."

The pitter-patter of feline paws sounded behind them.

Lara laughed. "Look who's here, Aunt Fran. Just in time for a crabby treat."

Nutmeg bounded over to Lara, her nose lifting at the scent she detected drifting from the countertop. Just as the tortie was about to leap onto the counter, Lara scooped her up and hugged her to her chest. "You're not supposed to be on the counter, remember? If you promise to be a good girl, maybe Aunt Fran will let you have a smidge."

Aunt Fran smiled at the cat. With a spoon, she placed a tiny bit of crabmeat onto a saucer and set it on the floor. Nutmeg attacked it as if she hadn't eaten in a week.

After the crabmeat rolls were put together, Lara covered them with plastic wrap and stuck them in the fridge. For dessert, Aunt Fran had made peppermint flan. Lara was already salivating in anticipation of the book club's holiday luncheon.

The front doorbell rang.

"Strange. No one ever comes to the front door. Must be a salesperson," Aunt Fran said.

"No worries. I'll take care of them." Lara wiped her hands on a dish towel and went through the large parlor to the front entrance. When she opened the door, her jaw dropped in shock.

A car Lara didn't recognize was parked in the driveway behind the Saturn.

And standing on the doorstep, a pile of gaily wrapped packages in her arms, was Brenda Caphart-Rice.

AKA Mom.

Chapter 17

Lara clutched the doorframe. She peered at her mother through the storm door. "Mom? What are you doing here? I mean...we didn't expect you!"

The woman standing on the doorstep shot an exasperated look at her daughter. "Lara, for criminy's sake, will you please open the door? It's freezing out here, and if I don't set these down I'm going to drop them."

"Yes! Gosh, sorry." Lara swung open the storm door and relieved her mother of the boxes. Balancing them with one arm, she grasped the sleeve of her mother's faux-leopard coat with the other and yanked her inside, shutting the door tightly behind her.

"What the—" Brenda sputtered, nearly stumbling into the foyer.

"Sorry, Mom. We have one cat who's always trying to escape, so we have to be careful about opening doors." She set the boxes on the floor behind one of the chairs.

Brenda rolled her blue-lined eyes. "Figures. Why don't you just let it go out? It's a cat, isn't it?"

"Our cats don't go out," Lara said, striving to keep her tone even. Her mother was not a fan of cats, so it wasn't a subject Lara wanted to get into with her. "But you...you look great! Why didn't you tell me you were coming?"

"I didn't know myself, until two days ago." Brenda peeled off her coat and handed it to Lara, who quickly hung it in the foyer closet. The last thing Lara needed was one of the cats to use it as a cozy bed.

"Thank you," Brenda said. "Is it okay if I keep these on?" She stuck out a brown, salt-encrusted boot.

"Sure, whatever you're comfortable in."

"I'm comfortable in a climate that's about fifty degrees higher," Brenda said tartly.

Lara gritted her teeth.

"Whew! Now that I've got my coat off, it's warm in here, isn't it?" Brenda pushed up the sleeves of her western-style red sweater, revealing evenly tanned arms. A chunky, turquoise bracelet encircled her right wrist, and a gold, chain-link watch dangled from the other. "Do I at least get a hug?"

"Oh, Mom, of course you do," Lara said. She gave her mother a clumsy squeeze, the cloying scent of gardenias curling around her.

After a few awkward seconds, Brenda pushed back on Lara's arms. "You look...really lovely, Lara. How long has it been, anyway? At least a couple years, right?"

Lara knew exactly how long. It would be two years in January.

She stepped back and studied her mom's face. Brenda's once auburn hair was now dyed to a straw-like blond. Worn long and loose, it framed Brenda's thin, sun-darkened face. Her blue eyes had faded a bit. A hint of sadness lurked in their depths.

Lara still recalled that wintry day when she'd escorted her mom and one of her mom's gal pals in a taxi to Logan Airport. They were catching an afternoon flight to Vegas for a week of fun, food, and gambling. One week later, the gal pal had returned *sans* Brenda, who'd been swept off her feet by a self-proclaimed country music virtuoso. Brenda married Rodney Rice three weeks later.

"Nearly two years, Mom," Lara said. "Hey, let me tell Aunt—"

"Brenda?"

Brenda whirled her head toward the voice. Her face pinched, and she twisted her hands. "Yes, Fran, it's me. Did you think you'd never see me again?"

Fran came into the large parlor and went over to Brenda. "How wonderful to see you. I had no idea you were planning a visit."

"Like I told Lara, neither did I until a few days ago. Rodney has a buddy in Portsmouth who has a gig every weekend at one of the high-end hotels. He invited us to join him."

Aunt Fran looked stymied. "A gig? What kind of gig?"

"Rodney's bud is with the Greenhorn Geezers," Brenda said. "You probably heard of them. They play light country, some bluegrass, stuff like that. We heard they're quite the attraction in this area." After a long pause she said, "Anyway, Rod and I"—she grinned, and her eyes sparkled—"we're going to be guest performers."

Performers? Since when had her mom had any musical talent? As for the Greenhorn Geezers, Lara had never heard of them, but that didn't mean much. Portsmouth was on the seacoast, and she didn't get out that way very often.

Lara waved her hand at the sofa. "Sit, Mom, and you can tell us all about it. Can I get you something to drink?"

Brenda eyed the sofa. "Is there cat hair on it?"

"Anything's possible. But I vacuumed it this morning, so you should be safe."

Smoothing her black slacks, Brenda sat carefully and perched on the edge. "Since you asked, I wouldn't mind a cup of hot chocolate, if you have any. With lots of whipped cream."

"We can do that," Aunt Fran said. "Be right back." She dashed into the kitchen.

"She never changes, does she?" Brenda said with a tight expression.

Lara felt herself tensing. The old rivalry her mom had always imagined between the two was rearing its ugly green head.

"If she changes, it's only for the better," Lara said. "She had both knees replaced this past year. I swear it took twenty years off her."

Munster strolled into the room, followed by Purrcival. Both cats stared up at Brenda, no doubt trying to fathom if she was friend or foe. Since everyone was a friend to Munster, he didn't hesitate to leap up on the sofa and plant himself beside her.

Brenda jumped up. "Oh, for the love of God, Lara. Look at that orange fur. I just had these pants cleaned. Can't you move him into another room and keep him there?"

Every nerve in Lara's body wanted to snap. For a brief second or two, she thought about sequestering the cats on the back porch for the duration of her mother's unexpected visit. Then she bolted to her senses. This was their home, their shelter.

"Munster, Purrcy, sit with me, okay?" Lara lured them over to the oversized chair and pulled them into her lap. Lara thanked her lucky stars that both cats seemed content to chill with her for a while.

Brenda looked appeased, at least for the moment. She sat down again. "I see you've turned this place into a shelter," she said flatly. "I saw the sign outside."

"We did, nearly a year ago." Lara smiled at the two felines curled in her lap. "It's been a blessing, for everyone involved. We've already rescued a number of cats, and—"

"Cats, shmats," Brenda said. "Tell me about you. Do you have a boyfriend?"

Lara breathed in slowly, then out again. She needed to calm herself. Her mom would never change, so it was best to simply accept it and move forward.

"I'm seeing someone, yes," Lara said. "In fact, you might remember him. Gideon Halley. He was in my class at school."

Brenda thought for a moment, then said, "God, yes. Skinny, nerdy-looking kid, right? Black hair? What's he doing now, selling pocket protectors?" She laughed as if she'd made a hilarious joke. When she saw Lara's face, she waved a hand at her. "Come on, Lara. I was only kidding. Don't look so serious."

Lara felt her blood boil over. *What century was this woman living in?*

"Mom, I'm sorry, but that was really unkind of you. Gideon is a wonderful, thoughtful, generous man."

Brenda's smile withered. "Honey, look—I'm sorry. I didn't mean anything by that. I'm sure he's very nice. Cute, too, I hope."

Lara swallowed back a lump of anger. She'd had enough.

Aunt Fran returned with Brenda's hot cocoa. She handed the mug to Brenda. "Be careful. Under all the cream it's steaming hot."

"Aunt Fran, do you still keep those letters in your bedroom closet?" Lara said, lifting both cats and setting them on the floor.

Her aunt stared at her for a moment, then suddenly understood. "No, Lara, don't," she pleaded. "It's water under the bridge."

"I don't care if it's under, over, or inside the bridge. I'm showing them to her."

Before her aunt could utter a further protest, Lara trotted up the stairs. She marched into Aunt Fran's bedroom and opened her closet door. The letters were exactly where her aunt had left them after she'd first shown them to Lara—on a top shelf inside a gold-speckled cardboard box.

Lara grabbed the box and carried it back downstairs. Her mom and Aunt Fran looked like a pair of deer caught in glaring headlights.

"Lara, please, this isn't necessary," Aunt Fran said in a shaky voice.

"I'm sorry, but it is necessary." Lara plopped the box on the sofa next to her mom. She lifted the lid and pulled out a handful of letters. "How do you explain these, Mom?"

Brenda stared at the letters, and her face paled. She pressed her fingers to her lips, then her eyes filled with tears. With a hand more wrinkled than Lara remembered, her mom reached toward the letters. "I—I sent them back. I didn't let you see them." With that she burst into a round of tears, crying so loudly that Munster and Purrcy fled into the kitchen.

Aunt Fran quickly retrieved the hot cocoa from Brenda so that she wouldn't spill it and burn herself. Then she looked at Lara and shook her head. After setting the cocoa on the fireplace mantel, she sat down next to Brenda and placed a hand on her back.

With that, Lara broke into a sob. She hadn't intended to hurt her mom, not like this. But she had to let her know that she knew about the letters.

Aunt Fran rose. She retrieved Brenda's hot chocolate from atop the mantel, then strode over and opened the door to the back porch. "I want both of you in here," she instructed in her stern, schoolteacher's voice. "You need to talk. I'll close the door so you won't have any cats in there with you."

Brenda lifted her teary gaze to Lara. "Okay," she said meekly and nodded.

The two went onto the back porch. Aunt Fran closed the door, grabbing Valenteena just in time before she scooted into the room.

Brenda giggled through her tears. "I think that black-and-white one wanted to join us."

"She did." Lara chuckled and swiped at her eyes. "Come on, Mom. You and I need to talk."

Chapter 18

Brenda twisted a tissue in her fingers. "I don't have any excuses, Lara. You were always closer to Fran than you were to me. I...I guess I was jealous of your relationship."

Instinctively, Lara had always known that. Even as a kid, she'd noticed the tiny barbs Brenda had inflicted on her only sister-in-law. They seemed to come out of nowhere, without warning. And for no reason. Lara had dealt with it the only way she knew how—by painting pictures and bonding with Aunt Fran's cats.

Lara blotted her eyes with her own tissue. "You know, Mom, I never really understood something. Why did you and Dad move to Mass? You both seemed happy here. Lord knows I was happy. I never got why we had to move."

"It was me," Brenda said hoarsely. "It was all my fault. I nagged at your father until he finally gave in. I knew he'd make a lot more money at the new job. I told him he had to do it—for us, for the family."

Lara was stunned at her mother's admission. It wasn't like her to confess to anything negative about herself. Maybe this was a catharsis for her. She smiled at her mom. She wanted to understand—she really did.

"Okay, I guess I can see that. You were thinking about the future. You wanted the best for all of us. But it was a pressure-cooker job, Mom. Even I could tell Dad hated it."

"I know." Brenda cried again, then pressed her mangled tissue to her eyes. "After you went off to art school, he changed jobs. By then it was too late. He was already getting sick. We didn't realize it then, but he didn't have that long to go."

A lump settled in Lara's throat. She still missed her dad. Every day. Colon cancer had been the enemy, her dad's early death the result.

"I'm so sorry about the letters. I thought"—Brenda swallowed—"I thought if you were cut off from Fran, that eventually you'd forget about her. Then you and I could be better friends."

Lara shook her head. She didn't need Brenda to be her friend. She needed her to be her mom.

And she still didn't understand why her dad had gone along with it. Aunt Fran was his only sister, and they'd always been close.

As if she'd read Lara's mind, Brenda said, "I know it made your father unhappy. Sometimes I wish he hadn't been so passive, but he went along with pushing Fran out of our lives. He did it for me. That's all I can say."

Because he didn't have the strength to fight you any longer, Lara wanted to retort. Elbows on the table, she dropped her face into her cupped fingers. She willed herself to stop crying.

A whoosh of air tickled her fingers. She lifted her gaze to see Blue sitting on the table, one paw resting on her mother's arm.

The past is the past. Live for the present.

Lara heard the voice clearly. Where had it come from?

Heart thrumming, she pulled in a deep, calming breath. She couldn't even imagine what her mom would say if Lara told her there was a spirit cat sitting next to her. And that her paw was touching her, cat hair and all.

In the next moment, Brenda looked all around the room and smiled. "It's so pretty in here. I'll bet you did all the artwork."

That simple compliment felt like the warmest of hugs. "I did, in fact. This room is where we introduce people to cats and try to match them up. I wanted it to be as charming and as welcoming as possible."

Brenda looked at her daughter, fresh tears resting on her blue-tinted lashes. Lara's heart turned over. In the short time since her mom had arrived, she'd aged. She looked every bit of her forty-nine years.

"Honey, I know you're passionate about cats. And I'm sorry I could never look at them the way you do. But I should have been more understanding."

"It's okay, Mom. Not everyone's a cat lover. I get that. Honestly I do."

"Thank you. That means a lot." Brenda sniffled, and then her damp eyes lit up. "Oh, Lara, I can't wait till you meet Rodney. I know it sounds weird, me going to Vegas and falling in love the second day. It's just that...Rod and I are so right for each other, you know? We both saw it right away."

And got hitched three weeks later in a Vegas chapel.

"I only want what's best for you, Mom. I want you to be happy."

"I am happy," Brenda said softly. "And...I'm so, *so* sorry about those letters. I broke your heart. I had no right to do that."

You broke more than one heart, Lara wanted to say. But as her aunt had pointed out, it was water under the bridge.

Everything her mom was saying was what Lara had been waiting to hear. Still, she couldn't help wondering if the fluffy Ragdoll with the turquoise eyes might have had something to do with Brenda's sudden unburdening of the soul.

Brenda tilted her head playfully. "You're going to love Rod—I just know it. He really is a good man. Just to show you how sweet he is, know what he did a few months ago?" She chirped like a teenager. The real Brenda was back.

"Nope. You tell me."

Looking more at ease now, Brenda said, "Well, his mom, Gracie, was dying—she was eighty-three—and she had to go into the nursing home for hospice care. The place was kind of a dump, but the hospice people were wonderful."

"Sorry to hear about Rod's mom," Lara said.

"Thanks. Anyway, Gracie had this dog, a fussy little poodle named Curly. Poor Gracie—she kept asking for the dog. It nearly broke Rod's heart, you know?" Brenda lowered her voice. "Gracie didn't have much time left, a day or two at the most. Rod asked the nursing home if he could bring Curly to see her one last time before she...you know."

"Did they let him?"

"They finally did, after Rod called them twenty times. Oh, and it just made Gracie's day. Curly got right in the bed with her and cuddled up. It was so sweet. Couple of the nurses didn't like it, but too bad about them, right?"

Blue, who so far hadn't budged from her cozy spot next to Brenda, inched closer to Lara.

"Right," Lara said distractedly, "too bad about them."

Was that what happened to the old woman in the nursing home? Had someone brought her cat there to comfort her in her final hours?

Brenda waved a hand in front of Lara's face. "Hey, you okay? You look a little spacey."

"I'm fine, Mom. What happened to Curly? I mean, after Gracie passed."

Brenda lowered her gaze. "Rod and I didn't really want a dog—well, I didn't— plus they're not allowed in our condo. Rod was going to bring her to a shelter, but then Gracie's neighbor offered to take her. Nice old lady. She already had a dog, but she said Curly would keep it company." She shrugged and smiled. "Far as we know, it's worked out great."

"Wow, that *was* lucky."

Brenda stood abruptly. "Honey, I've really got to get going. Rod's going to think I got lost or something." She flashed a nervous smile. "Those presents? In the living room? They're just a few things we picked up for you in Vegas. Rod even picked out one of them especially for you. He insisted."

"Thanks, Mom. If we ever get a chance to put up our tree, I'll tuck them all underneath."

Lara rose from her chair. She hugged Brenda again, this time longer and harder. When she felt her mom pull away, Lara released her. She looked down at the table and smiled. Blue was gone.

"Mom, I'm so glad you came here today. In the future don't be such a stranger, okay?"

"No," Brenda said, a catch in her voice. "I won't."

"When do you have to fly home?"

Brenda's face flushed. "I'm not really sure yet. But if we hang around through Christmas, I'll definitely let you know."

No more talk of meeting Rod, Lara noticed. Or of the guest gig with the Greenhorn Geezers.

Lara also wondered where her mom and Rod were staying. Could they afford to live in a hotel until Christmas?

Aunt Fran had discreetly remained in the kitchen. When she heard Brenda leaving, she came into the large parlor to exchange a hurried goodbye with her sister-in-law. Lara helped her mother out to her rental car to be sure she didn't slip on an icy patch. When she came back inside, her aunt was standing there, glaring at her.

"That wasn't like you, Lara," Aunt Fran said quietly. "You brought out those letters to embarrass her. I'm truly surprised at you."

"What? I didn't bring them out to embarrass her. I wanted her to know that what she did was wrong."

"I understand your anger. But your mother had only been here a few minutes when you shoved those letters at her. It's something that should have been saved for another time, if at all."

Lara swallowed. "I'm...sorry I disappointed you, Aunt Fran." She felt an ache settle in her stomach like a jagged rock.

Her aunt started to say something else, but Lara turned and ran upstairs, tears flowing down her face. She couldn't recall her aunt having ever spoken to her so harshly—not even when she'd questioned Lara's motive for returning to Whisker Jog after sixteen years.

The door to Lara's bedroom was halfway open. Swiping a knuckle over her wet cheeks, she pushed it open farther. Her mouth dropped open, and she covered it to suppress a gasp.

Nutmeg had tunneled under Lara's chenille bedspread, her tail sticking out like a furry baton. Ballou was pouncing on Lara's pillow trying to capture her tail. He rolled around joyfully, grabbing her tail in his paws and then releasing it again.

He was playing!

She felt more than heard her aunt coming up behind her. Aunt Fran touched Lara's shoulder. Lara turned and saw a smile light up her face.

They watched for a minute or so, until Ballou suddenly realized he was being observed. He shot them both a panic-stricken look, then bolted under the bed.

Nutmeg crept out from under the bedspread. She glanced around for her new pal, who'd fled without warning.

Lara and her aunt both broke out in laughter. "Oh, that was adorable. I could've watched them all day."

"I know," Aunt Fran said, grinning. "I think Ballou might have finally found his soulmate."

Found his soulmate.

Lara had long sensed that an odd dynamic was transpiring in their little shelter. Did Blue have anything to do with it? She wasn't sure. Whatever it was, it was bringing cats and people together in a strange and wonderful way.

Lara and her aunt spoke at the same time.

"Lara, I'm sorry. I—"

"Aunt Fran, I didn't mean to—"

"You first," Aunt Fran said.

"I was only going to say, I'm sorry for the way I handled Mom. I put her on the spot, big-time, didn't I? And I invaded your closet after you told me not to."

"You did," her aunt said. "But it's over now. It's time to move forward."

Lara smiled. *Live for the present.*

Aunt Fran went over to Lara's bed. She sat down on the edge, and Nutmeg instantly leaped into her lap. The tortie sniffed and licked at her fingers.

"She's a darling," Aunt Fran said. "I don't know why, but I have a feeling someone's going to show up to claim her."

"They might," Lara said. "We'll see." She went over and squeezed her aunt's shoulder. "Need any help getting the food ready for book club?"

"The food's all set. When the ladies get here, I'll put you in charge of the hot chocolate."

"You got it." She bent and planted a kiss on her aunt's cheek.

Chapter 19

Brooke Weston squealed with delight when she tore off the wrapping from the untagged gift. "Hmm," she said, sneaking a look at Mary Newman. "*Someone* must have noticed me admiring these earrings in her gift shop." She held up a pair of dangly red earrings that resembled a chandelier. "I love them!"

Mary, an attractive, thirtysomething brunette, gave an exaggerated shrug. "Don't look at me. Someone else could have bought them. Besides, Brooke, this is a Yankee swap. One of us might well take those earrings from you. Lara, don't you have number one?"

"I do," Lara said, wiggling her eyebrows.

No way would she take those earrings from Brooke. A freshman in high school, Brooke was their youngest member. Bubbly, fun, and smart, she was the darling of the book club. This month she'd highlighted her hair a dark burgundy for the season.

Aunt Fran was next, with number four. She chose the gift Lara had bought. "Oh my, isn't this perfect." She held up the green velvet change purse with a cat embroidered on the front.

"If you don't like it, you can take Brooke's earrings," Mary said gleefully.

Brooke swatted her arm playfully. "Hey, don't give her any ideas."

"Don't worry, Brooke," Aunt Fran said. "Your earrings are safe. This little change purse is perfect for me." She opened it. "Oh, and there's a lottery ticket inside. Who knows, I might strike it rich."

Brooke looked at Lara with a fake pout. "Please don't take my earrings."

Lara pretended to mull it over. "Well, then, I guess I'm stuck with this charming cat lady mug." She knew Brooke had bought it. "Actually, I love it."

Aunt Fran winked at Brooke. "Then I think we're done," she declared. "And we even managed to keep the cats out of the kitchen for an hour and a half."

"Yeah, but Nutmeg was definitely bummed about it." Brooke laughed. "She wanted one of our crabmeat rolls *bad.*"

"Don't worry, Brooke," Aunt Fran said. "I'll give her a smidge of crabmeat later."

"She'll love that." Brooke sighed noisily. "I guess I better start getting ready. Mom'll be swinging into the driveway any minute, and I've got an algebra quiz to study for. I'll help you put the dishes in the sink, Ms. C." She stood and began stacking plates in her arms.

Aunt Fran got up and hugged her. "You're so welcome, Brooke. All of you. I'm glad we decided to meet here today."

"You don't think it hurt Daisy's feelings, do you?" Mary asked, biting her lip.

Lara collected the empty hot chocolate mugs. "No, I chatted with Sherry earlier. I think they were actually grateful. The earlier they can close up the coffee shop, the better. Besides, we'll be meeting there next week."

"So, are we agreed on *Rebecca* for our next read?" Mary asked.

Everyone nodded their assent. "I am," Lara said. "I'll get my copy at the library. I have to go over anyway to return a book."

"I'll read it on my phone," Brooke said, a grim look crossing her face.

Lara understood. A little over a year ago, Brooke had had an unfortunate experience with one of the classic books she was reading. After that, she'd switched to reading electronically and never looked back.

"How are things at the high school?" Lara asked her. "Are the police still hanging around?" She followed Brooke to the sink, the empty hot chocolate mugs clasped in her fingers.

"They've definitely been there," Brooke said. "I saw one of them go into the cafeteria yesterday. Do you think they're still searching for evidence?"

"They might be." Lara set the mugs on the counter.

Brooke's face fell. "I feel so awful for Ms. Bowker. The cops need to leave her alone!"

"I know," Lara said. "We all feel bad for Daisy."

Something else was nagging at Lara. She had to find out more about the woman who died in the nursing home. Irma something-or-other.

Irma Hansen Tisley. That was it. The name came to Lara out of the blue.

Her mother's comment about her new hubby bringing his mother's dog to the nursing home had ignited the theory. What if one of Irma's loved ones had brought her cat to the nursing home before she passed away?

Lara needed to check into it further. Kayla was busy with her studies, so Lara didn't want to stress her out with any more research.

"Hey, you still with us?" Brooke waved and made a funny face at Lara.

"Sorry." Lara rinsed the mugs and stacked them in the dishwasher. "I tune out sometimes."

"It's okay," Brooke said with a worried look. "I tune out all the time."

* * * *

By the time Brooke and Mary left, it was nearly four thirty. The book club discussion and luncheon had been the highlight of the day, Brenda's visit notwithstanding.

"I don't think we'll be wanting any dinner," Lara said, patting her stomach.

"That's for sure." Aunt Fran used the remote to turn on the television. Dolce snuggled into her lap and rested his head on her knee. "Two crab rolls and that peppermint flan really filled me up. Want to watch the early news with me?"

"I think I'll catch it later, if you don't mind," Lara said. "I'm working on a watercolor for a couple in Colebrook. They live out in the wilderness, in a sprawling log cabin home they designed and built themselves. I'm painting it from the picture they gave me."

"Sounds like an ambitious project." Aunt Fran smiled. "I can't wait to see the finished painting."

"Yeah, me too."

In the small parlor—Lara's studio—she set up her painting supplies, including the tiles she used to mix colors. She'd started the painting a few days earlier but hadn't made much progress. So many distractions had cluttered her head. Luckily, the customer didn't need it by Christmas. They wanted it for the housewarming party they were throwing at the end of January.

The photo the customer had given her showed the log cabin nestled against a backdrop of newly planted fir trees. Touches of orange played at the horizon of a pale blue sky. Lara was applying a touch of burnt sienna to the painting when movement on one of the upper bookshelves caught her eye. She'd set a stack of papers there, intending to go through them at some point and either file or toss them as needed.

The top two sheets fluttered like paper airplanes, landing in the wastebasket Lara kept near the door.

"Now how the heck..." she muttered. She went over to the basket and plucked out both sheets. They were the two obituaries Kayla had copied at the library—Sarah Nally's and Irma Tisley's.

"Okay, that was weird," Lara said, reaching up to return them to the shelf. From behind her, a fluffy Ragdoll sprang over her shoulder. Startled, Lara jumped, and the papers flew from her fingers. She watched, stunned, as the cat pushed both sheets of paper back into the wastebasket. The cat sat inside the basket, her blue gaze fixed on Lara.

Lara's heart raced, and then it struck her.

"Those obits. They're both dead ends, aren't they?" she whispered.

Blue blinked once, then blinked again.

Lara closed her eyes and took several deep breaths, willing her heartbeat to slow. When she opened her eyes, Blue was gone.

Back to square one, she thought. *So where do I go from here?*

Chapter 20

Thursday morning dawned far too quickly after a restless, dream-filled night. In one dream, Lara was trudging through a piney forest in search of a lost cat. Her feet kept getting stuck in deep snow, preventing her from moving forward. At one point she fell, then spotted the cat in the distance. As it came into focus it morphed into a mountain lion, hungry and ready to spring.

"*Nooo,*" she groaned, feeling a paw squashing her eyelid. Her brain kicked into gear. "Give me a break, Teena. I'll feed you in a few minutes."

The paw stayed put. Lara lifted it gently and wrenched open her eyes. She was surprised to see Nutmeg's nose looming about an inch above her own. The little tortie made a *brrrp* sound and then licked her chops.

Laughing, Lara ruffled the cat's head. She was amazed at how quickly Nutmeg had adapted to the household. Only a few days ago the tortie had been wandering the woods. Thanks to Jason, she was now safe, warm, and well fed.

At the top of the cat tree, Ballou sat, watching. His tail switched back and forth. "I think he's sweet on you," Lara said, remembering how Ballou had jumped on the bed with Nutmeg the day before.

She grinned when Teena, Purrcival, and Snowball bounded into her room and leaped onto her bed in a wave. "Thanks, guys. Just what I need at six forty-five in the morning—a cat party."

A gust of wind rattled Lara's window, followed by an eerie, howling sound swirling through the distant trees.

It must be freezing out, Lara thought, slipping into her robe.

She was tempted to shower first, mainly to warm up her bones. Instead she went downstairs and performed her usual cat duties.

Feeding times had gotten more challenging, especially with some cats leaving the shelter and new cats coming in. Although each cat had a separate bowl, Lara wondered if some should be moved to another location. Where to put them was the question.

One more problem to resolve—and soon.

She and Sherry had agreed that Lara would skip her morning visit to the coffee shop. Instead, they'd meet right after closing time to come up with a plan for approaching David's mom. And Lara still wanted to go to the library. If there was an obit that Kayla missed—unlikely, Lara thought—she wanted a shot at finding it.

She also couldn't stop dwelling on Gideon. Something about their date Monday evening had felt off-kilter to her. If only she could pinpoint what it was, she might be able to troubleshoot.

As for what to get him for Christmas, she was still without a single idea. He had enough scarves, gloves, and earmuffs to sustain him through another ice age. In his rare spare time, he loved to read, but a book seemed too impersonal. She'd briefly considered a cashmere sweater, but Gideon was more of a casual guy. Cashmere was far too fussy.

If she thought about it long enough, she'd end up getting him nothing. *Not acceptable,* she chided herself.

Lara spent the morning catching up on smaller projects. Focusing on mundane tasks sometimes helped trigger an idea that wouldn't otherwise have come to her.

By noon, she was ready for lunch.

"Is there any of that crabmeat left?" Lara asked her aunt.

Aunt Fran, who'd spent her morning shopping, smiled and shook her head. "I used every last drop, including the smidgeon I saved for Nutmeg. I need to buy more, though. I'm going to make crab cakes, coleslaw, and steak fries for Jerry's birthday. His birthday's Tuesday, but we're celebrating it on Saturday."

"So, you finally caught up with him?" Lara asked her, rummaging in the fridge.

"I did. We had a long talk last night." She set down one of her grocery bags. "Lara, I have something to tell you. I don't want to get your hopes up, but it's almost certain that the police won't be charging Daisy."

Lara pulled out a block of cheddar and slammed the refrigerator door. "Oh my Lord, that's wonderful news! Not enough evidence, right?"

"Pretty much," Aunt Fran said.

"What a relief." Lara set the cheese on the counter. "Do Daisy and Sherry know?"

"They do, but it's not confirmed, so please don't repeat it to anyone," her aunt cautioned. "I'm sure Sherry's been dying to tell you, but the police warned them against sharing that information. The investigators still think foul play was involved. They just don't know how. From what I understand, at least two other cookies—not Daisy's—had traces of lobster as well."

Lara pulled a sharp knife out of the utensil drawer. "Then someone wanted to be sure Miss Plouffe got a good dose of shellfish. Who? *Who?*" Loretta Gregson's face flitted through her mind.

"I don't know." Aunt Fran set two plates on the counter. "But that's for the police to determine. Not us. Specifically, not you."

Lara smiled. "Don't worry. I can take a hint." She'd encountered enough killers—two, to be exact—to last her a lifetime and beyond.

She turned on the burner and prepared two grilled cheese sandwiches. Aunt Fran poured each of them a glass of cranberry juice. Lara told her aunt about their planned meeting with Loretta Gregson that afternoon.

"Sherry really should be meeting her alone," Aunt Fran said. "I'm afraid it's going to look like two against one. Loretta might think you're ganging up on her."

"I know, and I agree." Lara said. "But Sherry is terrified to face her alone. Which baffles me, because nothing ever really scares her. She's one of the bravest people I know." She tore off a bite of her grilled cheese and chewed it thoughtfully.

"It's a different kind of fear," Aunt Fran noted. She picked a shred of cheese from her sandwich and held it out to Munster, who was waiting in the wings. "She's afraid of being hurt. She's worried that whatever's going on with Loretta will impact her relationship with David."

"You're right." Lara sighed. "But whatever happens today, I'm determined to stay completely neutral. I'll be there for moral support only."

Famous last words, she thought.

* * * *

The bagel café was only a short ride from downtown Whisker Jog. It was located in one of the strip malls Lara had always found sterile and boring. The parking lot had been plowed clean, she was happy to see. Not a speck of treacherous ice remained on any portion of the pavement.

The café itself was crisp and clean, with checkered curtains and red plastic booths reminiscent of an earlier time.

Loretta Gregson, wearing a stylish knitted hat and a ski jacket, slid into the booth across from Sherry and Lara. "Hello, dear," she greeted Sherry. "Nice to see you again, Lara."

"You, too," Lara said. "How's Cookie doing?"

"Oh my—you remembered. She's doing wonderfully, back to her old self. Thank you for asking."

With that icebreaker, they all ordered coffee. Loretta pulled off her black leather gloves and gave Sherry a wary look. "So, what's this all about?"

Sherry leaned forward and smiled. "It's nothing bad, Mrs. Gregson. I just wanted to ask you something. I may as well get right to the point. A few people have noticed that you've had your hair cut exactly like my mom's. The color's the same, too, right down to the highlighting. And your makeup—" Sherry halted. Loretta's face had paled to a ghostly white.

Their server came by with their coffees. Lara gratefully snatched up her mug and took a hefty sip, burning her lips. She squelched a grimace.

They'd agreed in the car that Sherry should begin the conversation slowly and tactfully. Her friend had already ditched that plan in favor of blatant candor.

"I-I guess I don't understand." Loretta's voice was brittle. "Are you implying that I've been *copying* your mother?"

Sherry winced visibly. "Yeah, sort of. I guess so."

Loretta pressed her red-tinted lips together and shook her head. "I thought you were going to ask for suggestions on what to get David for Christmas. I didn't expect anything like this."

Sherry looked as if she wanted to shrink into the back of the booth and fade into oblivion.

"Mrs. Gregson," Lara said kindly, "there's nothing wrong with imitating someone's style. It's actually a compliment to Daisy." *Unless you're trying to pin a murder on her.* "It's only that it seemed to happen all at once, you know?"

Loretta's face crumpled. Ignoring Lara, she looked at Sherry through watery eyes. "David...he adores you, Sherry. I'm sure you know that. But I haven't been able to get close to you. I've tried, but you seem to hold back. Maybe I did copy your mother, subconsciously. But only so that you'd see me as more...approachable."

Lara thought about the altercation with Miss Plouffe that Loretta had been involved in. She couldn't help wondering—was Loretta trying to manipulate her way into Sherry's good graces? She didn't, for a moment, believe Loretta's claim that her imitation of Daisy had been subconscious.

"Okay, I get that," Sherry said, her shoulders drooping. "I'm kind of embarrassed now. I didn't realize you felt that way about me. To be honest, it takes me a while to warm up to people. And you being David's mom?" She laughed slightly. "It made me feel like I have to be perfect for you, you know? I hope that doesn't sound too crazy."

Sherry's playing the part beautifully, Lara thought. *If that's what she's doing.*

Loretta's features relaxed. She looked far more at ease than she had when she'd arrived, as if a huge weight had been lifted. "It doesn't sound crazy at all, dear. You're perfect for David, just the way you are." She gave Sherry a sly little wink. "In fact," she said, leaning forward, "I'm hoping you're going to be part of our little family one day."

For the first time since they'd arrived, Sherry was speechless. Lara buried her nose in her coffee mug and took a long, slow sip.

"Wow," Sherry finally said. "That's such a nice thing to say. Thank you, Mrs. Gregson."

"And dear," Loretta cooed, "I do hope I haven't upset your mother." She reached over and squeezed Sherry's fingers with her own. "That's the last thing I'd ever want to do."

A chill rippled down Lara's spine. Something about Loretta's response sounded cold and calculated, without an ounce of sincerity. If only there was a way to bring up her confrontation with Gladys Plouffe.

"Listen, don't worry about it, okay? I don't think Mom even noticed," Sherry said, easing her fingers free from Loretta's grasp. "Lately she's been too worried about the police and all the hoopla over Miss Plouffe's death."

Good job, Lara thought. Sherry had found a way to inject Miss Plouffe into their little chat.

Loretta's eyelid twitched. "That's certainly understandable. Believe it or not, I had a bit of a tiff with Miss Plouffe myself a while back. She was a very unpleasant woman, I'm sorry to say."

Sherry went wide-eyed. "Really? What happened?" Lara felt her friend's foot poke her under the table.

"It was embarrassing, really. She reported me to the police for something that wasn't my fault. All over a silly handicapped parking space. I ended up going to court and having to pay a fine. Ridiculous."

Sherry and Lara made the appropriate *tsk tsk* sounds.

Why was she suddenly so forthcoming? Lara wondered.

After an awkward pause, Sherry said, "I just hope the police close the Plouffe case soon. My honest opinion? It was an accident, pure and simple.

Someone handled the cookies with something Miss Plouffe was allergic to and didn't realize it."

No, Sherry. Don't tell her about the allergy!

Loretta's head snapped toward Sherry. Her eyes looked smaller now as they searched Sherry's face. "Is that what Gladys Plouffe died from? An allergic reaction?"

Sherry instantly realized her mistake. Her face flushed cherry-red. "Um, that's one of the theories, yes. But the police have others, too," she added, backtracking over her slip of the tongue.

Loretta stirred her coffee briskly. "I didn't realize that. About the allergic reaction."

If she was acting, it was an Oscar-worthy performance, Lara thought. But if she really hadn't known about Miss Plouffe's allergy, it could mean only one thing.

Loretta Gregson did not kill Gladys Plouffe.

* * * *

"So, what did you think?" Sherry said after they'd left the café.

"I don't know, Sher," Lara said. "I wanted to believe her, but something tells me she's not totally sincere. The main thing is, she couldn't have killed Miss Plouffe. Only someone who knew about her allergy could have tainted those cookies."

They both got into the Saturn. Sherry snapped her seat belt in place. Lara started the car and pulled out into the stream of traffic.

"I wanted to kick myself," Sherry said, "for stupidly letting it slip about the allergic reaction. The police have been trying to keep that quiet." She grimaced. "Think I'll get in trouble?"

Lara laughed. "With who? Chief Whitley?"

"Him, and the state police."

"It's too late now, so don't worry about it," Lara said. "The main thing is that your mom's off the hook, right? She must be so relieved." When Sherry didn't respond, Lara repeated, "Right, Sher?"

"Oh...uh, yeah right."

"You're lost in thought," Lara said. "Something else is wrong, isn't it?"

Sherry heaved a massive sigh. "David asked me again, about getting engaged for Christmas. He wants me to go with him to pick out a ring."

There was a part of Lara that wanted to scream "Yippee!" But another part told her Sherry needed a lot more time to make that life-altering decision.

"Sherry, don't get me wrong. I think it's wonderful that you and David found each other," Lara said. "But you shouldn't feel pressured into making a commitment if you're not ready. If you need more time, tell him."

"What if he says he can't wait? What if he says it's now or never?"

Lara braked slowly, then stopped for a traffic light. She turned and looked at her friend. "He won't say that if he loves you," she said softly. "Sher, this is the most important relationship you've ever had. And it all happened kind of quickly, you know? So don't feel rushed, and don't feel pressured. If you need to slow things down, then do it."

Lara wondered if she was talking to Sherry or to herself.

A sudden wave of melancholy washed over her. For reasons she couldn't pinpoint, she felt overwhelmed with sadness.

"Thanks, Lara," Sherry said tearfully. "You always know what to say. So, what do you think about me having Mrs. Gregson as a mother-in-law?"

Lara snapped her mind back to Sherry's problem. She didn't know what she thought about David's mother. Something about the woman bothered her. She reminded Lara of the mother-in-law in one of the old TV sitcoms who invaded her son's home several times a day on the pretext of "helping."

"I think you can handle her," Lara said. "The best advice I can give is to stay true to yourself."

Chapter 21

By the time Lara arrived at Gideon's office, darkness had fallen. The night sky was clustered with clouds, blotting out the stars. *The days are getting shorter,* she thought gloomily, *and my "to do" list is getting longer.*

It wasn't until after she dropped off Sherry at her home that she'd made the decision. She was going to do a "pop in" and surprise Gideon at his office. If he was too busy to talk to her, so be it. But something had been on her mind all day. She had to get it off her chest before her brain exploded.

Monday at dinner was the last time Gideon and she had seen each other, although they'd spoken a few times and texted dozens of times. The flatness in his words over the past few days gave Lara the sinking feeling something was wrong.

Gideon's office was housed in one of the stately old homes within walking distance of the downtown block. His apartment was located one story up, making his commute to work a dream. One other tenant, a financial consultant, rented the office space opposite Gideon's. The apartment above her office was occupied by an elderly woman, Mrs. Appleton, and her cat, Muffin. The same cat Gideon had offered to "borrow" if his company got too boring.

It was 4:45 when she rang the front buzzer. Lara knew Gideon didn't have an assistant—he did all his work himself, including answering the phone and typing up documents. Clients had to ring to be let inside—a system that allowed him to keep unsolicited vendors at bay.

After a minute or so, Gideon opened the door. He looked surprised but thrilled to see her, as if he'd waited a long time for her. "Hey there, come on in."

Her heart lodged in her throat, Lara stepped into the vestibule. The walls were paneled in a dark mahogany, giving the foyer a dreary feel. A small light hung from the ceiling—one of those art deco reproductions that attempted to imitate an earlier era. The combined scent of paper, furniture polish, and stale coffee hung closely in the air.

Gideon kissed her lightly on the lips, a strand of his straight black hair dipping slightly over his forehead. "I'm just finishing up with a couple signing a P and S for the new house they're buying. Can you wait for ten minutes or so?"

"Of course I can," she said. "I didn't mean to interrupt your work, Gid. Take your time, okay?"

He winked at her, touched her cheek lightly, then returned to the conference room adjacent to the foyer.

Tears pushed at the back of Lara's eyes. Thinking about it in the car, she'd figured out what was bothering him. The problem was: how was she going to broach the subject?

She sat in one of the hard-backed chairs, then loosened her scarf. When she checked her phone for messages, she saw one from Kayla asking her if she'd done any more snooping about the obituaries.

No, because a ghost cat told me they weren't the right ones, she thought bleakly. How could she tell that to Kayla? So much of her life, it seemed lately, was dictated by a Ragdoll cat no one else could see.

The conference room door opened. A thirtyish-looking couple, their faces alight with joy, strolled out hand in hand. "Thank you so much, Mr. Halley," the man said. "We'll chat with you again once the closing is scheduled."

Gideon wished them well, shook their hands, and saw them out the door. He turned to Lara. "I'm so glad to see you. You should have told me you were coming!"

"And you'd have baked a cake?" she joked, swallowing back tears.

Gideon's smile collapsed. "Honey, what's wrong? You look like you lost your best friend." He slipped his arms around her and pulled her close.

It felt wonderful, being wrapped in his arms. The scent of his soap, mingled with the laundry detergent he always overused, almost made her forget the nagging fear she'd come here to talk about.

Almost.

"Come on in my office," he said, taking her hand. "I have some coffee left over from about three o'clock, if you want to risk it. Even better, one of my clients brought me some peanut butter fudge." He waggled his eyebrows. "Can I tempt you?"

Lara smiled. "You can always tempt me."

Lara drifted over to one of the bookshelves to look at her favorite photo. Framed in vintage silver, it was a pic of Gideon at about twelve years old. One hand rested on his dad's shoulder as he gazed at the document clutched in his dad's hand. His dad, a lawyer, was seated at the desk he'd handed down to Gideon, his finger pointing at something he wanted his son to read. The desk was a jumble of papers, pens, and coffee cups, along with an old-fashioned green desk lamp. According to Gideon, his mom had taken the photo only a short time before his dad succumbed to kidney failure.

"Still staring at that picture, huh?" Gideon came up behind her and put his hands on her shoulders.

Lara smiled. "I've always loved it. It's the way I remember you right before my folks moved us to Massachusetts."

"It's my favorite pic, too," Gideon said, a slight catch in his throat. "Dad was such a professional. He loved pointing out little details to me. That day, I think he was showing me a clause he'd stuck in a will he drafted. He knew the heirs were going to contest it, so he wanted to make sure it was iron-clad. I guess he was hoping I'd follow in his footsteps."

"Which you did," Lara said, and her eyes blurred with tears.

"Honey, what's wrong?"

She folded her hands under her chin. "Let's see, where to begin." She started by springing her big news of the day—her mother's unexpected visit. Safe territory for discussion, at least for now.

Gideon took her by the arms and pushed her toward his high-backed chair, making her sit down. He perched on the edge of his desk and faced her, his brown eyes creased with concern. "You must have been shocked to see her. But pleasantly so, I hope."

"Gid, do you really have time to listen to all this?" Lara asked him. "I know I interrupted your work. I shouldn't have come over here without calling."

"Not true. I always have time for you, and I was getting ready to call it a day anyway."

"You always work until at least six," she chided.

"Okay, so I was *almost* getting ready to call it a day. Tell me, what happened with your mom?"

Lara launched into a recap of everything that transpired from the moment Brenda arrived until she zoomed out of the driveway in her rental car. She told him about her mom bringing the gifts, complaining about the cats, and about the letters Lara had forced her to look at.

Gideon listened without commenting. When she finished, he said, "It was an emotional roller coaster, wasn't it?"

"Boy, you said it."

"How do you feel now? Are you glad she made a surprise visit?"

Lara shifted in Gideon's chair. "I felt better after she left, but I also felt drained. I don't know what to think about this marriage of hers. Maybe after I meet Rodney I'll have a better comfort level." *Or not.*

"I hope I get to see her before she goes back to Vegas," Gideon said. "I think the last time I saw her was at our sixth-grade graduation. Remember when the flag toppled off the stage during Vice Principal Daley's excruciatingly long speech?"

"Oh my God, that's right. How did you remember that?" Lara laughed. "I think the universe was trying to send him a message."

"If it was, he clearly didn't get it. He droned on for another twenty minutes." Gideon rolled his eyes and grinned, then took Lara's hands in his. "Come on, Lara, something else is bugging you. I've sensed it for a couple days now. Did I say something wrong at dinner the other night?"

Lara shook her head. "No, not wrong. Just... Okay, here goes. Gid, do you remember when you invited me over for popcorn? You said that if I got too bored we could borrow Mrs. Appleton's cat to entertain me."

With a perplexed look, he shrugged. "Sure, but I was kidding. You usually know when I'm teasing."

"I know," she said. "And it wasn't your joking about Muffin that bothered me. I didn't mind that at all. Maybe I'm overthinking it, but...it was more about the *way* you said it, I guess. It made *me* think that *you* think cats might be too big a part of my life."

His expression serious, Gideon pulled over a rolling chair and sat down in front of Lara. He took her hands in his again, this time holding them tight. "Lara," he said in the quietest voice she'd ever heard, "that cannot be further from the truth. Everything about you, including your passion for cats, is what made me fall in love with you. I can't even imagine your life—our lives—moving forward without cats."

Lara gazed down at their joined hands, then directly into his eyes. "But you don't have a cat, Gideon," she said, choking out the words. "Which tells me that you never really wanted one."

"You're right, honey, I don't have one. But that doesn't mean I never wanted one. Growing up, I never had pets, so I never knew what it was like to have one in the house. The only cats I was exposed to were Uncle Amico's. It was one of the reasons I loved visiting him—I could roll around on the floor with his cat."

Tears flowed down Lara's cheeks. Gideon had always been honest with her. She had no reason to doubt him now. "Wow," she said and swiped at her face.

Gideon opened his desk drawer and retrieved a box of tissues. He pulled one out and pressed it to her cheeks.

"And let me add this," he said. "Someday, if we're living together, I expect cats to be a huge part of our lives. Without them, you wouldn't be you, you wouldn't be Lara. And Lara is the woman I fell in love with."

"What if you wake up some morning with a cat on your head?"

Gideon's eyes twinkled. "Then I wake up some morning with a cat on my head."

Lara leaped off her chair and threw her arms around him. "Thank you," she whispered. A tsunami of sheer relief flooded every nerve in her body.

"It's simply the truth," he said, hugging her.

She pulled back slightly and put her hands on his chest. "And now, I'm going to let you finish up whatever you were working on." When he started to protest, she said, "No arguments. I know you, and I know you have stuff to finish. Besides, there's some research I want to do at the library before it closes."

Gideon looked relieved. "I do have to get this P and S overnighted to the seller's attorney," he admitted. "And I have to do a cover letter. And I have to send a copy to the broker. What's your research about? Anything interesting?"

"Actually, I never had a chance to tell you about it. I found the oddest letter in a library book last week. Wait...I have a picture." Lara dug her phone from her bag and pulled up the photo she'd taken of the letter.

Gideon enlarged the pic on her phone. His curious smile morphed into a worried frown. "How about that...another murder," he murmured, reading the handwritten message. "What's even stranger is that a cat is involved—and you're the one who found the letter. I mean, what are the odds, right? Dozens of people must have checked out that book before you did!"

"Maybe not," Lara said wryly. "It's the book I used to find recipes for cat treats. I don't think it rocked the bestseller charts."

"Yeah, but still..." he said with a bewildered look. He shook his head. "Anyway, I don't suppose there's much danger in looking into a murder that's almost thirty years old. But—hey, wait a minute. This letter is dated March 9, 1990. Isn't that a week after you were born?"

She should have known his eagle eyes would miss nothing. "Another weird coincidence, right?"

"Or not," he said. "Lara, I don't like this. Too many things about it hit home." He frowned at her.

"I had a feeling you might say that," she said. "Gid, I promise I'll be extra careful. And like you said, who cares about a murder that old? Even if it really did happen, everyone involved is probably long gone."

"I wouldn't make that assumption," he said. He tapped a finger to his chin and thought for a long moment. "You know what we need? Some kind of code. Something that'll let me know if you're in trouble and need help."

Lara suppressed a groan. He was carrying things too far. Yes, she'd encountered two murderers in the past. But how likely was that to happen again?

Although, she reminded herself, only five months ago Gideon had shown up just in time to help her subdue a killer. That time, however, a certain blue-eyed Ragdoll had made sure Gideon knew she was in trouble.

"Okay, well, that might not be a bad idea," Lara said, relenting. She snapped her fingers. "Gideon, I've got it. Code Blue."

"Code Blue," Gideon repeated. "How did you think of that?"

Lara scrambled for an answer. "I had a roommate in art school whose dad was a cardiologist. It's hospital slang for 'cardiac arrest...all hands on deck'...or—well, you know what I mean."

"I get the drift." Gideon smiled at her. "Okay, then. Code Blue it is."

Lara breathed out a sigh. She hadn't lied. Her roommate's dad had been a cardiologist.

But it was getting harder every day to keep her secret about Blue. *It wasn't a lie so much as an omission,* she thought. Which, unfortunately, didn't make her feel any better about it.

Right then, Lara promised herself something. If they decided to make their relationship permanent, she would tell him. And if he said she was crazy and dumped her, so be it.

One thing Gideon hadn't mentioned—the code system would only work if Lara had quick access to her phone. She decided not to mention it; the less he worried, the better.

"Hey, before you go, you heard about Daisy, right?" Gideon said.

"Yup. Aunt Fran told me she's no longer a suspect. I feel like I can breathe again."

Gideon nodded. "The police are lying low on this one. They still believe someone tainted those cookies on purpose. If that's the case, they want the culprit to feel secure in thinking that someone else will take the heat for the crime. That way he, or she, might relax and make a mistake."

"I can't imagine killing someone and then letting an innocent person take the blame. Then again, I can't imagine killing someone at all."

"Neither can I," Gideon said. "Lara, I know you're sick of hearing this, but please, *please* be—"

"Careful," she finished. "I know. And I will. I promise." She kissed him lightly. "Hey, do you have a bottle of water I can take for the car?"

"I'll get one from the fridge. Be back in a sec."

The moment he was gone, Lara went over to where the picture of Gideon and his dad sat atop the bookshelf. She held up her phone and took a quick, close-up photo.

Gideon returned with her water and a plastic bag. "Here's your water and some peanut butter fudge. More calories for you, fewer for me."

Lara opened the bag and sampled a tiny smidgeon of fudge. "Gid, this is delicious—thank you. This will be my dessert tonight." She resealed the bag and tucked it into her coat pocket.

They indulged in a rather lengthy goodbye, after which Lara hurried out to her car, slammed the door, and locked herself in.

From where she'd parked, she could see the downtown block. On both sides of the street, immense plastic snowflakes sat atop the light poles. Wrapped diagonally around the poles were garlands of faux greenery festooned with red bows. The scene made Lara smile, until the red-and-green lights twinkling in the windows of the library reminded her of the letter.

On the day she was born, someone witnessed a murder. Someone who was afraid to go to the police.

Someone who also saw the spirit of a blue-eyed cat float off to take care of a new life.

Lara started the car, shifted into gear, and headed over to the library.

Chapter 22

Lara was surprised at how many workstations were occupied in the library's microfiche room. At least five of the occupants were teenagers, probably doing research for a school project. Most looked bored, but a few stared at their monitors as if they were witnessing an alien spacecraft landing.

Edith Daniels, her spectacles hanging around her neck on a multicolored chain, directed Lara to the area where newspapers from all over the state were stored. She pointed a gnarled finger at the gray metal shelves resting against the rear wall. "The year you're looking for is 1990? Well, now, isn't that interesting. Another young gal was in here a few days ago looking for the same year. Same newspaper, too."

"That was probably my friend Kayla. She was helping me out."

Edith nodded sagely. "Then I gather she didn't find what you needed."

"She found some obituaries, but I don't think they were the right ones. The thing is, we don't know the exact name." *Or the name at all.* "We know the date of death, though. Isn't it strange that the obit wouldn't have been published within two or three days of that?"

"No, in fact, it's not," Edith said, leading Lara over to one of the free microfiche stations. "Why don't you put your jacket on the chair, dear. That way no one will steal the machine while you're looking for the reel you want. As I was saying, the publication of obituaries can get delayed for various reasons. Sometimes, the family doesn't want to publish until they're sure the deceased's loved ones have all been notified. Can you imagine returning from a ski vacation, opening the newspaper, and finding out that dear old Uncle Rudy died while you were away?"

Lara removed her jacket and draped it over the back of the chair. "Did that actually happen?"

"It did, although I changed the name to protect the innocent." Her faded blue eyes twinkled over an amused smile. "If I were you, I'd search for at least a month after the date of death. Just to be sure you don't miss it."

"Thanks. That helps a lot."

"And if you make any copies, tell Ellie you used machine seven."

"Will do," Lara promised.

Edith toddled off to help another patron. Lara set her tote on her chair and went over to peruse the rows of microfiche reels. The print on the labels was tiny—and sideways. Her eyes were nearly crossed when she found the one she wanted. The label read: *February 23, 1990 –April 3, 1990.*

Lara sat down and shoved the reel into the microfiche reader. She did a fast-forward to March 2, 1990—the known date of death—and went from there. She retraced Kayla's steps, though she felt sure she hadn't missed anything. Kayla was a stickler for detail.

The job was more tedious than she thought it would be. Stop, read, go forward. Stop, read, go forward—until she was sure her eyeballs were going to pop out of her skull. And since she didn't know the name of the deceased, the task was even harder. She'd just squelched a massive yawn when an obituary jumped out at her. She clapped a hand over her mouth. *Oh my Lord,* she mouthed through her fingers.

The newspaper was dated March 19, 1990. The deceased: Eugenia Kay Thryce, nee Vigeant.

Date of death: March 2, 1990.

Thryce!

Heart pounding in her ears, Lara scanned the obituary. *Eugenia, age 82, died at Pine Hollow Nursing Home in Whisker Jog on March 2, 1990.* Pine Hollow.

That sounded familiar. Where had she heard it recently?

She continued reading through the obit.

Eugenia was survived by her grandson, Todd Thryce, and her son, Tate Thryce. Her other son, Holland Thryce, Jr., and her husband, Holland Thryce—philanthropist and founder of The Bakers Thryce—had both predeceased her.

The remainder of the obit blurred before Lara's eyes. How did Holland Thryce's widow end up dying in a nursing home? Surely she'd had the means to be cared for at home? Even if she'd required nurses around the clock, the family hadn't exactly been struggling to make ends meet.

Lara swallowed. She perused the rest quickly. The obit went on to cite numerous charities with which Eugenia had been involved. Children's hospitals, cancer research groups, and her parish church had all benefited from her generosity. It was the last one that made Lara's breath halt in her throat.

Eugenia was also a frequent contributor to charities for homeless cats. Her own cat, Angelica, was her source of inspiration as well as her constant companion.

There was no mention of a cat being with her when she died. But then, why would there be? She died in a nursing home.

Lara pressed the button to copy the page with the obituary. Once she got home she could read it again, slowly and more thoroughly. She slipped her arms through her jacket, then reached over to retrieve the copy from the output tray. A black nose attached to a golden head suddenly plopped into her lap. The nose sniffed her pocket, and a furry paw clawed at her jacket. "Oh my gosh!"

"Sorry, so sorry." A young woman with a nervous look, a dark braid trailing down her back, tugged at the dog's halter. "Lucy Goosey, you know better than that. We don't help ourselves to people's pockets."

Lara patted her pocket and laughed. She'd forgotten that the peanut butter fudge was in there! She pulled it out and showed it to the woman. The dog, a gorgeous golden retriever, eyed it hungrily. "No wonder she was curious. I'm sure she smelled the peanut butter."

"Again, I'm so sorry," the woman said. "Lucy is my therapy dog—I'm an epileptic. She's still in training, but she sure does love her treats."

"She's fine," Lara said. "May I pet her?"

The woman grinned. "Oh, she'd love that. Scratch between her ears and you'll be her buddy for life."

With two fingers, Lara rubbed the golden fur between Lucy's ears. The dog's liquid brown eyes gazed up at her with pure adoration. "She's beautiful," Lara said. "I'd give her a piece of fudge, but I'm sure it isn't good for her."

The young woman reached into the pocket of her corduroy slacks. "Here, give her this." She handed Lara a dog cookie shaped like a mailperson.

Lara fed the dog treat to Lucy. The dog swallowed it in one gulp and swished her golden tail, then began to whine.

"What's wrong, Lucy?" her owner cooed. She tightened her grip on the nylon leash attached to the retriever's halter.

Lucy tugged at it and whined even louder, jerking the leash away from her owner.

"Stop that, Lucy," the woman scolded, then looked at Lara. "She probably has to pee. I'd better take her outside. It was nice meeting you!" Lara waved goodbye with a confused smile, then removed her copy from the machine.

Another furry face gazed up at her—this one with turquoise eyes. Lara jumped. She understood now what had alarmed Lucy.

"You frightened that poor dog, you know," she whispered to Blue. Blue reached up and clawed at the obituary, then sat and stared directly into Lara's eyes.

"This is the right one, isn't it?" Lara said softly. Blue blinked, then lowered her head to her forepaws.

Lara glanced around. Seated at one of the microfiche machines, a curly-haired teenage boy gawked at her as if she'd grown a second head. She gave him a disarming smile, shoved the obituary into her tote, and scurried off to the front desk to pay.

* * * *

"Find what you were looking for?" Ellie Croteau said flatly, with an air of clear disinterest.

"I think so." For once Lara was grateful that Ellie wasn't the nosy type. She didn't want anyone to know whose obituary she'd copied.

"Let's see. You were at machine number seven, right? That'll be fifty cents for the copy."

Lara dug two quarters out of the change purse she kept in her tote.

"Need a receipt?"

"Yes, please." Lara hoisted her tote back onto her shoulder.

"Lara?" A voice from behind startled her.

She swerved to see Whisker Jog High School's principal standing behind her.

"Oh, hi...Andy Casteel, right?" She took the receipt from Ellie, then slid over to one side so he could check out the book he was clutching—the latest Dean Koontz thriller, Lara noticed. She herself was on the library's waiting list for it. Judging from its popularity, Aunt Fran's tulips would be poking through the ground before she'd ever get the chance to read it.

The barest hint of a woodsy aftershave wafted over Lara. Casteel set the book on the counter and gave Ellie his library card. "It's certainly nice seeing you again. So, you're friends with Gideon Halley."

Something about his tone irritated Lara. Was he fishing? Trying to find out how close she was with Gideon? She stepped slightly away from him.

"That I am," she said. "He mentioned that you're the principal at Whisker Jog High. That must be a stressful job."

Casteel nodded a quick thank you at Ellie, then took his card and snatched up the book. He moved away from the counter, then stopped and peered down at Lara from a height of at least six feet three. His sheer bulk, along with his shock of white hair and piercing gaze, made Lara wonder if his students were intimidated by him.

He laughed, displaying a mouthful of overwhitened teeth. "I guess it is, but I've been doing it for so long I don't notice anymore. Just part of the daily routine."

"Still, it must have been so horrible when that poor woman died at the cookie contest Saturday. Not that it had anything to do with the school," she added quickly, "but I heard Miss Plouffe used to teach there."

Andy looked at Lara for a long moment, as if he were memorizing her features. "The school is cooperating with the police in every way possible. Naturally, if Gladys's sad death was *not* a tragic accident, we want to get to the bottom of it."

His spiel sounded too careful, as if he'd practiced it, Lara thought. "Mr. Casteel—"

"It's Andy," he said. "I hope you don't mind that I called you Lara." Again, the bright white smile.

"No, not at all. Andy, do you think we could chat for a few minutes? Something's been bothering me a lot. Now that I've run into you, I'm hoping you can help clear up a few things for me."

Andy's jaw tensed slightly, as if he were debating with himself. Then his face relaxed, and he said, "Certainly, Lara. I'd be glad to answer any questions I can, so long as confidentiality isn't required."

It sounded like he was hedging, but Lara would take what she could get. "Of course. I understand."

Andy glanced around the library. "I'm just trying to see if there's a free table. Oh—there's one over in the periodical area no one's using. Shall we grab it?" He held out one bear-like arm in the direction of the magazine section.

"Oh, sure, that would be great. Thanks."

Lara went ahead of him into the periodical area. The table was in an alcove of sorts, which made it perfect for a private discussion. She draped her tote over the back of a chair and sat down. Library patrons occupied the remaining three tables. They tapped away at laptops or flipped through magazines.

Andy set his Koontz book on the table, then sat facing her. "Now, what can I help you with, Lara?"

Now that she had his attention, she wasn't sure how to begin. "Andy, I didn't go to high school in Whisker Jog, so I never got to know any of the teachers. My friend Sherry Bowker did, though."

"I remember Sherry. She and her mom run the coffee shop." He frowned, the lines in his face deepening. "Her mom baked the cookie Gladys supposedly died from. I say supposedly because, despite what the police say, I think the whole horrible mess was an accident."

"That's...very interesting." Lara paused. "So, you have every faith in Daisy Bowker's innocence?"

"I do, indeed," he said.

Keeping her voice low, Lara leaned toward him. "Andy, what bothers me is that so many people seemed to have had a grudge against Miss Plouffe. I got the impression she wasn't too well liked."

Casteel remained stone-faced. He folded his hands on the table. "There's some truth to what you're saying, Lara. But I'm sure you're aware that some teachers treat school like a popularity contest. They joke with the kids. They make their classes *fun*." He made air quotes around the word. "If it works for them, and their students learn, then that's great. More power to them. But for other teachers it's not that easy. Miss Plouffe, I'm sorry to say, was one of the less popular teachers. Given that status, she took a much different approach to teaching—she had to be firmer than most."

"Firmer," Lara said quietly. "Wasn't it a little more than that? Wasn't she more of a bully? Especially to the boys?"

The principal's face reddened. He stared down at the Koontz book. "All right look, Lara, I'll come right out and say it. Without question, Gladys was always tougher on the male students than she was on the girls. She didn't want boys taking her class, period. She was just too old-fashioned."

"Then why didn't she just resign? Retire early? Find a different career? This is the twenty-first century."

Andy smiled, then shook his head. "Come on, Lara—you're a smart woman. You know it's not that simple." He slid his hand across the table and touched her fingers. The gesture made her want to snatch back her hand, but she didn't want to interrupt his momentum. "And, not that it was fair, but she didn't have any patience for the girls who couldn't sew, either. Sewing was Gladys's first and only love. The culinary part of the class was just to satisfy the curriculum requirements. She couldn't have cared less about cooking."

That had to be why Miss Plouffe had poked fun at Sherry's sewing skills. Sherry hated sewing, and therefore wasn't a student worth teaching. Lara pulled her hand back and clasped both hands in her lap. "You seem to have known a lot about her."

Andy gave her an odd look, then glanced off at an imaginary spot on the wall. "I've known Gladys, *knew* Gladys, since I was a teenager," he said, so softly she barely heard him.

He suddenly looked vulnerable, like a lost little boy. Gladys had meant something to him. Lara was sure of it.

Had they been involved romantically? Was that why Andy's wife left him? Somehow Lara couldn't picture the two as a couple. But, as she'd learned the hard way, anything was possible.

Either that or Gladys was blackmailing him over something. Everyone had a secret or two, didn't they? Lara's was a cat no one else could see. Did Miss Plouffe know something about Andy Casteel that he didn't want revealed to the world?

"There's one thing I don't understand," Lara said. "Even with all the complaints against Miss Plouffe, she never lost her job. Why was that?"

Andy glanced around to see if anyone was within earshot, then gave a quick shake of his head. Lara waited. She sensed he was wrestling with a decision. *To tell or not to tell*—is that what he was thinking?

His eyes became glassy, and he cleared his throat. "Lara, I'm a fairly good judge of character. In my job I have to be. My gut tells me you're a trustworthy person. Someone who can keep a confidence."

Uh-oh.

"I'm going to tell you something I've never told anyone, and I'm serious when I say that."

"Okay," she said, her pulse throbbing in her veins.

Andy apparently sensed her hesitation. He smiled. "Don't worry, it's nothing bad. It's just a glimpse into Gladys's history—and mine—that'll help you see where I was coming from."

Lara felt every muscle in her body relax. "Sure. Go ahead, Andy."

"I grew up in the same neighborhood as Gladys. My folks didn't have much, but they were hard workers. There was a nine-year age difference between my younger brother and me, so I always got stuck babysitting him after school. I hated it. To make matters worse, Artie was the most hyperactive kid you ever saw. He was like a jumping bean, always in constant motion. I swear, I wanted to put a leash on him."

Lara smiled, encouraging him to continue.

"Anyway, being your typical, self-centered teenage boy, I always did the least amount of work I could get away with. So this one day, after school, I dragged Artie with me to the park. Some of my buds were there, shooting hoops. I plunked Artie on the grass with a couple of his action figures and told him to play quietly and stay put."

"Oh boy."

"Yeah, oh boy. So anyway, I'm having a great old time shooting hoops with my friends. We got kind of rowdy, like we always did. I never even saw Artie disappear. Next thing I know, there's a squeal of brakes that made my heart jump into my throat. I look toward the street and see this pink box flying through the air like a missile. And there's Gladys Plouffe—she's racing across the roadway toward Artie, who's walking directly into the path of an oncoming car. Lara, you should have seen her. She tackled him like she was an NFL linebacker. They both landed on the grass at the edge of the park. That car missed my brother by a cat's whisker." He held up his thumb and forefinger and pinched them together.

"I think my heart would have stopped!"

"Mine dropped into my sneakers. Worst of all, I couldn't even see Artie. Gladys's compact little body was covering his entirely, except for one shoeless little foot that stuck out from under her leg."

Lara pictured the scene in her head. "You must have been so terrified. I can't even imagine it."

"I was beyond terrified." He chuckled and shook his head. "My insides froze up like one big Popsicle. And the driver of the car, when he finally got out, was shaking uncontrollably. 'Who's supposed to be watching that kid?' he screamed at me. By that time, my buddies had all rushed over to check out the commotion."

"It must have been sheer chaos," Lara said.

"What scared me most was that Gladys hadn't moved. For one horrible moment I thought she and Artie were both goners. I reached down to pull her off Artie when she stiff-armed the ground and hoisted herself upward. I'll never forget her face. It was red with fury. She reached down and jerked Artie up by the collar, pushing him around until his feet were planted on the ground. 'Which of you morons is supposed to be watching this little twerp?' she sputtered out."

Lara couldn't help smiling. Miss Plouffe's snarky personality had apparently been cultivated at an early age. "What about Artie—was he okay?"

"Oh, he was fine, the little monster. A bit numb from shock, with two badly scraped knees." Andy's expression sobered.

Wow, Lara thought. Miss Plouffe as lifesaver—who'd have imagined it?

"You mentioned a pink box. What was that all about?" Lara asked him.

Andy sighed. "Poor Gladys. It was her precious sewing box. I found out later she'd been on her way to catch the bus to Mrs. Thryce's house. She did a lot of sewing for the old woman."

That got Lara's attention.

"Did her sewing box survive the ordeal?"

Andy winced, as if the memory hurt. "I retrieved it from the side of the road and handed it to her. She snatched it out of my hand like I was going to contaminate it. I'll never forget her face that day, Lara—it was actually kind of pretty back then. She opened the box so tenderly I thought the crown jewels must be in there. When she saw the jumbled mess inside—needles, threads, you name it, all clumped together—her face collapsed, and tears fell down her cheeks. I asked if I could help her straighten it out, but she slapped my hand away and told me to go...well, you can fill in the blank."

Lara could. Easily. "Did she at least have a decent home life?"

"No, I'm afraid she didn't. It was just her and her mom, and her mom drank. A lot. If Gladys hadn't taught herself to sew, they'd have probably been homeless. Gladys kept the family together, such as it was, doing alterations and making clothes for people. Sad part? Everyone said the mom was a super nice lady. She just couldn't get sober, no matter how hard she tried."

"That *is* sad," Lara said. She suspected that Mrs. Thryce had paid Gladys well for her sewing services. Was it the generosity of the Thryce family that had kept the Plouffes' heads from sinking below the water?

"Andy, how old would you say Gladys was when she rescued your brother?"

Andy mulled over her question. "Well, let's see. I was about fifteen. I'd say she was twenty-three, twenty-four?"

And she was still sewing for Mrs. Thryce.

"When did she start teaching?"

"Now that," he said, "I'm not sure of. I went off to Plymouth State when Artie was in fifth grade, I think. Frankly, I lost track of her. I heard she left town for a while, too. I'm not sure how she even paid for college. There were rumors floating around, nasty ones. Some people thought she'd had a secret lover, but I doubt it was true. No one got close to Gladys. *No one.*"

Lara was stunned at how much she'd learned from Andy. Not that it had anything to do with Miss Plouffe's death. That was still a mystery. But knowing Miss Plouffe's history, what she'd endured as a kid and as a young woman, helped Lara gain a better perspective of her. She felt guilty, now, for having condemned the woman based only on the opinions of others—even if some of those others were Lara's nearest and dearest.

"Make no mistake, Lara," Andy said, his voice hoarse. "Gladys saved my brother's life that day. If he'd been killed or crippled, it would have been my fault. And it would have torn my family apart." He swallowed, his eyes burning into hers with a silent plea. "Does that help any? Does it help you understand?"

"It tells me everything," Lara said. "I heard you mention to Gideon that you lost your brother recently. I'm so sorry."

"Thank you. And Lara, I want to say one last thing. Please...*please* don't think that I didn't try reasoning with Gladys about her attitude. God knows I did, more times than I can count. And each time, she'd be better for a while. But then she'd backslide, right into her old ways. As I mentioned, she was unforgiving with the boys. But keep in mind, not everyone hated Gladys. A few of the girls, the ones who loved to sew, praised her name to holy heaven. Some of them said she was the best teacher they ever had. No matter what Gladys did, she always had a small cadre of kids who stuck up for her. For every student who hated her, there was another one who adored her."

"All girls, I assume."

He nodded. "All girls. Several years ago, one of the kids put a garter snake in her hand-sewn purse. The purse was a colorful, flowered thing she designed herself, with all sorts of hidden pockets and snaps. I wasn't in the room when she found the snake, but I heard the scream from all the way down the hall. Afterward, I found out she burned the pocketbook. But even after all that, she didn't quit. She switched to using a fanny pack, or whatever they call it, so no one could get to it. I never saw her carry a purse again. Gladys always found ways to put up walls to protect herself."

Like eating alone in her classroom to avoid shellfish contamination.

Lara understood, now, why Andy had never been able to bring the hammer down on Miss Plouffe.

It also confirmed the connection between Gladys and Mrs. Thryce.

Mrs. Thryce—who died in the nursing home. Had any of her family members been present? Had Todd been there when she passed?

Lara glanced at the wall clock. Andy had been generous with his time. He answered all her nosy questions, and more. Nonetheless, she felt guilty for having corralled him into spilling his private story.

"Andy, did you know any of the Thryces?"

"Not really. They didn't exactly travel in our circles. But there wasn't much to the family, when I think about it. Todd's dad and mom both died sort of young, and Todd ended up living with his grandmother. There was an uncle, as I recall, but he lived out of town. Rumor had it the old lady threw him out, but who knows? People love to gossip about rich people."

"That they do." She glanced again at the clock. "Oh good glory, I've taken up twenty minutes of your time."

His gaze grew distant. "Ah, Lara, not to worry. I spend my evenings reading reports and answering complaints from parents. This has been a welcome diversion." He rose from his chair and held out his hand.

The loneliness in his eyes trickled into his handshake. "Gideon is a very lucky man. I hope he knows that."

Lara felt a surge of heat suffuse her face. "That's a nice thing to say, Andy. May I ask one last question?"

"You surely may," he said gallantly.

"Who teaches home ec at the school now?"

"No one. One of the reasons I encouraged Gladys to retire when she did was that I knew the school board was going to drop it from the curriculum. Most schools don't even teach it anymore. Or if they do, they call it something like Life Skills. Anyway, I sure as heck didn't want to be the one to tell her the class was being eliminated. Easier to let her believe the board dropped the class because they knew that once she retired, she'd be irreplaceable."

"You're a kind man, Andy Casteel."

"Nah. Just a former teacher who's grateful for the good things life has given him."

Lara thanked him again, and they parted. Aunt Fran was probably wondering what she'd been doing all this time. Not that she had to explain herself. Her aunt was good about respecting her privacy.

She had two final tasks to complete before leaving the library. With Andy having interrupted her at the desk, she'd nearly forgotten. She located a copy of *Rebecca* in the fiction section and pulled it off the shelf.

"Hey, Ellie, I'm back," Lara said, sliding her borrowed book across the counter. "I'm turning this one in and checking this one out."

Ellie tapped her wristwatch and scowled. "God, is it only seven thirty-five?" She gave Lara an embarrassed smile. "Sorry. I'm extra tired tonight." She eyed the cover of *Treats for Your Cat* and rolled her eyes. "I'll bet this was a real page-turner."

"It was actually helpful, but I want to ask you something. Would you be able to check your records to see who borrowed it in March of nineteen ninety?"

"Nineteen ninety? You mean like, almost thirty years ago?"

"Yeah, I know it's a long shot."

"Not just a long shot," Ellie said. "Even if we could track it back that far, there's a state law prohibiting us from giving you the info. Any special reason you need it?"

"Not really," Lara fibbed. "Curiosity, mostly."

Ellie took Lara's card and checked out *Rebecca*, then returned her card to her. "Then I guess you're out of luck. Sorry."

"Hey, thanks, Ellie. I tried, right?"

"Yeah, no harm in trying."

Lara thanked Ellie, then bundled up her jacket, tucking her scarf tightly around her neck. The weather app on her phone said it was nine degrees outside.

When she got into the Saturn, she cranked the engine. It groaned, but it started. *Thank heaven.*

She was putting on her seat belt when her phone dinged with a text. She dug it out of her tote, pulled off a glove, and tapped it open. The message, accompanied by a photo, was from Aunt Fran:

No need to open the gifts from your mom. Valenteena did it for you.

Lara enlarged the pic, then laughed until tears spilled down her cheeks. The photo showed Valenteena stretched out on the floor, the spaghetti strap of a lacy red negligee draped over one furry ear. The rest of the garment was wrapped around the little cat like a flimsy, see-through blanket.

"Oh, Teena, my sweet little valentine, you definitely made my day."

She could only imagine the mess Teena had made ripping open the boxes.

One more thing to do, she told herself.

Lara stuck her phone back in her tote and headed for home.

Chapter 23

Lara held up the flimsy bit of nylon to the golden glow of the lampshade. She swung it back and forth like a flag. "Good glory, Aunt Fran. What was my mother thinking? I could read the paper through this thing!"

She'd rescued the nightie from Teena's clutches, only to find it embellished with dozens of punctures.

Aunt Fran sat on the sofa with Dolce curled in her lap. Snowball's head and forepaws nestled on her aunt's shoulder, her back end resting on the top of the sofa. She gazed at Lara with her distinctive eyes, as if she were listening to every word.

"I wouldn't have thought it possible," Aunt Fran said with a chuckle, "but Teena made that nightie even more see-through than it was."

Lara folded the nightie into a neat square, which ended up about the size of a business card. A horrible thought gripped her. "Aunt Fran, the nightie was definitely from Mom, right? You saw the name on the tag?"

"Don't worry, it was. There's a gift labeled to you from Rodney, but it's fairly heavy. There are two other boxes from your mom, but I rescued those before Teena got her teeth into them. I stuck everything at the top of the coat closet for safekeeping."

"Oh, that's a relief. Thanks." Lara plopped onto her favorite chair and dangled her legs over the side. "I guess I'll have to thank Mom...eventually. Maybe I'll wait till after Christmas."

Purrcival meandered into the room, assessed the seating arrangements, then leaped onto Lara's chest. "Oomph. You're getting heavy, baby boy. I think you've been eating too many of my Cat Nips." She rubbed his head, triggering a sweet, guttural purr.

"Did you have any luck at the library?" Aunt Fran asked.

"I did. Not only did I find the obituary I think we've been looking for, but I also had a very informative chat with the high school principal."

"Principal Casteel?" Aunt Fran looked surprised. "Do you know him?" Lara tickled Purrcy under the chin. "I met him on Monday when Gid and I were having dinner at The Irish Stew. He was on his way out when he spotted Gideon, who just happens to be his attorney."

"Ah, and then you bumped into him at the library."

"My timing was perfect. I was paying for my microfiche copy just as he was checking out the Dean Koontz book I've been waiting an eternity to read. I brought up Miss Plouffe's horrible death, you know, as kind of a conversation starter. Turned out he had quite a lot to say about her." Lara didn't want to relate the conversation. Andy had confided in her only because he'd had faith in her discretion. "Suffice it to say, he'd had his reasons for not getting her fired. But he did admit that most of the kids despised her, especially the boys who took her class."

"I never taught at the high school, so I didn't know her," Aunt Fran said. "But she did have a reputation, and it wasn't a glowing one. Did the principal offer any insights as to who might have wanted to poison Gladys?"

"No, but he's sure Daisy had nothing to do with it. He's not even convinced it was foul play. In his mind it was a tragic accident."

"I see. Well, I hope he turns out to be right. That would be best for everyone involved. Tell me about the obituary you found."

Holding Purrcy close, Lara swung her legs around and plunked them on the floor. "You're not going to believe this, but the obit I found was for Mrs. Eugenia Thryce."

Aunt Fran's eyes flicked to Lara. "Old Mrs. Thryce? Holland Thryce's widow?"

"Yup. She was eighty-two when she died."

Aunt Fran reached up and cupped Snowball's head. The cat closed her eyes and rubbed against her hair. "I'm curious, Lara. What made you go back and search for more obituaries? I thought you were going to investigate Sarah Nally first."

Lara shifted her weight in the chair so that Purrcy could get more lap space. "Something told me she wasn't the right one. It's hard to explain. It was just a feeling I had. Anyway, the woman at the library suggested I research the newspapers beyond a few days after the date of death. And sure enough, Eugenia Thryce died on March second, but her obit wasn't published until March nineteenth."

"Seventeen days later," her aunt murmured. "I still don't get—"

"Aunt Fran, it doesn't matter how I found it. The obit says she was a big supporter of cat charities. Her own cat, Angelica, had been her inspiration."

Aunt Fran's face paled. She closed her eyes and rested her head back. She remained that way for so long that Lara wondered if she'd dozed off. Then she sat up abruptly and stared at Lara.

"Lara, there's something very wrong about all of this," her aunt said, and ticked off points on her fingers. "A letter written in 1990, which by some serendipitous accident happens to fall into your hands, describes a murder, victim unknown, that took place on the day you were born."

Lara nodded, her heart drumming her ribs.

Her aunt continued. "Nearly thirty years later, Gladys Plouffe dies from a tainted cookie at a competition sponsored by Todd Thryce's company. And Todd's grandmother, Eugenia Thryce, died on the day you were born."

And she loved cats.

"I know," Lara said in a shaky voice. "It's *Twilight Zone* material, right?"

"No, it has nothing to do with the *Twilight Zone.* Something else is going on, Lara. Is there something you're not telling me? Is there something else I should know?"

And so it all came down to it—a lie.

A big fat hairball of a lie Lara had no choice but to tell.

"If I could explain it better, I would," Lara said. She tried to suppress the tremor in her voice, but she knew that it squeezed through. "Aunt Fran, sometimes I...sense things. That's the best way I can describe it."

"You mean you have premonitions?" her aunt asked, her eyebrows dipping toward her nose.

"No. A premonition is a feeling that something is about to happen. What I get is more like...a feeling that something *has* happened."

Aunt Fran sat back and stared at her niece, her eyes brimming with worry. "How many times has this happened to you, Lara?"

She shrugged, her stomach churning with discomfort. "I don't know. A few, I guess. I never really stopped to count."

Aunt Fran looked as if someone had slapped her. "I'm sorry, Lara. I didn't know. There were times when I wondered, but… In a way, it explains a few things. Like Hesty."

Lara nodded. "Exactly," she said quietly. "Like Hesty."

Hesty was a kindly, local man who'd applied to adopt one of their cats, Frankie, at the beginning of the summer. Lara had sensed from the beginning that the adoption was doomed, but she couldn't explain why to Aunt Fran. A certain blue-eyed Ragdoll had warned her against the match, but there was no way she could tell that to her aunt without sounding insane.

Blue had been right—the adoption wasn't to be. Frankie ended up in a different home with a loving mom, where he'd been thriving ever since. It was another successful placement for the shelter.

"Lara, I really wish you'd told me all this before," Aunt Fran said. "If we could have talked about it..."

Lara gave a slight shrug. "I know, and I understand your feelings. But there were times when I thought I was going crazy. It's not the easiest thing to talk about, especially to someone who's close to you."

She was relieved when Valenteena sprang onto the arm of her chair. Lara deflected any further questions by turning her attention to the cat. "And you, miss lacy pants." She tickled the black heart under the cat's chin. "What kind of trouble are you getting into now?"

Valenteena plopped onto Lara's lap and batted a paw at Purrcy. Instead of giving in to the demands of the princess and leaping down, he feigned sleep. After a few more swipes, Teena settled in beside him, licked his ear, and curled a paw around his neck.

Her aunt smiled at their antics, and they switched conversational gears. Lara was relieved that her aunt wasn't going to dwell on the topic. It was hard enough to make sense of a ghost cat, let alone explain her to someone else.

After several more minutes, Lara remembered she hadn't eaten a single bite for dinner. She went into the kitchen, dug out one of the leftover pizza slices from a few days ago, and popped it into the microwave.

Balancing the plate with her pizza slice in one hand and a glass of cola in the other, Lara poked her head into the large parlor. "I'm going to work in my studio for a while," she told her aunt. "Yell if you need me."

Aunt Fran turned to her niece, her eyes shiny. "Thank you, Lara, for confiding in me. I know that wasn't easy to talk about."

Inwardly, Lara winced. She hadn't confided in her aunt, not really. She'd held back the biggest puzzle piece—the part about her spirit cat. She nodded, then ducked into her studio.

Someday, she told herself.

Lara set her meal down on one side of her worktable. She bit off a slab of pizza, then slugged it back with a swig of cola. Over the past few hours, the idea for the watercolor had taken shape in her head. Almost without realizing it, she'd been creating it in her mind's eye.

She prepared her easel with a fresh sheet of paper, then set up her tools—water, brushes, tiles for blending colors—and, of course, the paints themselves. The predominant shades would be brown, ivory, and sage. Touches of lilac, maroon, and gold would brighten the faces and add depth and texture to the setting.

Lara flexed her fingers, eager to begin.

Two hours later her pizza sat cold, but she had the basic shapes completed. Faces were formed, though the expressions were still bland. The eyes were the most challenging—they had to reflect the trappings of the heart. She needed time, and a decent night's sleep, before she tackled the project again. If she could pull it off and complete the final touches by Christmas, it would be a miracle.

It would also be the best thing she'd ever painted.

Chapter 24

Friday was an adoption day, so Lara needed to be prepared. Daisy usually baked the cookies they served to prospective adopters, but only a half dozen remained in the freezer. Since they were never sure how many visitors would show up, Lara liked to be prepared with at least a dozen, with an extra dozen in reserve.

After performing her usual cat duties, she bundled up and headed down to the coffee shop. A pale sun struggled to break through the dense clouds. The sidewalks had been shoveled, but treacherous icy patches remained.

Lara hadn't talked to Sherry since she'd heard about Daisy's good news. She hoped the two had spent the prior evening celebrating with a bottle of bubbly. Lara intended to ask Daisy about supplying more cookies, but first she wanted to gauge her mood. After the horror of the past week, the poor woman might never bake cookies again.

She smelled them even before she opened the door. The aromas of vanilla and almond swirled around her—a mouthwatering hint that everything was back to normal. She hoped.

Relief swept through Lara when she spotted Daisy bouncing from table to table taking breakfast orders. She smiled and waved, and Daisy grinned and waggled her fingers in return.

"Oh my gosh, that smells good," Lara said, dropping onto her usual stool.

Sherry looked especially nice today. Her raven-colored hair had been blown into soft curls, and her cheeks glowed with a rosy shade of blush. Her eyes had a sparkle that had been missing for several days. Lara was glad to see that her friend's chipper personality had resurfaced.

"As you can see, we're slammed today," Sherry said, beaming like a newly discovered star. She poured coffee into a mug for Lara.

"I smelled the cookies from outside," Lara said. "Any chance you can put a dozen aside for me?"

"Already done," Sherry said. "Mom was in here at four thirty this morning, baking her tail off. Want a blueberry muffin?"

"Does a bear want salmon?"

Sherry returned a minute later with a warm muffin, two pats of butter melting beside it. "David and I are going to have 'the talk' tonight," she said in a low voice. She made finger quotes around the words. "I've got my speech all prepared."

"It's good to be prepared," Lara said. "But there's also something to be said for spontaneity."

"Yeah, I know. I'll probably forget my speech anyway and say something dopey."

"If it's sincere, then it's not dopey." Lara broke off a piece of her muffin and popped it into her mouth. "Mmm, heavenly."

Daisy came up behind Lara and gave her a squishy hug. "Oh, I'm so glad to see you. You should have brought Fran with you!"

Lara grinned. "I left her in charge of the cats. Tough job, but someone has to do it."

"Speaking of cats, I baked you a fresh batch of cookies especially for adoption day. Gotta run!"

"Wait till you see them," Sherry said with a sly look. "I'll go get 'em."

Sherry returned a half minute later with a foil pan protected by a snap-on plastic top. The feline-shaped cookies inside the pan made Lara gasp. Each cookie was frosted with a different whimsical design. "Oh...my gosh," she squeaked. "These are unbelievable."

"I know, right?" Sherry set them down carefully next to Lara's plate. She pointed to a black-and-white one. "I told Mom about the heart under Teena's chin. Didn't she do it perfectly?"

"Oh, yes she did. And this one with the kaleidoscope design must be Purrcy!" Lara pressed the heel of her hand to one leaky eye. "If you guys don't stop doing such nice things for us, I'll have to buy stock in a tissue company."

"Oh, just chill, will ya? We love you and Fran." Sherry's smile faltered, then flattened into a frown. "Mom should have won that competition, Lara. It's not fair. She could've used that prize money."

"I know, Sher, and I agree. But after what happened, there was no way they could judge the cookies fairly. It's no one's fault except—" She stopped and looked at Sherry.

"Except the killer's," Sherry finished, and shook her head. "Sorry, I don't mean to be a downer, but I am still seriously ticked about the whole freakin' thing."

Lara wasn't exactly thrilled herself. If the cookies had been intentionally tainted, then it was a diabolical act. It meant someone had been determined to harm Gladys.

Harm her or kill her? Not that it mattered. The result had been the same. She took a long sip of her coffee, her mind skittering over all the things she wanted to accomplish today. Adoptions would start around one—that is, if anyone showed up. And she was itching to get back to the painting. She'd even awakened during the night with ideas for how to improve it. Last of all, she hoped to find time to visit the nursing home where Eugenia Thryce had died. It wasn't likely anyone would remember her, or her death, but she wouldn't know until she tried.

Another thought nudged her. Wouldn't Todd Thryce remember his grandmother's death? By Lara's estimation, he looked to be in his late forties or early fifties. He'd have been a young man, perhaps even a college student, when she passed.

The problem was, what excuse could she use for asking him about her?

Sherry waved a hand in front of Lara's face. "Earth to Lara," she said.

"Sorry." Lara laughed. "I was in outer space."

"Yeah, no kidding. What I was saying is that Mom and I already decided we're not going to use The Bakers Thryce flour anymore. Which is a shame, because it's a quality product." Sherry snatched up the coffeepot and topped off Lara's mug. "Someone dropped the ball at that stupid event, Lara. I mean, who was supposed to be in charge? Did you see anyone who looked like they were running the show? No," she sputtered. "It was a flippin' free-for-all."

Lara waited for her friend to finish her diatribe, then took another sip of hot coffee. She had to admit—there hadn't seemed to be any one person in charge that day. Maybe the teacher who'd broken both her ankles was supposed to be the coordinator? The woman's job as judge had been dumped, at the last minute, in poor Miss Plouffe's lap. But who'd been initially selected to run the event?

"Hey, sorry," Sherry said. "I didn't mean to unload my anger on you. But you do make a good sounding board."

"That's my job. BFF and sounding board." Lara polished off her muffin and wiped her lips with a napkin. "Sher, I'm going to run. Today's an adoption day, so there's lots to do."

"Mom said not to let you pay for the cookies. Those are her gift to you for helping out in the kitchen. Your breakfast is on the house, too."

Lara sighed. She knew it would be fruitless to argue. For today, she'd accept the cookies and the free breakfast.

Somehow, she'd make it up to them in the future.

* * * *

Back at the house, Lara scooped and freshened all the litter boxes and cleaned and replenished the cats' water bowls. She was nearly finished when she got a call from Kayla.

"Hey, I'm in between classes, but I wanted to ask if I could work for a few hours this afternoon instead of tomorrow. I can come over right after my twelve thirty chemistry exam."

"Uh...sure," Lara said. "Any reason for the switch?"

"My gram wants me to take her Christmas shopping tomorrow at the mall in Concord. I figured I'd better do it with her this weekend while the weather's looking clear. We never know when the next blizzard might hit."

"You got that right. I'll be glad to have you. We can work on next Sunday's reading day."

"Oops. Good idea. I almost forgot about that."

Reading day at the shelter was held on the third Sunday of every month. It was an event that ran from noon to four, in which kids came with a book—or borrowed one from the shelter—and read aloud to one of the cats. In the three months since they'd started the program, it had gained popularity so quickly they'd had to limit the reading times to half-hour segments. Munster, with his friendly persona, was a favorite of the kids, but Purrcy and Twinkles had also been willing participants. Each child was required to be accompanied by an adult. The only glitch so far? Space. With only the back porch available, only one child at a time could participate. It was a problem Lara had been wanting to discuss with her aunt, but she was putting it off until after the holidays.

She forced her thoughts back to the present. "Wait till you see the cookies Daisy made!" Lara told Kayla.

"Cookies?" Kayla gasped through the phone. "I'm surprised you even want to *look* at a cookie, let alone eat one. Speaking of which, how's the investigation going?"

Lara told Kayla about Daisy being officially crossed off the suspect list.

"Oh, that's such good news! Do the cops still think someone poisoned Gladys Plouffe?"

"I'm not sure," Lara said carefully. "Either way, it's not something I want to get involved in." *Been there, almost got killed through that.*

"Yeah, I don't blame you for that," Kayla said. "Hey, I'll try to get there by two or so. Let's hope we get some possibles today."

They disconnected, and Lara went into her studio. She studied the painting she'd started the night before. Sometimes, when she began a project in the evening, it looked like a mess to her the next day. This time was different.

Her heart clenched when she looked at the partially completed watercolor. She'd captured the mood she was aiming for—warmth, security, and a touch of mystery. The faces had to be filled in, and the background needed more detail. But the work she'd done the previous evening had been spot-on.

Lara breathed out a sigh. Should she work on the painting for another few hours? Or try to get information from the nursing home where Eugenia Thryce had died?

She opted for the nursing home. There were too many coincidences for Lara to ignore.

Todd's grandmother had died on the day Lara was born, and then the letter fell out of the library book only days before Miss Plouffe was murdered.

A sudden chill washed over Lara. Had a certain blue-eyed cat been responsible for Lara finding that letter?

Only Lara, Aunt Fran, Kayla, and Gideon were aware of the letter. What harm would it do to make a visit to the nursing home? The chances were overwhelmingly high that no one who worked there when Eugenia Thryce died was even still employed there.

Lara pulled Eugenia's obituary out of her tote. She made another copy on her printer, then left it on her worktable.

Pine Hollow. She Googled it and pulled up the address. It was located on the outskirts of Whisker Jog, near the Moultonborough town line. She'd probably driven past it dozens of times but hadn't paid any attention. Lara programmed the address into her phone, then went into the kitchen to let Aunt Fran know of her plan.

Her aunt was standing at the counter, whipping up some pumpkin-colored batter in her favorite Pyrex bowl. Dolce snoozed on her sneaker.

"Be careful. Cat underfoot," Lara said.

Aunt Fran smiled. "There always is. How were Daisy and Sherry this morning?"

"About a thousand times better than they were yesterday. What a change of mood in the coffee shop! Daisy was chirping like a spring robin. And wait till you see the cookies she made for us."

"My hands are full, but I'll look at them later. I'm making those pumpkin squares you all liked so much at Thanksgiving."

"For the chief's birthday dinner?"

"Exactly."

Lara inhaled the air, as if she could already smell the finished product. "Save me a couple, okay? Those things were out of this world."

"You got it." With her forefinger, Aunt Fran swiped the excess batter off her spatula and set the utensil in the sink. "So, what are you up to now?"

Lara gave her a rundown of her planned events for the day, including Kayla switching days and working in the afternoon.

"It's always a joy to have her here," Aunt Fran said. "We should get her a small something for Christmas, don't you think?" She pulled out a rectangular pan from the drawer beneath the oven. "She's our only employee, and she's been a godsend."

"I agree," Lara said. "Let's try to think of something fun, but not too expensive. Otherwise she might feel she has to reciprocate."

Aunt Fran set the pan on the counter. "Lara, I'm wondering if I should go with you to the nursing home. This whole thing with the letter, and now the obituary, has been so strange."

Stranger than you know.

"I hear you, but honestly, there's really no need for two of us to go. You've got a lot of Christmasy stuff to do today, and besides, I'm sure it will end up being a wild goose chase. Think about it—almost thirty years? Who's going to be there who'll remember anything? And remember, people die in nursing homes all the time."

"That they do," Aunt Fran said. "But Mrs. Thryce was a so-called pillar of the town. Even I remember that much, and I was only in my twenties when you were born."

"I got thinking about that, too. It surprised me that she died in the nursing home. I'd have thought that the Thryces, with all their dough, could've paid for twenty-four seven care for her at home."

"There could be any number of reasons. She might have been there for rehab if she'd broken a hip, or something like that."

"Yeah, I suppose."

Aunt Fran snapped her fingers. "Lara, on your way home, would you stop at the market for me? I want to get another package of that crabmeat to make the crab cakes for Jerry. I'll give you the money."

"Sure thing. And you can pay me later. Don't interrupt what you're doing."

Lara grinned when Purrcy strolled into the kitchen. He padded over to Lara and rubbed against her leg. Lara lifted him into her arms, and he put a paw on her shoulder. She pulled him close. "I'm going to cry the day you leave here," Lara said, and planted a smooch on his forehead. "But don't worry, Aunt Fran and I will make sure you get the best home possible."

"You've really gotten attached to him, haven't you?" Aunt Fran said.

Lara smiled. "Yeah, something about the way Teena kept pushing him around made my protective instincts kick in. But you know what? He doesn't let her get away with all her bullying anymore. He figured out that if he ignores her, she'll either bother someone else or curl up and snooze with him."

Lara set Purrcy on the floor, then dressed to go outside. "I shouldn't be too long," she told her aunt, looping one end of her scarf through the other. She tugged on her knitted gloves. "I want to be back by twelve thirty or so to get ready for adoption day."

"See you in a bit, then," Aunt Fran said. "And Lara?"

"Yes?"

"Be aware of who's around you, okay?"

"I will," Lara promised.

Chapter 25

Pine Hollow Nursing Home was located exactly as its name promised—nestled in a hollow set back from the road and surrounded by a thicket of fir trees.

On the way over in the car, Lara thought about how she should approach the nursing home administrator, assuming anyone would even talk to her. She'd already decided not to tell the truth. Any mention of a murder, regardless of how old, might make someone nervous...and put her at risk. She had to dream up a believable story, something that would tug at the heartstrings.

By the time she arrived at the facility, she'd concocted her tale.

The residence itself was an L-shaped, one-story clapboard building, painted white with black trim. A humongous pine-cone wreath with a bright red bow hung over the entrance door. Rhododendron bushes hunkered in a row along the front of the building, their leaves curled against the winter chill. A flagstone walkway led from the parking area to the front of the building, no doubt to give the place a homey feel.

The parking lot, which sat on the left side of the building, was nearly packed with cars. Lara figured that weekends were prime visiting hours. Lara squeezed the Saturn into a narrow slot near the rear. Luckily the lot had been plowed and sanded and was down to bare pavement.

Inside the building, the scent hit her immediately. It was a blend of disinfectant, air freshener, and whatever the home was serving for lunch that day. *Some kind of fish,* Lara guessed, with a slight wrinkle of her nose.

At the front desk, she was greeted by a receptionist with butter-colored hair twisted into a topknot, a red-lipped smile drawn widely across her face. "Good morning," the receptionist said, then glanced at her watch. "Oh my, not really—it's almost lunchtime. How may I assist you today?" "Good morning," Lara said. "I'm wondering if I could speak to the administrator for a few minutes." *Darn, why hadn't she looked up the name on the internet first?* "I won't take up too much of his, or her, time." The woman's smile shortened a bit. "May I ask what this is about?" This was the part Lara dreaded. "It's a bit hard to explain. It's about a former patient, a female patient. She lived here almost thirty years ago, and I just have a few questions."

"Thirty years?" The woman looked aghast. "I was in high school thirty years ago."

And I wasn't even born, Lara wanted to retort.

"I know, it's a long time ago. I don't know how far back your record-keeping goes—probably not that far. I thought I'd give it a try anyway."

The receptionist rose from her desk chair, which swiveled slightly as she backed up. "Wait here. I'll find someone who can help you. May I have your name?"

"Sure. It's Lara Caphart."

The woman nodded, then stalked away down a rear hallway. Lara sighed. This wasn't going to be easy.

As she waited, she glanced all around at the bland furnishings. A sage-colored sofa, flanked on either side by what looked to be maple end tables, sat in a central part of the reception area. A needlepoint pillow emblazoned with a Santa face rested at one end. In the far corner of the room, a round table boasted a Christmas tree about two feet tall, clustered with tiny bulbs and glowing with colored mini-lights.

"Ms. Caphart?"

A stout woman with a gray head of curls and wearing a navy pantsuit strode crisply toward Lara. The receptionist, whose name Lara still didn't know, scuttled meekly behind her, and then reclaimed her seat at the desk.

"Hello, I'm Olga Tully, the acting administrator."

Lara shook the woman's hand, which felt dry and powdery. "Lara Caphart. My aunt and I run the High Cliff Shelter for Cats."

The woman's brown eyes lit up. "Really? How interesting. Why don't you come down to my office? We can chat more privately there."

Lara followed the woman down the same hallway. At the end, they turned left into a narrow corridor that apparently housed the administrative offices. Olga Tully's office was the first one on the right. The door was open. "Have a seat, Ms. Caphart."

Leaving the door open, Olga Tully sat behind her smallish desk. She waved Lara into the chair opposite hers. "In case you're wondering, I have an open-door policy. My predecessor always kept her door closed. Even if she was in here, she rarely answered if someone knocked. Occasionally I'd tap on her door with a quick question, then poke my head in. She'd glare at me and snap, 'I can't talk to you now. I'm busy.' She was...a very difficult woman."

Probably why she's no longer here, Lara thought.

"Anyway, that's why I keep my door open, unless I'm discussing something confidential. I want people to feel free to come in and talk to me. I'm...hoping the directors will make this my permanent position."

"I wish you luck," Lara said.

The office was cramped but tidy, with papers and folders sitting in neat, organized piles. Scads of family pictures lined the bookshelf behind the desk. Lara squinted to get a better look, but she was too far away to make out any of the faces. She thought she spied a cat in one of the pics, but it could also be a tiny dog.

Olga Tully folded her hands on her desk and smiled. "Are you looking at Sparky?"

"Sparky?"

Olga turned and removed one of the smaller picture frames, then handed it to Lara. "My daughter's cat. I figured since you work at a shelter, you must be a cat lover."

Lara smiled at the photo. A family of five—mom, dad, three girls—sat lined up along a picnic table bench, grinning into the camera. The smallest child clutched a pure white kitten in her arms. It reminded her of Snowball. "What a nice family—and of course, an adorable kitten." She set the frame on the desk.

"Sparky turned sixteen last year, but she didn't make it to seventeen. We had to put her down because her kidneys—well, everything was failing." Her eyes glistened, and she swallowed. "I had to call my daughter in her dorm room in Maine to let her know. It was one of the hardest things I've ever had to do. And I see death on a regular basis." She pulled a tissue from a box on her desk and blotted the corner of her eye.

"I'm so sorry, Ms. Tully. I can't even imagine how difficult that was."

"Please, call me Olga."

"Olga," Lara said, "I don't want to waste too much of your time. My great-aunt Dottie, who I was very close to, died recently. Before she passed, she asked if I would try to find her half sister, Eugenia. I was shocked, frankly, because I never knew she'd had a half sister. Evidently, Eugenia had a falling out with the family when she was quite young and was cut off from all communication. Anyway, I did some Googling and found out that Eugenia died here at Pine Hollow in nineteen ninety."

"I see," Olga said. "Nineteen ninety. That's almost thirty years ago. What is it you're hoping we can do for you?"

"Well, my aunt was devastated that Eugenia never tried to get in touch with her. At one time, I guess, they'd been very close. What I'm hoping is that, well, maybe someone who took care of Eugenia back then might still work here. If so, I'd like to ask her, or him, if Eugenia ever mentioned my great-aunt Dottie. It would give me and my family comfort to know Eugenia still cared about my great-aunt. Is it possible you'd still have a file on her?"

Olga stared at Lara. "Ms. Caphart, I have to say, that's really grasping. Even long-term employees don't remember patients that far back. Besides, it would be a miracle if we could locate a file on her. By law, we're required to maintain resident files no longer than six years after their discharge."

Discharge or death, Lara thought dolefully.

Lara tried to look dejected. "Oh, dear. I was so hoping..."

The sound of squeaky wheels rolling over the carpet drifted in from the hallway.

Olga pulled her laptop over and tapped at the keys. "Thirty years is a long time, but I'll see what I can find. Can you give me her full name?"

Lara spelled Eugenia's name, including the middle name of Kay.

"Thryce," Olga said thoughtfully, tapping at her keyboard. "Not exactly a common name. I don't suppose she was related to the Thryces who founded the flour company."

"Well, that's just it, I'm not sure," Lara said. "But if I have any distant cousins out there that I've never met, I'd love to connect with them."

Olga's lips pursed. "Yes, I'm sure you would." She tapped a few more keys, then pushed her laptop to the side. "Her name isn't coming up, Ms. Caphart. I'm afraid I can't do anything for you."

Lara wondered why Olga's tone had suddenly cooled, but then she got it. Olga Tully thought Lara was trying to prove she had a distant, and very rich, relative.

The creak of wheels rolling over the carpet drew closer, then stopped abruptly in Olga's doorway. Lara turned and saw a painfully thin woman, who had to be in her seventies, holding on to a portable trash bin.

"That time again, Wanda?" Olga swung her legs out from under her desk.

"Yep." With a nod, Wanda scuttled over and scooped up the plastic wastebasket from underneath Olga's desk. She emptied the contents into her oversized barrel, then stuck the wastebasket back in place. She gave Lara an odd look—a cross between a wink and a scowl.

"Don't forget, Mrs. T—spaghetti's the alternate today. You don't wanna miss out on that."

"Thanks for reminding me, Wanda. I've been smelling those fish sticks all morning. I forgot about the spaghetti."

On her way out of the office, Wanda paused and looked at Lara. This time she definitely winked. "Ma'am, I just scrubbed the visitors' bathroom, in case you need to use it. Right down the hall." She studied Lara for what seemed like several seconds, then shuffled out the door and moved her cart in the direction from which she'd come.

Olga swiveled her chair to one side and then rose. "I'll see you out, Ms. Caphart. As I said, we really can't do anything to help you."

Lara nodded. Clearly, she was being dismissed.

"Sorry I troubled you. But...if you don't mind," she added meekly, trying to look humble, "I will pop into the bathroom. I've been drinking coffee all morning."

Olga nodded and held out her arm in that direction. Lara hurried down the hallway. When she reached the door labeled Restroom, she glanced over to be sure Olga wasn't watching her. The acting administrator was striding off in the opposite direction, apparently in pursuit of her spaghetti lunch.

Lara ducked inside the bathroom. In the next instant, she felt a strong hand shove her toward the sink. Then the door locked behind her with a metallic click.

She whirled and saw Wanda grinning at her. "I knew you looked smart."

Chapter 26

"Good glory, you scared the beans out of me," Lara said, her heart banging her ribs.

"Sorry," Wanda said. "I didn't mean to. When I heard what you were talking about to Mrs. T, I knew I better get you alone while I had the chance." She nodded toward the toilet seat. "Why don't you sit? This'll take a few."

"Thanks, but I'll stand right here," Lara said.

With that, Wanda plopped onto the commode with a grunt. "Lordy, feels good to get off my feet."

Lara instantly felt bad for the woman. At her age, shouldn't she be retired?

"I been working here almost forty years," Wanda said. "Not much room for advancement in this job, but they been good to me. Even gave me a fancy title: Chief Housekeeper. The pay sucks, but I'm up to three weeks' vacation a year. Not bad for an old dame with a tenth-grade education."

Lara smiled at the woman. In spite of her rough edges, she seemed genuine and honest.

It suddenly occurred to her how ridiculous the two of them would look to an outsider—locked in a tiny bathroom of a nursing home like a pair of conspirators.

"Anyways," Wanda said, "I heard you talking about old lady Thryce. I might be losing my teeth, but I still got great hearing." She tapped her right ear.

"Do you remember her?" Lara said, excitement rising in her voice.

"Ohhh, yeah," Wanda said. "Believe me, you would too if you'd a worked here back then. Man, she was a real pain, that one. 'Course I felt sorry for her, what with her tummy troubles and such. It's prob'ly why she was so miserable to people all the time. Got this one poor gal fired for callin' her

Eugenia instead of Mrs. Thryce. Yep, that woman sure thought she was the queen—"

"Wanda, do you remember the day she...passed?" Lara asked, issuing her a silent plea to cut to the chase.

Wanda nodded, her dull blue gaze darting off to one side. "I remember. I wasn't in the room when she crossed over—I was down the hallway. But all of a sudden, I saw the nurse on duty shut the door to her room. Which wasn't exactly unusual in this place, but then two of the aides went running in, and then the doc. Next thing I know, the paramedics come rushing in and then they're wheeling her out on a stretcher. I thought she was on her way to the hospital." Wanda shook her head soberly. "Turned out she was already gone, on her way to meet Jesus." She crossed herself. "At least I hope that's where she went."

"Do you remember the names of the aides who were working that day? Or the nurse?"

Wanda blew out a long breath. "That's what I been trying to remember. One of 'em was a skinny gal, barely weighed a hundred pounds. Pammy something-or-other, I think. Sorry, the last name escapes me. But I knew the other aide pretty well—Janice Weller. The two of us used to take our breaks together and go outside to smoke—back when I was still indulging, that is. Don't go looking for her, though. She died a couple years ago."

"What about the nurse?"

Wanda shook her head. "Nurses come and go like flies around here. None of 'em last. I'm afraid I don't have a clue who it was."

Lara sagged. She was asking this poor woman to dredge up names from nearly three decades ago. It was only natural she wouldn't remember most of them.

"You know," Wanda said, "there *is* someone else I oughta mention. I almost forgot about her. There was a young gal used to work in the kitchen. Came to the US of A with her folks from Italy when she was only a teenager. I remember, she got real friendly with old lady Thryce. For some reason the old bat liked her."

"Did the kitchen staff normally spend time with patients?"

"Nah. They delivered the meals, but that was about it. That's why it was so odd that Rosalba—" Wanda slapped her forehead. "That's it! Her name was Rosalba! Now how the heck did that jump into my brain so fast?"

Lara closed her eyes, then opened them again. A fluffy Ragdoll cat rested on Wanda's white sneakers.

"Wanda," Lara said softly, "do you remember Rosalba's last name?"

Wanda shook her head. "Gallo, Gallino...something like that. I can't be sure."

"Did you ever see anyone try to harm Mrs. Thryce? Threaten her? Raise their voice to her?"

"No, never. 'Course she didn't have many visitors that I ever seen. I saw the grandson a couple times—he visited kind of regular—but that was about it. One time I even saw him reading to her. But like I said, I only went in her room to clean. The aides woulda known a lot more."

A voice in the hallway made Lara's heart jump.

"Wanda, can I meet you someplace after work?" Lara whispered.

The woman shook her head. "Sorry. I gotta babysit my great-grands after work. Besides, there's nothing left to tell. I just emptied my brain of everything I remember." She grabbed Lara's wrist and spoke in a low tone. "But listen, I gotta tell you one last thing. That day, after they found the old lady and took her out of the room, the doc told me there was a plastic bag in the closet. He told me not to look inside, but to store it someplace cold till the grandson could get there to pick it up."

The grandson—Todd Thryce.

"Did...you look in the bag?"

"No, I did like the doc said. I knew something weird was going on, and I didn't want any part of it."

Blue had already vanished—faded like a whiff of smoke. Lara had a sinking feeling she knew what had been in the bag.

Someone twisted the door lock. A woman's voice called out, "Hello? Is this occupied?"

Wanda jumped off the commode and gave Lara an exaggerated wink. "Follow my lead."

"What...?"

Wanda swung open the door, startling the poor woman who was waiting in the wings. She turned and gave Lara the stink-eye. "Yeah, well next time don't be such a slob. You think I got nothing better to do than clean up after people like you?"

If Lara hadn't known Wanda was acting, she'd have been totally fooled. "Thank you again...and sorry," she muttered, rushing toward the lobby.

She waited until she got into her car, then burst into a fit of giggles.

Wanda had truly made her day. In more ways than one.

* * * *

Lara set a small stack of holiday-themed paper plates, cups, and napkins on the table in the meet-and-greet room. She wanted the room to look especially festive for any potential adopters. She'd already hung a balsam wreath on the entrance door to the shelter. Its huge red bow was emblazoned with tiny cats. Lara had purchased the ribbon online—a find, if there ever was one—and made the bow herself.

Daisy's cat-shaped cookies were in the kitchen, still sealed in the foil container. She'd bring them out only if someone showed up to meet the cats.

Lara's head was still reeling from what she'd learned at the nursing home. In spite of Olga Tully's curt dismissal, the delightful Wanda had supplied her with some juicy tidbits of intel.

Todd Thryce. Had he been involved in Eugenia's death? He'd been the only regular visitor, according to Wanda. The thought that he might have harmed his own grandmother made Lara's insides roll over. Had he been wild in his younger days? At odds with the woman who Wanda had said was a "real pain"?

Lara hated thinking of him as a killer. For starters, he loved cats—a big checkmark in his "plus" column. In Lara's experience, which she confessed was limited, animal lovers tended to be peaceful types. That was a big generalization, but nevertheless, she thought it was true.

Wanda had made Mrs. Thryce sound like a tyrant. Had she refused to give Todd money? He'd have been around college age when she died. Maybe she'd told him she was cutting him out of her will—giving it all to cat charities, or something like that. But why would she do that if he'd been the dedicated, caring grandson who'd visited her in the nursing home?

Any number of reasons, Lara thought with a groan. Family politics were often complex—she'd learned that firsthand.

Eugenia's will. Now that was a thought. Where could Lara find it? Were wills always made public?

A good question for Gideon. She'd text him later, after she decided how much to tell him about her strange visit to Pine Hollow.

So much to think about. She put it aside and concentrated on getting ready for adoption day. Munster, Twinkles, and Dolce had to be outfitted with blue collars for the afternoon. The collars indicated that they were in-house cats and not available for adoption. Munster, who loved meeting new people, would have been adopted several times over if he hadn't been one of Aunt Fran's original cats.

"Hey, I see you're ready for the holiday," Aunt Fran said, stepping onto the back porch. "That wreath is so pretty. Maybe we should put one on the front door, too."

"We haven't really done much decorating yet, have we?" Lara noted. Her aunt laughed. "It's just as well we don't have a tree up. Valenteena would've probably torn it to shreds by now."

"I love that little girl," Lara said wistfully. "I'm kind of worried about placing her. She really needs a special kind of home, don't you think?"

"I agree," Aunt Fran said. "The little monkey. She sure can find ways to get herself into trouble, can't she? But isn't that a typical cat? Anyway, it won't do any good to fret over it. We agreed early on that we wouldn't place any cat in a home that wasn't perfect for them."

Lara reached over and gave her aunt an impulsive hug. "Thanks, Aunt Fran. You know, I never had time to stop at the market for your crabmeat. I'm going to pop over there as soon as adoption hours end, okay?"

"Sure, but I can go if that's easier. I'm heading to the, ugh, mall, but I can drop by on my way home."

"Nope. I know you have a lot planned for the afternoon. I promised to do it, and I'm going to. Soon as you get back with the car, of course."

Her aunt held up both hands. "Then I'll leave you to it. You said Kayla might stop over?"

Lara reached over and straightened the colorful table runner. "Yup. She wants to work for a few hours today instead of tomorrow. I told her it was fine."

"She's been a blessing, hasn't she?" Aunt Fran said.

"Yeah, you said it. Best part is, she loves being here. I swear she'd move in if she could."

"If I see anything at the mall that we can give her for Christmas, I'll pick it up. Is that okay?"

"Lord, yes. I trust your judgment completely."

Lara debated whether or not to tell her aunt what she'd learned at the nursing home, but she decided to wait. They both had full afternoons planned. Evening would be soon enough to talk about everything.

She bade her aunt goodbye, warning her to be careful on the icy roads. Then she went into the kitchen to prepare a pitcher of spiced cider for any potential visitors. Not surprisingly, her thoughts drifted to Gideon.

So far, he hadn't asked her to do anything with him after work. On Friday nights they typically had dinner out, and sometimes took in a movie. Today, however, she hadn't heard from him at all. He hadn't even sent her a text. Was he that busy?

That insecure voice, like a nagging elf, danced again in her head. She tried shoving it aside, but it kept waltzing back. Kayla's face peeking through the kitchen door pane pulled her out of her funk.

"Hey, you're early!" Lara said, unlocking the door. "It's not even one yet."

Kayla stepped inside and shivered. "The temperature's already dropping. It's not even Christmas, and I'm *so* sick of winter." She pulled off her jacket and scarf and draped them over a chair. "I'll hang those in a minute. I came in this way because I knew the shelter door would be locked. Anyway, so listen to this. I was supposed to have a chemistry exam at twelve thirty. So we all get there, and there's a note on the classroom door. Exam canceled. Professor Gormley has the flu. Rescheduled for Monday, same time." She dropped into a chair at the kitchen table.

"Well that's a pain," Lara said. "You probably studied half the night for it."

"I did. Anyway," Kayla said, rubbing her hands, "I'm here early. What can I do to help?"

"Um, maybe start by putting the blue collars on Munster, Dolce, and Twinkles. And then do some grooming?"

"You got it. How's Nutmeg doing?"

Lara poured a glass of spiced cider for Kayla. "Taste this. Let me know if it needs more cinnamon. To answer your question, Nutmeg is doing great. And I think Ballou is starting to bond with her."

"That's so good to hear," Kayla said. She sipped the cider. "It's perfect as is. Doesn't need anything. You know, this could open up a whole new world for Ballou."

"My thoughts exactly. The thing is, I don't want to get my hopes up. Slow and steady wins the race, right?"

"Right." Kayla grinned.

Lara glanced at her watch. The shelter was scheduled to open in ten minutes. That didn't mean anyone would show up at one o'clock. Lara wondered if she had time to tell Kayla what she'd learned that morning at the nursing home.

"Kayla," Lara said, sitting down adjacent to her friend. "I visited a nursing home today. It was a spur-of-the-moment decision, but I'm glad I went. I found out some interesting stuff."

"Oh my God, did you check out Sarah Nally? Did they remember her?" Kayla took a long sip of her cider, then wiped her lips with her finger.

"No, not Sarah Nally. Something told me she wasn't the lady we were looking for, so last night I went to the library to look for more obituaries."

Kayla's lips puckered. Disappointment flickered in her gaze. "Okay. So, what did you find out at the library?"

Lara told her everything—how she'd searched way past the date of death to find Eugenia's obituary, and how her date of death matched up exactly to Lara's birth date. The fact that she was a cat lover added fuel to the belief that she was the woman they'd been trying to find.

"But...Lara," Kayla said, her face draining of color. "She was one of the Thryces, the same people who sponsored the cookie competition. Don't you find that, like, way weird? I mean, how did you find that letter when you did? The letter was the same age as you! Is there something you're not telling me?"

Yes, but not about the letter. The hurt in Kayla's eyes made Lara's heart twist.

Kayla didn't wait for an answer. "You know, Lara, if you didn't think I found the right obituary, why didn't you just tell me? I'd have been glad to go back to the library. You didn't have to re-do my work."

Lara rubbed her hand over her forehead. She felt light-headed, floaty—beads of moisture populating her upper lip. "Kayla," she said, her words sounding distant in her ears. "Would you please get me a glass of ice water?"

Without hesitating, Kayla jumped off her chair. She returned seconds later with the water. Lara snatched it up and drank thirstily, then rolled the glass over her forehead.

"Lara, what's wrong? You're scaring me." Kayla's voice quaked. "Are you going to faint?"

After a long moment, Lara shook her head. "No, I'm okay. I'm fine." She set down the glass and took several slow, deep breaths.

She couldn't go on this way. It was time—time to tell someone. Someone she trusted. Someone who had an open mind.

Lara glanced over at the chair next to the one Kayla occupied. Until a moment ago, the chair had been empty. Now, a blue-eyed Ragdoll cat sat there staring at Lara. The tranquility in those turquoise eyes was like a living thing—so defined that Lara felt she could reach out and touch it. The cat blinked, then rested her chin on the table, her gaze shifting to Kayla.

Lara felt a sense of peace flow over her like a cleansing waterfall. She knew what she had to do.

"Kayla, there's something I have to tell you. Something I've never told anyone, not even Aunt Fran or Gideon. But you have to promise to keep an open mind, okay?"

Kayla nodded. "You know I will."

"I...need to tell you about one of the cats," Lara murmured, then swallowed.

"Oh no, is one of them sick?"

"No, nothing like that," Lara said quickly. "Don't worry. It's nothing bad, okay?"

"Okay," Kayla said, relief smoothing her face. "Well, which cat is it?"

Lara looked across the table and nodded at Blue. "The cat sitting on the chair right next to you."

Chapter 27

Kayla looked at the chair, then peeked under the table. "There's no one here, Lara. Strange, because even Munster hasn't come in to greet me today."

"The cat's name is Blue," Lara said quietly. "She was the cat I had as a child."

"A child?" Kayla shook her head. "Lara, isn't that pretty much impossible? Are you sure you're okay?"

"No one except me has ever seen her. Aunt Fran doesn't believe she ever existed."

"Oh my God," Kayla whispered. "I think I'm getting it now. You're saying she's a...ghost cat?"

"Exactly."

Kayla looked at the chair again. "Is she still here?"

Lara smiled. "She is, and she's looking right at you. With approval, I might add. Oh, Kayla, she's a gorgeous, fluffy Ragdoll, with creamy fur and chocolate-colored ears, paws, and tail. Her eyes are so blue—I think that must be why I named her that."

For a long time Kayla was silent. Then, "When did you first see her?"

"Best I can recall, it was when I was a kid, playing near the river. She stopped me from trapping a poor little salamander and sticking it in a cage. I didn't know any better. I thought I could keep it as a pet."

From there, Lara told her everything. How Blue had helped Darryl read, how she vetted people who came to the shelter to adopt. Most important, how she gave Lara cryptic clues that helped lead her to murderers.

"Is that why you went back to the library?" Kayla asked.

"Exactly. You know those obituaries you copied from the microfiche room? Blue pushed them right into the wastebasket in my studio. It took me a few seconds to figure out what she was trying to tell me, but then I got it. That's why I knew I had to keep looking."

"And look what you found," Kayla said soberly and took another sip of her cider. "But...why doesn't she just tell you who the killer is? You know, like write it on a piece of paper with her paw or something."

Lara smiled. "I don't think it's that easy. It's a good question, though, and I've asked myself that many times. Best I can figure, it takes a good deal of energy for her to even let me see her. I think she has to reserve that energy for crucial times. Like right now—I knew she was telling me to share her with you. It won't be long before she fades."

"I feel kind of honored to be the first one to know." Kayla paused before saying, "Lara, has it...occurred to you that Blue might be the cat who was mentioned in that letter? The one whose spirit floated off to care for a new person."

"Actually, Kayla, that did occur to me. The thing is, I wasn't the only soul born that day, so why should it be me? Why not someone else?"

"Maybe you were the closest baby born that day. Or maybe the cat saw your future with your aunt and all *her* cats."

Lara laughed. "I don't know if we can extrapolate it that far. But I guess if a ghost cat is possible..."

"Then anything is possible," Kayla finished. "Can I see the obituary?"

"Of course." Lara fetched her tote from her studio and returned with it half a minute later.

Kayla read through it, then dug her cell phone out of her jacket pocket. She tapped at a few keys, and then sucked in a gasp. She held out her phone to Lara. "Lara, could this be Blue?"

Lara stared at the photo on Kayla's phone, and then choked out a cry. "Oh my Lord, Kayla. How did you find that?"

"It's her, isn't it?" Kayla said softly.

Lara nodded, and a lump filled her throat.

"All I did was Google Eugenia Thryce. First off, it's kind of an odd name, so I lucked out that way. And with all her family dough, I figured she might have had her picture in the paper a time or two."

Lara took the phone from Kayla and enlarged the pic. A proud-looking senior with a wide smile, her hair secured away from her face with two elaborate combs, sat holding a stunning Ragdoll cat. The caption beneath it read: *Eugenia Thryce with Angelica*. The photo accompanied an article about a fundraiser for cats for which Eugenia had helped raise thousands of dollars. She'd then matched the funds with her own contribution, making it a whopping donation. The article had appeared in a newsletter published by one of the area animal shelters. Given the time frame, Lara was amazed that the article had popped up on the internet.

With a shaky hand, Lara gave the phone back to Kayla. "I'm not sure what to think," she said.

"Well, you're definitely tied to the Thryce family, in some strange kind of way." She looked at Lara. "Do you suppose...I mean, could that Todd Thryce guy have been involved in his grandmother's murder?"

It was the question Lara had been asking herself since she left the nursing home. According to Wanda, Todd was about the only visitor Eugenia had ever received there. That is, if you didn't count the nurses and the aides, and the mystery woman named Rosalba.

What about Gladys Plouffe? Had she ever visited?

Rosalba. The name bugged Lara. It reminded her of something, someone...somewhere.

"Kayla, at this stage I'd say anything is possible. I hate to think of him that way, though. He has such a kindly smile and a nice way about him, plus he did give us that big fat check for the shelter."

"He can well afford that donation," Kayla scoffed. "And a lot of psychopaths have a pleasant smile and good manners." As an aficionado of true crime, Kayla had read a lot about psychopaths. She'd been saving articles about crime since she was a kid.

A buzzer sounded at the door to the back porch. Kayla bolted off her chair. "Lara, someone's already here for adoption day." She looked down at the chair beside her. "Is...Blue still here?"

Lara glanced over at the vacant chair. "No. Not anymore." *For now.*

She leaped off her own chair, and they both scrambled into the meet-and-greet room. They hadn't even had time to attach the blue collars to the three in-house cats.

Kayla got there first and unlocked the door to the back porch. Lara saw her stumble to the side, and then she realized why.

Todd Thryce stood on the doorstep, beaming at them with a pleasant, friendly smile.

Chapter 28

For a few seconds, Kayla stood frozen in place, but then her well-honed manners kicked in. "Um, hello," she said with a smile. "Welcome to the High Cliff Shelter for Cats."

Todd took off one leather glove and offered his hand to Kayla. "Good afternoon. Todd Thryce, at your service."

Kayla gave him a funny look. "Pleased to meet you. I'm Kayla Ramirez." She shook his hand, then moved aside quickly to let Lara take over.

Outside, the sleek black limo idled in the shelter's parking lot, its tail end spewing exhaust into the frigid air.

"Lara, so good to see you again," Todd said as if he hadn't seen her for a year. "Hey, am I a bit too early? Is it too soon to come in?"

Lara wanted to bop herself on the head. She'd totally forgotten that he'd made noises about visiting the shelter on Friday. She'd been so upset over Sherry's meltdown that day at the coffee shop, she'd pushed it off her mental calendar.

"Of course not, Todd. It's great to see you. Come right inside and have a seat."

Todd helped himself to a chair and pulled off his other glove. He set both gloves on the table. "Wow, I'm impressed already," he said, bouncing his gaze all around. "But this can't be the whole shelter, right?"

Kayla piped right in. "No, the shelter is actually the entire home. That's what's unique about it. The cats have full run of the house. No cages, fresh water all the time, top-quality food. And all the kitty litter boxes get scrubbed thoroughly and often." She held out both arms as if conducting a tour. "This is only our meet-and-greet room, where people and cats discover each other, and hopefully meet a great match."

Impressive, Lara thought. Kayla was not only terrific with the cats, but she was getting to be pretty good at public relations.

"Well, that's a great intro," he said, clapping his hands lightly. "I love this place already. I have two monsters of my own, you know—both Siamese. Little devils, but I'm nuts about them." He pulled out his cell phone from the depths of his coat pocket, then brought up a color pic of a pair of slender Siamese cats. "Meet Rambo and Lacey."

"Oh, they're adorable!" Kayla squealed, taking the phone from him. "Look at those faces." She gave Lara a telling glance. "And those blue eyes."

Lara peeked over Kayla's hand at the phone. "They're so sweet-looking. Do they live up to their names?"

"Rambo does," Todd said, taking the phone from Kayla. "Thinks he owns my townhouse. Struts around like he's got a shotgun slung over his shoulder." He smiled and touched the pic with a forefinger. "Lacey's a dainty little creature. But she doesn't hesitate to give me a solid swipe if she doesn't like what I'm serving for din-din on any particular day."

The guy's a charmer, Lara thought. *Is he for real? Or is he one of Kayla's sociopath types?*

"You're so lucky to have them," Kayla said. "You're a real cat person, aren't you?"

He cocked a finger at her. "You got me there. Can't help it, though. I was raised that way. My mom and dad both died when I was young and my uncle Tate traveled all over the globe, so I grew up with my gran. Man, that lady loved her cats."

"What kind of a cat did she have?" Kayla said.

"Mostly she had Siamese, like mine. Her last cat—the one she had right before she died—was a Ragdoll. Gorgeous baby. Looked somewhat like a Siamese, but her coat was fluffier. Had a more docile personality, too. A real lovebug."

"I'm familiar with Ragdolls," Kayla said, looking directly at Lara. "Was she sort of a cream color?"

"Exactly!" Todd was animated now. "But her ears, and I think her paws, were kind of a dark brown. Prettiest little cat—" He stopped himself abruptly. "Well, anyway, I'm sure you don't want to hear me ramble on about my boring childhood," he said, in a more serious tone. "I came because I wanted to say goodbye before Alice and I left for New York. I have some things to finish up in town, and Alice wanted to spend some time with her brother. We're leaving tomorrow afternoon."

"Oh, so Alice still has family around here?"

Chapter 29

Todd stayed for a while longer and got acquainted with more of the cats. He claimed that since he hadn't been home for a week, he needed his "feline fix." Kayla excused herself and disappeared into the house, saying she had grooming and kitty litter chores to attend to.

"I'd better go," he said finally, setting Snowball down on his chair. "Alice wants to take the limo to the outlet shops in Tilton this evening."

"With all the great stores in Manhattan?" Lara laughed.

He shrugged. "A bargain's a bargain. She never stops reminding me of that." He pulled his checkbook out of his shirt pocket. "I'm giving you another donation, Lara. The other one was from the company. This one's from me."

"Todd, you don't have to—"

"Nope." He held up a hand. "Seeing what you and your aunt are doing here seriously impresses me. The least I can do is help out a little." He tore out the check and handed it to her.

Lara gasped when she saw it. "All I can say is thank you. I'm glad you paid us a visit." *Unless you're a murderer.*

She thanked him again, then gave him two of Daisy's cookies to take along with him.

Shortly after his limo pulled out of the parking area, an elderly woman arrived, accompanied by a male friend. The woman was hoping to find a kitten she could present as a Christmas gift to her four-year-old granddaughter.

Lara invited them both inside and sat them down at the table, offering each one a glass of spiced cider and a cookie. After describing the cats currently ready for adoption, she explained why the shelter didn't have any kittens.

In the Northeast region, kitten season typically began in early spring, when female cats were most likely to breed, and lasted throughout the summer. During those times, shelters were often overloaded with kittens. It was a challenge to properly care for them, or even to find enough homes able to foster. Over the summer, the High Cliff Shelter had taken in a number of kittens. Lara was thankful that, except for Snowball, all had been successfully adopted.

The woman, who'd identified herself as Mrs. Hudson, plopped her handbag on the table and frowned. "I see." She snatched up her cookie and took a tiny nibble, then wiped her lips with her fingers. "And you said the white cat is about six months old, but has two odd-colored eyes?"

Lara tamped down her annoyance. "She has two different-colored eyes, but she's warm and sweet and loving." *And you're not getting her. No way. No how.* "Mrs. Hudson, I haven't quite finished. We don't encourage the adoption of cats as gifts, especially to young children. Bringing a cat into your home is a huge commitment. For the adoption to be successful, a cat or kitten can't be treated as toy. It's a living creature with feelings and specific needs."

"I'm aware of that," Mrs. Hudson huffed. "I'm not an idiot. And I can assure you, my son and daughter-in-law are both very smart. I'm sure they can take care of a cat."

Lara's patience, which she normally had in abundance, was thinning down to a nub.

"Mrs. Hudson, let me ask you something. Do they know you're planning to give their daughter a kitten?"

The woman flushed. "Well, no, not yet. I guess they'll all get a surprise on Christmas, won't they?" She jabbed her male friend with her elbow. Like a wind-up doll, he shoved his cookie into his mouth and nodded. "Besides, I was going to see if we could leave it here and pick it up on Christmas Eve. I don't have...any way to care for it at home."

Of course you don't.

"This is my suggestion," Lara said. "After the holidays, if your son and daughter-in-law are interested in adopting, we'd be glad to have them bring their daughter here for a visit. They can spend as much time as they'd like getting to know some of the cats. In the meantime, I can give you one of our welcome packages. It explains everything you need to do to make your new cat's home—"

With a dismissive flap of her hand, Mrs. Hudson hoisted herself off her chair, snatched up her cookie and her satchel, and flicked her knuckles at her companion. "Let's go."

Lara watched them sweep out the door without even a goodbye. *Yeah, happy holidays to you, too.*

Kayla popped in from around the corner, Snowball balanced on her shoulder. "I heard most of that," she said tartly. "I purposely stayed out of here so I wouldn't be tempted to go for that witch's throat."

"She was so clueless," Lara said, straightening the table runner. "If we had twenty kittens here, I still wouldn't have let her adopt." She plucked a few cookie crumbs off the chair the woman had vacated, then dropped onto it.

Kayla sat down beside her and took Snowball into her lap. The kitty closed her eyes and curled up for a snooze. "You look glum," she said to Lara.

"I feel so bad about interrogating Todd Thryce the way I did. He looked so sad about Alice. He's loved her forever. Then I had to go and remind him of all their troubles."

Kayla ran her fingers through Snowball's fur. "Yeah, I get what you're saying. But remember, he could've been acting. That's what sociopaths do—they're manipulators. They suck you into making you feel sorry for them. I read a whole book about it."

Lara shook her head. A man who loved cats that much couldn't be a sociopath. Could he?

"Hey, look, Lara, I gotta go," Kayla said. "Everyone's been groomed, and all the litter boxes have been changed."

Lara got up and gave her an impulsive hug. "Thank you. I can't imagine how we ever got along without you. By the way, Todd Thryce gave me another check before he left. This time from his own personal account, not a company donation."

Kayla rolled her eyes. "Yeah, okay, but remember—he's got plenty of dough to go around. It's probably pocket change for him."

Lara smiled. Kayla was still applying her sociopath theory to Todd. "Message received, but it's pocket change we can use. Anyway, adoption hours are over. After Aunt Fran gets back, I'll see if she still needs me to go to the market."

* * * *

Aunt Fran returned loaded with shopping bags, looking tired and ready for a nap. "I remember, now, why I hate holiday shopping," she said. She dropped her things in the front hallway and removed her tweed jacket and gloves.

"Can I help you put stuff away?"

Aunt Fran snatched up the bags so Lara couldn't peek. "Absolutely not. You mind your business, young lady," she said with a wink.

Lara chuckled. She hoped her aunt hadn't overdone buying gifts for everyone, especially for her. "Don't worry. I wasn't going to peek. You still need me to go to the market?"

"Oh, that would be wonderful. I almost headed over there myself, but the traffic was a nightmare. The light at Elm and Second was backed up to the North Pole. I think there was a fender-bender clogging up the works."

"That's okay. I'll take the back road and go into Shop-Along's rear entrance."

Grocery list in hand, Lara put on her things and jumped into the car. It was still warm. She turned on the radio and found a station playing traditional holiday music.

She groaned when she swung into the rear parking lot at the Shop-Along. The place was packed tighter than sardines in a tin. After cruising around the lot twice, she finally spotted a good-sized SUV pulling out of a parking space. She quickly nabbed it before someone else got it. Reaching into the back seat, she retrieved her reusable shopping bag.

Inside the store, the aisles were crowded with shoppers. Instead of grabbing one of the large carts, she pulled a handheld basket from the pile near the door and looped it over her arm. She checked her aunt's list. *Yellow onion, wheat bread, crabmeat (8-ounce package), can of pumpkin (15-ounce).*

Not bad. If she hustled, she could get through the list quickly. She started with the nonperishables, then headed toward the section of the store where the deli meats and seafood were located.

The line at the deli was mind-boggling. Luckily, the crabmeat was in a large refrigerated unit where the packaged seafood was displayed, so she didn't need to take a number. She perused her choices. She thought her aunt had mentioned a brand name, but if she had, the name had escaped her. Her breath caught when she saw the bags of cooked lobster meat. Is this where the lobster had come from that killed Gladys Plouffe?

"Need some help?"

Lara swiveled around. Jason Blakely was standing directly behind her, a jaunty elf hat sitting atop his head. His white apron, imprinted with the store name, was dotted with stains. "Jason, this is a surprise!"

"Hi, Lara. This is my other job," he said, his smile revealing yellowed teeth. "Helps pay the bills and keeps me off the streets."

Lara laughed. "Well, that's a good thing, I guess."

"What are you looking for?" he asked.

"My aunt sent me for an eight-ounce package of crabmeat. Any idea which brand is best?"

Jason opened the glass-front door and pulled out a silver package. He closed the door. "I'd go with this one. Most of our customers prefer it to the others. Pricey, though."

Lara winced at the price, then dropped the package into her basket. "In this case, I think it's okay. My aunt wants it for a special occasion. Thanks, Jason."

Jason's gaze shifted to the person standing behind Lara, then Lara felt a light tap on her shoulder. She turned, and recognition dawned instantly. It was the woman who worked with Jason in the school cafeteria. Strands of her dark brown hair curled around her face from beneath a red crocheted hat.

"I remember you," the woman said in her lilting tone, one hand resting on the handle of her cart. "That pretty red hair. Who could miss it? You're Lara."

"And you're Rose Stevens. So nice to see you again."

The woman sighed and looked at the list in her hand. "Jason, you need to help me. I can't find the ground chuck in the case—only the ground round. Can you grind some for me?"

"Sure, Rose. How much you need?"

"Two pounds."

Jason grinned at her. "Spaghetti and meatballs for the fam, right? Every Friday," he said.

"You got it. You never forget." She winked at Lara.

But Lara barely noticed. She was gawking at Rose's grocery list. That handwriting. It looked like the writing on the mystery letter! A bit more refined, but with the same tilt to the letters.

After Jason went off to grind the meat, Rose shoved the list into her pocket. "Thank the Lord, after this I'm done. I'll be glad to get home. Long day." She stared at Lara as if sizing her up. "That Jason, he's such a nice boy, isn't he?"

"Yes, he is," Lara agreed, only half listening. She wanted to see that grocery list again!

"If only he could meet a girl as nice as he is," Rose went on, shaking her head. "But these days, everybody wants to meet online. No one wants to meet in person anymore. Or meet at church, like they used to."

"Yes, I know what you mean. Well, it was nice seeing you again, Rose,"
I am said. "Have a great holiday!"

Rose started to say something, but Lara dashed off before she could
finish her sentence.

Something tickled her brain.

She hurried to the checkout and paid for her purchases. Rose had said
the burger was the last thing on her list, which meant she should be in
one of the checkout lines within a few minutes. If Lara timed it right, she
might be able to catch her in the parking lot.

Her tote over her shoulder and her shopping bag clutched in her hand,
Lara headed outside into the freezing night. She stood near the entrance
to the store, close enough to spot Rose leaving, but not so close that she
blocked the shoppers who were streaming in and out. She fished her cell
phone out of her tote and pretended to check her messages.

When she spotted the red hat bobbing toward the parking area, she
hurriedly shoved her phone in her pocket and tailed the woman.

Rose walked slowly, her shoulders drooping from the weight of her two
bags. She wove her way among the cars, then stopped when she reached
a dark-colored sedan. The parking space on the driver's side was vacant,
giving Lara plenty of room to approach her.

Shifting one bag to the other hand, Rose dug her car key out of her
pocket. She'd just clicked open the trunk lock when Lara came up behind
her. Lara didn't want to frighten her, but she had to know.

"Rosalba?"

Rose Stevens dropped her keys and whirled around. She crossed herself
hurriedly. "Oh, my dear sweet Lord, I didn't hear you. You scared me."

"I'm sorry," Lara said, picking up Rose's keys and handing them to her.
"I didn't mean to. I only wanted to talk to you."

"I...you knew my name."

"I wasn't sure. Not until now."

Rose's face, half hidden in shadow, looked frozen in fear. "I can't talk
to you. I have an appointment with someone." She hurried over to her
trunk, shoved the door open higher, and dropped her bags inside. She
slammed the trunk shut.

"That's okay. I just wanted to ask you a quick question—about Pine
Hollow."

Rose sucked in a loud gasp. Even under the dim glow afforded by the
parking lot lights, Lara saw the woman's face go ash-gray. "That was a
long time ago. I don't remember anymore. Please, I have to go. Someone's
waiting for me."

"I thought you were making spaghetti for your family," Lara said.

"I am! But first I have to meet someone."

Lara heard a vehicle swing into the vacant spot next to Rose's car, but she ignored it. The driver got out and slammed the door. Lara waited for a few seconds, then moved closer to Rose. "Rose, I found the letter. You wrote it, didn't you?"

Rose backed up hard against her car and folded her hands over her mouth. She shook her head and gave out a choked sob.

"Did you now?" The voice came from behind Lara.

Lara whirled and saw a large black pickup parked next to Rose, so close that she felt trapped between the two vehicles. She had only seconds to register the face before the world went dark.

Chapter 30

Lara shivered and forced open her eyes, her head throbbing from the effort. Something had struck her, forcefully. That was the last thing she remembered.

She lay on her side, on a rock-hard surface. Her hands were secured in front of her with enough duct tape to build a tank, and her ankles were bound tight. She tried to take in gulps of fresh air, but something scratchy and rank-smelling, like a moldy blanket, covered her entire body.

Where was she?

She turned and twisted, every muscle screaming, but the blanket—or whatever it was—wouldn't budge.

Wherever she was, it had to be outside. The temperature had dropped considerably since she'd left the house. If she stayed like this much longer, she'd die from hypothermia.

Or suffocation.

The pain in her head worsened with every second, as if someone was pounding barbecue forks into her ears.

A metallic clang behind her made her heart jump. Then someone was crouching next to her, pulling off the covering and shoving her into a sitting position. "One word and I'll kill you and Rosalba. Do you hear me?"

Lara nodded, tears stinging her eyes. She knew the voice.

Lara felt herself being dragged to the edge of the truck's bed. In the next instant, two strong hands shoved her out of the truck. She shrieked when she hit the frozen snow.

"I told you to keep your mouth shut," Alice Gentry said.

Looking around, Lara tried to get her bearings. Everything looked fuzzy. The building in the distance, however, looked dimly familiar. She'd been here before. Recently.

To her left, she saw Rose Stevens propped against a shed of some sort, her hands secured in front of her and her ankles bound. Her eyes closed, Rose listed to one side. *Please, let her be alive,* Lara silently prayed. The only light came from the reflection of the night sky off the frozen snow. Lara risked a glance at Alice. Her burgundy cape was buttoned up to her neck, her scarf slightly askew. Her pretty features had hardened into an enraged mask.

"Where are we?" Lara said. "We're going to freeze out here."

"Where's the letter?" Alice demanded.

Lara frowned at her. "Letter? What letter?"

"Don't play coy. I don't have time."

"Why, are you going somewhere?"

Alice reached down and slapped her, then marched over to the truck. Lara's face stung from the blow, and she forced back tears.

Her phone—it was in her coat pocket. She'd shoved it there back at the market after she'd pretended to check for messages.

Seconds later, Alice returned, a rifle propped in her arms. From the way she was holding it, Lara suspected she knew how to use it.

"You own a rifle, Alice?" Lara said, willing her voice not to tremble.

"I don't have to own it. My brother does. He's a game warden. I was a kid when he taught me how to shoot. He was younger than me, but a crack shot." She laughed. "I might be a bit rusty, but I can't miss at this range."

That's where she got the pickup, Lara realized. "Todd said you were going shopping at the outlet stores."

She smirked. "Todd talks too much. I gave our driver the evening off. Told him I wanted to have a cozy little visit with my baby bro."

"That's a pretty nice truck," Lara said. "Goes through snow really well, doesn't it?" Lara swallowed. "As for that nifty rifle, don't you think the neighbors will report a gunshot blast?"

"This close to the woods?" Alice shrugged. "Doubtful, especially at this time of year. Let's cut the crap, Lara. We can do this the easy way or the hard way. The easy way will be painless. I just need to know where the letter is."

"Why do you care?"

"Because my name is probably in it."

Lara shook her head. "Trust me, it's not. If it was, I'd have already taken it to the cops."

Alice hesitated, appearing to mull over Lara's words. "How do I know that?" she said finally, with a glance toward the building Lara thought she'd recognized. Lara realized, now, where Alice had taken them—to one of the playing fields at the Whisker Jog High School. The shed against which Rose was slumped was probably the outbuilding where all the sports equipment was stored.

"Did Rose tell you she named you in the letter?"

"Rose said she didn't name me, but why should I believe her? Maybe she's lying, like when she said she didn't want money. She only wanted me to confess, she said, to cleanse my soul, as she put it. What a crock."

Lara blinked, and then reality sank in. "And she told you she'd hidden the letter, but that she knew where it was. That even after all these years, she could find it if she had to. It scared you, didn't it? To think she might just be telling the truth."

"I'm only going to ask you once more," Alice said. "Where is it?"

"My attorney has it," Lara said. "There's a copy on my tablet, of course." *And on my phone. If only I could reach it.* "Did you go to school here, Alice?" Lara asked, trying to keep her voice from shaking.

Alice's nostrils flared. "Of course I went to school here. Where else would I go? My folks couldn't afford a fancy private school like the snooty Thryces could. Even though I was just as entitled as Todd was." She cocked the trigger on the rifle and pointed it at Lara. "Is my name in the letter?"

Lara shook her head, unable to stop the tears. A groan penetrated her senses. She looked over at Rose and saw the woman trying to jiggle her hands free. "Help me," Rose said softly. "Someone, please..."

"Rose, are you okay?" Lara called out.

Alice stomped over to Rose and aimed the rifle at her. "You—you caused all this trouble," she screamed. "Why couldn't you leave it alone?"

"Alice, don't do this," Rose pleaded. "I don't want anything from you. I never did. I only want to go home to my family."

"Your family," Alice taunted. "What about my family? My *real* family?"

"I had nothing to do with that," Rose said. "But you...I saw you hold the pillow. You kept it there, so she would stop breathing. And then that beautiful cat, she tried to stop you, but you didn't care. You just kept pressing the pillow—" Rose broke into a sob.

"That cat nearly scratched the skin off my hands. I had to tell Todd I'd gotten a violent rash and scratched it myself!" Alice sucked in a hard sob and swabbed at her cheek. "Then suddenly they both stopped moving— the old witch and the cat. They died together, like some freak show act.

The vet told Todd afterward the cat died of a broken heart because she'd watched Eugenia pass."

Lara felt tears streaming down her cheeks. *She died trying to stop you, trying to save the lady she loved.*

"Why, Alice? What did Eugenia ever do to you?"

Alice's lip curled. "She was going to tell Todd everything—about his uncle. Lovable, charming rogue Uncle Tate, who seduced a young woman during one of his rare trips back home. He was much older, of course. The poor woman—I heard she fell hard for him, head over heels. When she told him she was pregnant, he refused to marry her. She had the baby, and Eugenia secretly arranged for a private adoption. Right here in town."

Lara closed her eyes. *Oh...my God.*

She remembered what Todd had said only a few hours earlier. *Alice's mom and dad were in their forties when they got her.* That's what he'd meant, that Alice was adopted. At the time, Lara had wondered, but then decided it would be rude to ask.

"The baby. It was you, wasn't it?"

"Eugenia knew Todd and I were in love, that we planned a future together. During every one of his school vacations, we were inseparable. She said if I didn't break it off, she'd tell him everything—every last sordid detail about my parentage."

"When did you know," Lara asked, her voice quivering, "that you and Todd were first cousins?"

Alice lowered the rifle slightly, but her expression burned with fury. "I found out when I was still in high school. My adoptive mom was dying. She didn't want to go to her grave without my knowing."

"That's why you never wanted children, isn't it?" Lara said.

Alice's eyes blazed at her. "Who told you that? Todd?"

Lara nodded.

"Todd should have kept his big mouth shut. We're fine the way we are. Why did we need kids cluttering up our lives?"

"Fine the way you are? Separate but equal?"

Alice shifted her rifle to one side, then reached down and slapped Lara. This time Lara felt her teeth rattle. Fresh tears pricked her eyes and trickled down her cheeks.

She shivered violently. She was so cold, she couldn't feel her fingers—or much of anything else. Rose must be frozen, too, and her family had to be worried sick.

Was Aunt Fran wondering what had delayed Lara? Probably not. She'd figure Lara had stopped to see Gideon, and they'd decided to head out for dinner.

Except Aunt Fran knew Lara always kept her in the loop, especially if she made last-minute plans. So why hadn't her cell phone rung? And where was Gideon? Why hadn't he called her to make plans for Friday night? On second thought, Lara was grateful the phone hadn't rung. If Alice heard it, she'd snatch it away from her and shut it down—or destroy it. This way, at least she had a chance.

Her cell was in her coat pocket, but with her hands and wrists bound so tightly, she couldn't reach it. She leaned over and lay on one side, her cheek resting on the frigid snow, hoping she could stretch her hands far enough to slide her fingers into her pocket.

A sudden flurry of movement caught Lara's eye. Blue, right there beside her, her paw digging frantically at her coat pocket. Lara leaned her hands away as far as she could, hoping to give her guardian cat a better angle.

Alice swung the rifle and aimed it directly at Lara. "What are you doing?"

"I-I'm just so cold," Lara said. "I'm trying to get warm. Please, Alice, it doesn't have to end this way. You did a crazy, impulsive thing when you were practically a kid. Don't make it worse by killing us, too. You won't get away with it. Didn't you ever watch those forensics shows on TV? The police always figure it out."

Alice hesitated, then she turned the rifle back toward Rose. "None of this, *none* of this would be necessary if this little gold digger over here hadn't started it. Did you think I'd just keep paying, *Rosalba?* Did you think you could just keep draining me?"

Rose sobbed openly now. "I never asked you for money. I only asked you to turn yourself in, to confess to the police what you did. But you just kept sending me cash—money I never asked you for!"

Lara heard their voices fade into the background, as if they were moving away from her. Was her mind shutting down from the cold? Was this how it was going to end?

She blinked, trying to stay awake. Then a rectangle of light beside her jolted her senses. A spark of hope flickered through her.

Her cell phone—it rested next to her now. Alice, who was unleashing her wrath on Rose, was temporarily distracted. With her bound hands, Lara pulled the phone closer. She saw several missed calls and texts. Strange, why hadn't she heard them? She found Gideon's most recent text. Without reading it, and with a finger she could barely feel, she tapped out a response: **Code Blu hi school.**

Then something soft and warm filled the curve of her chest, suffusing her body with unexpected heat.

She pushed the phone beneath her coat and prayed.

* * * *

Voices. Somewhere in the distance.

How long had she lain there?

Lord, she was cold. She'd give anything to have that moldy blanket back. Moldy blanket...the pickup truck...she was starting to remember. Where was she?

Lara lifted her head. Pain seared through it like a hot blade. She dropped it back to the frozen snow, then turned her body slowly, until she lay on her back.

Stars, above her. Were they in the sky, or in her head? Was she in heaven or a hot place?

No, definitely not a hot place. She still felt chilled straight down to the marrow of her bones.

Once more, she tried lifting her head. This time, in her fuzzy line of vison, she saw Alice Gentry struggling with Rose. Trying to shove Rose into the back of the pickup, screaming at her to move faster or she'd shoot her.

Racked by a harsh shiver, she dropped her head to the snow.

"Lara!"

The sound came from far, far away. Had she imagined it?

Footsteps, pounding toward her like horses' hooves. This time, she fought the pain and lifted her head higher. Dark-clothed figures raced toward her, their boots crunching through the snow as they closed the distance.

"Lara!" someone yelled.

"Drop the rifle!" someone else ordered.

A man dropped down beside her in the snow and draped himself over her. She recognized the clean scent of the soap he always used. Over and over, he said her name. Then he sat up and rubbed her arms briskly with his gloved hands. "Give me that blanket, now," Gideon said urgently to someone.

Something warm was pulled over her and tucked around her. "You... got the text," she whispered.

"I called you a thousand times, but you didn't answer," Gideon cried.

Lara couldn't explain it. Somehow, the sound on her cell had gotten turned off. "Rose...sh-she okay?" she said, her teeth chattering.

"I think so. You're both going to the hospital now. I just heard one of the cops call for ambulances."

"No." Lara shook her head, which felt as if golf balls were being tossed around inside. "I'm okay. Wanna go home."

Somewhere off to her left, she heard Alice sob as her rights were being read to her. As two uniformed officers led her past Lara, Lara reached up a hand. "Wait! Please...I need to ask. Alice, why...did you kill Miss Plouffe?"

Alice stopped dead in her tracks. Her face looked like something from a horror film, her once lovely features twisted from hatred and rage. "Are you stupid?" she spat out. "I didn't kill Miss Plouffe. Why would I? She was my mother."

Chapter 31

Lara lost the battle over going to the hospital. Minutes after Gideon and the police arrived, she was whisked away in an ambulance, the siren whining in her ears. In the emergency room, after a battery of tests, she was diagnosed with a mild concussion. The doctor insisted on keeping her overnight for observation. Her instructions for the next several days: rest, rest, and more rest.

Rose Stevens, Lara later learned, had also been rushed to the hospital. After treatment for hypothermia, she was released later that evening. Her husband had been frantic when he'd found her car in the lot at the Shop-Along, groceries in the trunk but no sign of Rose. When he'd gotten the call from the police that his wife had been located, he'd sped to the hospital, nearly collapsing at her side by the time he reached her.

Lara sat up in her bed, plump pillows propped behind her, Teena and Purrcy wrestling for position beside her. "If the doctor tells me to rest one more day I'm going to scream," Lara said, tickling the heart under Teena's chin. "I need to work, and I need to paint."

The watercolor she was anxious to get back to had languished in her studio for three days. The doctor had advised against performing any action that required straining her brain. "Mental rest is as important as physical rest," he'd sternly lectured, then given a reluctant nod. "I know you're an artist, and I know you're anxious to paint, but I'd suggest you hold off for at least a few more days."

"He doesn't get it, does he?" Lara complained to the cats. "Painting is as natural to me as breathing, so where does the mental strain come in?" She huffed out a frustrated sigh.

"Talking to yourself?" Gideon said, tapping his knuckles on the slightly open door.

"Gid! Oh, good glory, I'm glad to see you."

He went over to Lara and reached down to envelop her in a hug. The hug lasted a long time, but Lara didn't mind. As far as she was concerned, it could last forever.

When Gideon felt Teena's claws sink into his Christmas sweater, he said, "Ow," and gently unhooked himself. He rubbed her furry head, and she squeaked out a meow.

He looked so handsome in his green knitted sweater, the one with a grinning reindeer embroidered on the front. Despite his cheery smile, his brown eyes held a deep well of concern, and his face was more drawn than usual. Lara knew that the incident with Alice Gentry had frightened him. Badly.

Lara patted the bed. "Sit. Talk to me. I feel like a prisoner in here."

"Yes, ma'am," he said, and sat close to her. He took her hand in his. "I finally have some news I can share, but that doesn't mean you don't have to rest."

Lara closed her eyes and pulled in a deep breath, releasing it slowly through her mouth. She repeated the action and then said, "There, I'm relaxed, just like the doctor said. Now tell me everything you know."

Gideon snugged in closer to her. "Okay, I'll start with Rose. The police impounded her car and got a warrant to search it. They found a FedEx box addressed to Rose from Alice Gentry. The box had been opened, and it was stuffed with cash—to the tune of eighty thousand dollars."

Lara gasped. "Eighty grand?"

"Yup. Rose had apparently been receiving cash from Alice over the past three years. It started when Rose contacted her and begged her to confess what she'd done. First, she received an envelope with ten thousand, then twenty, and on and on until she had eighty grand. She tried telling Alice she didn't want the money, but it kept coming. Rose was afraid to send it back—she didn't know what to do."

Lara dragged her mind back three days earlier, to that awful scene behind the school. "I remember Rose saying she'd never wanted the money. She only wanted to go home to her family."

Gideon shifted to let Purrcy climb onto his lap. "As it stands now, the police are inclined to believe her. That night, she claims, she'd asked Alice to meet her around six at the vacant strip mall across the street from the Shop-Along. She was going to give the money back, all of it, and beg Alice one more time to confess to suffocating Eugenia Thryce."

"Poor Rose," Lara said, shaking her head. "Imagine the torment she's been going through all these years. Not to mention the danger she put herself in by meeting Alice alone."

Gideon looked troubled. "It never occurred to her that Alice might be dangerous. Rose is a wonderfully kind woman, but she's also more than a little naïve."

"What I still don't understand," Lara said, frowning, "is why she didn't go to the police when she first witnessed it."

A smile swept across Gideon's handsome features. "Actually, Rose would like to explain that to you herself. She's downstairs with Fran. You feel up to joining them?"

Lara squealed and shoved her hand at Gideon's thigh. "Get up. Let me get dressed."

Ten minutes later, wearing a pink fleece sweater, black sweats, and fuzzy slippers with cat faces on the toes, Lara shuffled into the kitchen. Rose had been sitting at the table, sipping from a mug emblazoned with polar bears. When she saw Lara, tears filled her eyes, and she got up and gave her a huge hug.

"Please sit, Rose," Lara said.

Her aunt came over with a plate of pumpkin squares. "The recipe makes about four thousand of these things, so there'll be plenty left for Jerry's birthday dinner. Meanwhile, you can all taste test them for me." She poured a mug of tea for Lara.

"Thanks, Aunt Fran," Lara said.

Rose dabbed at her eyes with the holiday napkin Aunt Fran had given her. "I wanted to explain...about the letter," she said. "That day, at the nursing home, the grandson had gotten permission to bring her beautiful cat there to see her. Her stomach"—Rose patted her own abdomen—"it hurt so much. That's why she was so mean to everyone. The pain made her half-crazy."

"Why didn't they take her to the hospital?" Lara asked.

Rose shook her head. "She'd been, many times. They always brought her back. There wasn't much more they could do, and she insisted she didn't want to die in the hospital. She wanted to go home, but she was too sick."

"So Todd Thryce brought her cat in."

"Yes, he brought in the fluffy cat in a carrier. Oh, that woman was so happy! You should have seen her face. The nurse said the cat could stay for a few hours, but then it had to go home."

"Rose, before you go on, what part of the nursing home did you work in?" Lara asked.

She took in a deep breath before answering. "The kitchen, helping with food preparation. I also delivered meals to patients. That's how I got to know Mrs. Thryce. Her doctor had given orders to feed her special meals six times a day, because of her condition. It was a strain on the kitchen workers—there was never enough help—but I was happy to do it, even if I had to work a little extra for no pay. I was young then. I had more energy than I do now." She laughed slightly.

Lara easily imagined this compassionate woman putting in overtime for no pay. "I'm sorry I interrupted. Go ahead, Rose."

"I know you're all busy, so I'll try to be quick. In Italy, where I was born, some of the old people used to make drinks called *amari* to help with digestion. In Italian, *amaro* means bitter. My great-grandfather was a big believer in them. And they are bitter, made from things like quinine and anise, sometimes with herbs. I thought maybe I could help Mrs. Thryce by giving her a little each day. You know, to help with the stomach troubles."

Oh boy. Lara saw where this was going.

"We had some at home. The one my father used was mostly brandy, but with a few other things mixed in. Every day, when I knew no one was looking, I gave Mrs. Thryce a tiny bit. She hated the taste, but then for a while she'd feel better." Her eyes brimmed with tears. "I only wanted to help."

Lara reached over and lightly squeezed her wrist. "I know you did, Rose."

"The grandson, he was so good to his grandma. That day, he left the cat with her. He told her he would be back for the cat but had errands to run first. I heard him say he was moving to New York the next day." She blotted her eyes again. "After he was gone, his girlfriend came in. Mrs. Thryce had asked to see her alone. I know, because I heard her talking on the phone. She insisted on seeing Alice when her grandson wasn't there."

Gideon caught Lara's eye. He obviously knew the ending to the story.

Rose took a fortifying sip of tea, then tasted a bite of her pumpkin square. "Mrs. Clarkson, these are delicious. But let me continue. That day, I had just given Mrs. Thryce a tiny sip of the amaro before her early afternoon meal. When I went back to get her tray, I saw them, Mrs. Thryce and the girlfriend. They were fighting, screaming at each other. I hid behind the door, afraid to let them see me. I prayed to the Lord, 'Please make her go away, please make her leave Mrs. Thryce alone.' I didn't know what to do."

"You must have been terrified," Lara said.

Rose nodded. "Finally, everything got quiet, so I looked through the crack in the door. That woman, she was pressing the pillow to Mrs. Thryce's face. Poor Mrs. Thryce—she wasn't even moving. But that beautiful cat, she was clawing at the girlfriend's hands, trying to make her stop." Her face took on a strange expression, and her voice grew soft. "The cat, I saw her spirit leave. I know, you think I'm crazy, but to me it was as real as I am sitting here telling you."

Lara felt a lump setting up a roadblock in her throat. She choked it back. "No, I don't think you're crazy, Rose. I believe every word you're saying."

Aunt Fran looked over at Lara, her eyes misty. She ran her hand over Dolce's soft fur. Was she beginning to understand?

"Was anyone else around, Rose?"

Rose shook her head dismally. "No. There were never enough aides, so the hallways were often empty. Oh, you must think I'm a beast for not trying to stop her." She tapped a fist to her heart. "But I knew, deep in my heart, Mrs. Thryce was ready to go to the Lord. She told me many times she wanted it to end, that the pain was too much. I think that's why she didn't fight. I told myself, *This way she won't suffer anymore.* I was so selfish, but also so afraid. If I told the authorities what I saw and they did tests on her body, they might find the amaro I'd given her. I had only been in this country for a year. I didn't know how the police worked."

"You were worried that you'd get blamed for her death," Lara said.

Rose smiled through her tears. "You are exactly right. As for the money Alice kept sending me, I never wanted it," she added. "Wait, let me go back. About three years ago, I wrote to her in New York. She wasn't hard to find. I used Google. Anyway, I wrote and begged her to confess. Next thing I know, a packet of cash arrives. I told her to stop, but she kept sending more."

"Rose, there's one thing I don't understand. The letter you wrote, how did it end up in the library book?"

She smiled. "That nice grandson, he left the book on Mrs. Thryce's night table. He tried to cheer her up one day by showing her the book he borrowed so he could make treats for her cat. After Mrs. Thryce died, one of the nurses found it. When the nurse realized it was a library book, she was annoyed because someone would have to return it. She was glad when I offered to do it, and that's when I thought of writing the letter."

Lara sat back, absorbing everything Rose had told them. She couldn't imagine living with a secret like Rose's. No wonder it had eaten away at her until she finally decided to contact Alice.

When she looked over at Gideon, she saw Blue sitting beside him, her chin resting on the table. Blue stared at Rose. Was she remembering?

"I have to tell you one more thing," Rose said, with a nervous glance at Gideon. "That awful night, Lara, when Alice tried to hurt us both, I had the strangest feeling that Mrs. Thryce's cat was there. I can't explain it, but the feeling was strong. At one point I thought she was keeping me warm."

Lara's heart felt lighter than a helium balloon. Rose understood. That meant everything.

"Rose, believe it or not, I sensed the same thing—that a furry angel was watching over us that night, trying to keep us both warm. Maybe Mrs. Thryce was looking down, sending help when she knew we needed it most."

Gideon shot Lara a look, then smiled at her. Did he think she was humoring Rose? *Oh, Gideon, wait till I tell you everything, and then see if you're still smiling.*

Blue had already faded, but she'd gotten her message across. Lara reached for her tea, but Snowball thwarted her by leaping onto her lap. Lara rubbed the cat's head, then bent to kiss her.

"Oh, that is such a beautiful cat," Rose said. "My mama had one like it. She had it nearly eighteen years." She pushed aside her empty tea mug and ate the last bite of her pumpkin square. "Mrs. Clarkson, before Christmas I'm going to make you a panettone and bring it over to you and Lara."

"Oh, I love panettone. Thank you, Rose," Lara said. "And someday I hope to meet your family."

Rose stood and winked at her. "I think you will. No, I'm sure of it."

She hugged Lara again, thanked Fran for her hospitality, and left.

* * * *

After Gideon walked Rose out to her car, he came back into the kitchen.

"Now, are you up to hearing about Alice?" he asked Lara, slipping an arm around her.

"Totally," she said. "I've been waiting for more information. I had the feeling you two were keeping things from me so that I'd rest."

Aunt Fran looked anxious. Did she want Gideon to leave so they could talk alone?

"We weren't keeping things from you," Aunt Fran said. "We only wanted to give you a few days to get your bearings again. Let's go into the large parlor. That way you can stretch out on the sofa."

Lara didn't fight it. She knew her aunt was worried about her, but the pampering had to end. "Okay, but after today I go back to my normal routine," Lara insisted. "I feel fine, and my head is fine."

"Agreed," her aunt said, although she didn't look thrilled.

Lara sat on the sofa, but instead of stretching out she sat cross-legged and took Snowball onto her lap.

Gideon lowered himself next to her and was immediately assaulted by a lovable orange ball of fur. "Hey, Munster, you're getting to be my best bud, aren't you?" Gideon rubbed the cat's head and then sat back.

Aunt Fran sat in Lara's favorite chair. "I heard part of the story from Jerry, but I think Gideon knows more."

"I do. I'm going to try to summarize, but more details are coming out every day. Alice Gentry was adopted by Clifford and Diana Gentry in 1971. Nice folks, lived here in town all their lives. Cliff worked at one of the mills, and Diana was a bank teller. Never had any luck having kids, but everyone close to them knew they'd always wanted a child. Then one day, Eugenia Thryce approached them. A newborn girl, whose mother was unmarried and couldn't keep the child, needed a loving home. Eugenia offered to pay for the private adoption, and the Gentrys eagerly took her up on it, no questions asked. All they wanted was a baby."

"Did the Gentrys know who the mother and father were?"

Gideon ran his hand over Munster's fur. "No one's sure about that, but I don't think they did, at least not initially."

Lara suspected there was more to that thread. "So how did Alice end up with a brother?"

"After they adopted Alice, the Gentrys were so happy that they applied to adopt a baby boy. That time they went through the proper channels. It took a few years, but they ended up adopting Carl Gentry in 1975."

So, Carl was the "baby bro" whose pickup truck and rifle Alice had commandeered.

"Going back to Alice," Aunt Fran said, "Eugenia must have been apoplectic when she found out that her son had seduced Gladys Plouffe."

"Exactly. According to what the police learned, Eugenia was very protective of Gladys. She tried to pressure Tate into marrying her, but instead he left town—permanently."

"Coward," Lara said.

"He was that, and more," Gideon said darkly. "That's why Eugenia got involved and quickly set up the adoption. She knew Gladys had endured a difficult home life, with an alcoholic mother. It was Eugenia who urged her to attend college. With an education, Gladys could put her sewing skills to good use, and end up with a pension after she retired. No one knows for sure, but we suspect Eugenia paid her tuition at UNH."

"Eugenia was like a second mother to Gladys, wasn't she?" Lara asked.

"She was. What Eugenia didn't anticipate was that her grandson and Alice would meet and fall in love. She assumed that sending Todd away to private school would keep him away from 'townies' as she called them."

"The best laid plans," Aunt Fran said wryly. "No wonder she was so furious when she learned of their relationship. She knew their fathers were brothers."

"At that point, Alice didn't care. She loved Todd and would stop at nothing to keep him. He was her life, and her future."

"I can't help wondering," Lara said, "what Todd would've done, all those years ago, if he'd known Alice was his cousin."

Gideon sighed. "I guess only he can answer that."

"When do you think Alice found out that Gladys Plouffe was her birth mother?" Aunt Fran asked him.

"No one knows, but it was probably Gladys herself who told her. Gladys's shellfish allergy was legendary at the high school, so Alice obviously knew about it. Alice, by the way, took home ec from Gladys. Got two Cs and a D. That was before she knew who Gladys was."

"Did the police ever find the lobster meat package?"

"They haven't yet. Alice still maintains that she didn't kill Gladys, but the district attorney is pressing ahead with the indictment. They located Gladys's will, and it was most enlightening."

Lara sat up straighter. "Did she leave anything to Alice?"

"Oh, yes," he said. "She left Alice exactly one dollar. The rest was bequeathed to a textile museum in Connecticut."

Lara reached over and grabbed his arm. "Wait. Did you say *one* dollar?"

Gideon smiled. "Exactly. Under New Hampshire law, a child who isn't named in a parent's will still inherits his or her rightful share of the estate. The statute phrases it differently, but that's the gist. By naming Alice and leaving her a pittance, it proves that Gladys was aware of the child but chose to leave her nothing."

"Wow," Lara said, shaking her head. "Gladys Plouffe was an enigma, wasn't she? From everything I've heard, she did some charitable things, but she also hurt a lot of people. But Gid, assuming Alice killed Gladys, how would she have known the contents of her will? Doesn't someone have to die before their will is probated?"

"You're exactly right. The police think that Gladys either told Alice or showed her a copy of the will. They're still investigating the extent to which the two corresponded. My hunch? They'll find out that Gladys taunted Alice by telling her she'd inherit nothing. Alice fumed and found a way to get revenge on her birth mother. Gladys's shellfish allergy was the perfect vehicle, so to speak."

Lara rested her head on the back of the sofa. Maybe her brain did need more rest. She still struggled to make sense of Alice's motive.

According to Todd, Alice made a fabulous salary. Plus, Alice was smart. No doubt she had some plump retirement accounts waiting to keep her comfy in her old age. Killing for money, unless Gladys had been a billionaire, didn't ring true.

Then again, it might have been simple retaliation—payback for Gladys having given her up as an infant, for allowing her to be raised in a modest home when she should rightfully have shared the Thryce fortune.

"You're probably right, Gid. Either way, the police will sort it out. I feel bad for Todd, though. I suspect he was blindsided by all this."

"He's pretty shaken," Gideon said. "I didn't talk to him, but Jerry did. He had no idea Alice was his first cousin. I think he's still trying to absorb it all."

"How is this all going to end?" Lara said, feeling the words lodge in her throat.

Gideon pulled Lara's head gently onto his shoulder. "It's too soon to tell, but at least the worst is over." Munster snuggled up between them, but then suddenly the cat got up and trotted out of the room.

Gideon chuckled. "Where's he going in such a hurry?"

Lara felt tears flowing down her cheeks, and she glanced down. Blue sat between her and Gideon, her chin resting on Gideon's knee. The Ragdoll cat gazed up at Lara, her turquoise eyes shining. *It's time,* she seemed to be saying. *Time to tell them everything.*

"Honey, what's wrong?" Gideon said, hugging her close.

Lara pulled away and sat up. She blotted her face with the back of her hand. "Aunt Fran, Gideon...you'd better fasten your seat belts. I have something to tell you that's going to blow your minds clear out of the room."

Chapter 32

Lara started with the first day she'd arrived at her aunt's. That fateful October day that had changed her life forever.

She'd first noticed Blue sitting in the small parlor with Darryl Weston, Brooke's younger brother, who'd struggled mightily with reading aloud. Though Aunt Fran had been tutoring him, the child's progress had been plodding. When suddenly he began reading at the level of a high school student, Aunt Fran had been shocked. Lara tried to explain about the Ragdoll cat she'd seen reading over the child's elbow, but her aunt had insisted that she'd never owned a Ragdoll cat.

That was the beginning.

After that, Blue showed up at odd times, usually when Lara needed her most. She'd pointed out things to Lara that had helped her nail murderers, and she'd been there to intervene when she was in dire trouble.

"I can't explain what happened three nights ago," Lara said. "Somehow, that tiny lever that controls the sound on my cell phone got turned off. If it hadn't been for that, Alice would have heard it ring in my pocket."

"*Blue,*" Aunt Fran said, almost in a whisper, her green eyes moist with tears.

Lara nodded. "That's the only thing I can think of. One minute my phone was in my coat pocket, and the next it was lying in the snow. The moment Alice turned her back on me, Blue must have wrestled it out of my pocket."

"Code Blue," Gideon said, his face pale. "It was the perfect distress signal, wasn't it?"

"It was, but at the time I couldn't tell you why. You know what else I remember? That day Alice came here to deliver the company's donation check, Blue appeared, and she was very agitated by Alice's presence. I thought she was telling me that Alice was not a friend of felines, but I realize now that it was much more."

Aunt Fran looked as if she'd shrunk into herself. Lara's heart wrenched. "The other day, Lara, when you told me you sometimes *sense* things, I knew there had to be more. I wish you'd told me all of it."

"I didn't know how to tell you—either of you. I was afraid you'd think I was having delusions. The only other one who knows is Kayla. I told her when she was here on Friday. It was easier to tell her because she's not as close to me as you both are."

Gideon clasped her hand, then lifted it to kiss her fingers. "Lara, I would never have doubted you, not for a second. And I never would have said you were crazy, or delusional."

She leaned into him, the feel of his arm warming her to the core. "Good to know," she joked, "in case I ever have any real delusions in the future." Lara looked off to the side, her gaze unfocused. "In my head, I keep going back to that night. I kept wondering why Blue didn't go after Alice. After all, she was Eugenia's killer..."

"Because Blue has to be Angelica," Aunt Fran supplied, "Eugenia's beloved Ragdoll."

Lara nodded at her aunt. "But now that I've had time to turn it over in my head, I think I understand why. I think it takes a massive amount of energy for Blue to make her presence known. She never lingers for long, because she can't."

"And maybe, that night," Gideon said, picking up the thread, "she had to choose between keeping you and Rose warm or going after Alice." He squeezed Lara's fingers and leaned over to kiss her temple. "She made the right choice."

Lara laughed. "Thanks. I think so, too."

Aunt Fran had regained a bit of her color. "Well, if you two will excuse me, I have crab cakes to make. Jerry's birthday dinner is this evening, and I want everything to be just right."

"Crab cakes. Wow. Lucky guy." Gideon winked at Lara. "And that just gave me an idea. Lara, why don't you come over to my place this evening so we can let Aunt Fran and her favorite dude have the place to themselves. I mean, to themselves and the cats."

Lara grinned. "Counselor, I like the way you think."

"Have to admit, I'm partial to it myself." Gideon leaned over and kissed her nose, then leaned his forehead on hers. "Thank you for trusting me, Lara. I'm glad you told me about Blue."

"I am too," she said. "It was a secret I didn't enjoy keeping from you, or from Aunt Fran. I feel as if a tank has been lifted off my chest."

He squeezed her hands in his. "I'm going to head back to the office to play catch-up. Pick you up later, okay?"

After Gideon left, Lara headed back to her bedroom while Aunt Fran puttered in the kitchen preparing the crab cakes. When she reached her bedroom doorway, Lara stopped short.

Nutmeg and Ballou were snuggled up together on her unmade bed, the tortie's paw curved around Ballou's neck. So far, they were unaware of Lara's presence. She watched for a few minutes, then carefully backed away.

Very quietly, Lara descended the stairs. She went into her studio and closed the door all the way. The painting was waiting for her.

She set up her watercolor supplies and went to work.

* * * *

The watercolor was coming along magnificently. The shading, the expressions, and the details that made it unique were all working in tandem to create the emotion Lara wanted to capture.

When she glanced at her watch, she realized she'd been working for several hours. Aunt Fran, no doubt, thought she was upstairs resting. *Sorry, Aunt Fran, but I had to paint.*

She pushed back her chair about six feet and studied the painting from all angles. After sharing her secret with the two people she loved most, Lara felt her spirit uplifted. Their belief in her made all the difference.

She rolled her chair forward again. Grinning to herself, imagining the finished painting. Lara had just swabbed her brush over the sepia-toned paint when a crash from the kitchen made her jump. She threw her paintbrush onto her work table, vaulted off her chair, and shot into the kitchen.

In front of the counter, near the sink, Aunt Fran's favorite bowl lay in pieces on the floor. Chunky shards of Pyrex were mingled with globs of crabmeat mixture.

"Aunt Fran, what happened?" Lara cried. "You didn't cut yourself, did you?"

Her aunt threw up her arms. "No, I'm fine," she said, surveying the mess. "Don't come close. There's broken glass. I'll get it all with some paper towels." She shook her head and chuckled. "I only left the kitchen for two minutes, but apparently she smelled it. Poor little girl, I think it scared her more than it did me when the bowl went crashing to the floor."

"What poor little girl?"

Aunt Fran nodded toward the kitchen table. Nutmeg crouched under one of the chairs, her eyes wide with worry. When Lara bent down, the cat gazed up at her as if to say, *I'm sorry, really. I didn't mean to do that. I only wanted a snack.*

"Come here, sweetie, it's okay. I want to be sure you're not hurt."

At Lara's soothing tone, the tortie crept toward her. Lara rubbed her head to reassure her, then checked her paws for cuts. "She's okay, she's not...hurt." Her last word fell away as she dropped down hard onto the floor, her heart breaking in two. Lara pulled Nutmeg into her arms and held her close.

Chapter 33

Andy Casteel sat behind his desk, absently twirling a pencil. His expression grim, his face a sickly shade of gray, he waved a hand at the three chairs lined up on the opposite side. "Please, both of you, have a seat."

Lara lowered herself onto an end chair. The chief took a seat at the other end, leaving an empty chair between them. Lara's stomach felt weighted with sadness. She'd barely slept all night.

"Thank you for allowing us to meet here, Andy," Chief Whitley said quietly. "This is very irregular, I know, but the state police and I are honoring Lara's request. They have a police escort waiting outside."

Casteel nodded, making eye contact with neither of them. "No problem, Chief. It was the least I could do." He reached over and pressed a button on his phone. "Abby, you can send him in now."

Lara patted her pocket to be sure she'd tucked some tissues in there. A minute later, Jason Blakely stepped through the open door. His gaze bounced from one to the other, and his eyes dimmed with confusion. "You wanted to see me, Mr. C?"

"Yes, Jason, and please close the door. You can have a seat next to Chief Whitley."

Jason closed the door softly and shuffled over to the chair. He gave Lara an odd look but said nothing.

Casteel cleared his throat. "Chief?"

Whitley nodded. "Jason, we've done some checking into your file here at the high school, and—"

"My file?" Jason said, looking baffled. "What for? I've never even been late for work."

"Not your employee file, your student file," the chief clarified.

"But I only went to school here two years."

"Yes, we understand that, but it's those two years that concerned us. I regret that we didn't look into it sooner, but after you were interviewed by the state police we saw no reason to consider you a person of interest."

"A person of—" Jason swallowed, and his face reddened. "What's this about?"

"Jason," the chief continued, "we believe you tainted the cookies that caused Miss Plouffe's death. You knew about her allergy. Everyone in the school knew."

He shrugged. "Yeah, so what? That means there's, like, at least a couple hundred suspects, right? Everybody I know hated her."

Lara spoke up. "Jason, when you said the stray cat you were feeding was fussy, I didn't think much of it at the time. It wasn't until I got her to the house, to the shelter, that I realized what you meant. She has a strong preference for shellfish, any kind of shellfish. Yesterday, she knocked over a bowl of crabmeat that my aunt had left on the counter."

"Again," he said peevishly. "So what?"

"So I wondered, where did you get the shellfish you gave Nutmeg? I didn't think the school cafeteria served it. Too expensive, for starters, plus there's the whole allergy thing."

"Last evening," the chief said, "Mrs. Stevens confirmed for us that the school cafeteria never uses any form of shellfish in the students' meals."

Jason went silent, his ears flushing red. "Okay, big whoop—you got me. I helped myself to a package of frozen lobster at the Shop-Along. I thought the smell would attract the cat more than the stuff we had in the school fridge. The store wasn't going to miss it."

"Jason," Lara said, "when I asked you how you knew Miss Plouffe carried injectable allergy medicine, you told me that the last year she worked at the school you saw one sticking out of the gaudy flowered purse she always carried."

"Yeah, so?"

The principal spoke up. "Gladys Plouffe hadn't carried a purse like that for years, Jason. Not since one of the students put a garter snake in it. She'd switched to a fanny pack. The sad part is, she wasn't even wearing it that day. The police found it later in her car. I can only assume she locked it there for safekeeping. Gladys trusted no one."

Jason's mouth formed a grim line, and his shoulders sagged. "I only said that to make myself look good. It was stupid of me. When the school put me in charge of setting up the displays for the cookie contest, I remembered I'd hidden that lobster for the stray cat in the back of the fridge in the kitchen." He shook his head and his eyes misted. Lara pulled a tissue from her pocket and gave it to him.

"Gladys Plouffe always hated me," Jason said bitterly. "She knew I wanted to work in the food business after I graduated, so she sabotaged me every way she could. If I made a mistake in her class, she never let me forget it. She always used me as an example of what not to do. Even her pet students—the nasty girls, I called them—used to join in humiliating me. And she just let them do it."

"You were the student who switched schools because of her, weren't you?" Lara asked him.

Jason nodded. "I didn't want to switch. I loved this school because it's small. I hated the one I went to for my last two years of high school. Plus, it ticked off my folks royally because they had to drive me there. My dad wrecked his car one morning driving me to school in a rainstorm. He's never let me forget it." He swabbed a tissue over his cheeks.

"I blame myself for much of this, Jason," Casteel said soberly. "Over the years, I disciplined Gladys many times, for many reasons. And I filed all the appropriate reports required by the school district, and by state law. But the parents, they almost always supported her—that was part of the problem." He leaned forward and folded his hands on his ink blotter, his face the picture of misery. "The other part? I was biased. Long ago, Gladys Plouffe saved my younger brother's life. I foolishly allowed that to color my actions, or rather, my inaction. I apologize to you for all the harm it caused you. You should never have been so unhappy here that you felt forced to change schools."

A heavy silence fell over the room.

Jason let out a sob, his fingers covering his eyes. "I wanted to make her sick, but I didn't want to kill her. At the end I tried to revive her, but it was too late." He looked at Lara, his face blotchy and his eyes red. He looked like a cross between an old man and a child. "You know what's really funny? I've been thinking about what I'd do if I had to go to jail. Do you think they'll let me train animals, like those prisons on TV do? Maybe I could work with feral cats."

Lara swiped at her own tears. "If they do, I'll help out any way I can."

Casteel pushed his chair back and rose. "I'm going to help you as well, Jason. Right now, please don't say anything further. You need a good criminal attorney. Gideon Halley gave me a recommendation. With your consent, I'm going to call her for you."

Jason nodded, and the chief stood. "You and I will walk out together. I see no need for a state police escort. One of them will read you your rights when we get to the car."

Jason turned to Lara. "Please say goodbye to Rose for me, okay? I'm going to miss her."

"I will," Lara said, crying openly now.

She watched him leave with the chief, her heart breaking for him.

Casteel looked shaky, but he forced a smile. "I've said it before, Lara, but it bears repeating. You're a very smart woman. You're also a very caring one, and for that I'm most grateful."

Her throat too tight to respond, she nodded. The idea of Jason locked in a prison cell made her stomach clench. She thought back to the tender way he'd handled Nutmeg, the way he'd worried about the little stray being cold and hungry.

How sad that he'd never gotten over Miss Plouffe's horrible treatment of him. Over the years, it had eaten away at his psyche. When he saw her again at the cookie competition, the bad memories must have flooded back.

Lara blotted her eyes one last time, then shoved her tissue into her coat pocket. "Thank you, Andy. Shall we pay Rose a visit now? I'm sure she's wondering what happened to Jason."

Chapter 34

A pan sat on the stove, simmering with a blend of cloves, cinnamon, and orange peel. The delectable aroma wafted into the large parlor.

Above the mantel hung a pine wreath adorned with a massive red bow. Sitting on her heels in front of a small stack of gifts, Lara rubbed her hands together. She felt as if she were six again, eager to tear the wrapping off the packages to see what Santa had delivered.

Gideon sat cross-legged beside her, his brown eyes beaming. He tugged lightly on her curly ponytail, which was secured with a red velour scrunchie. On her ears Lara wore the whimsical blue tree bulbs she'd bought at Mary Newman's gift shop.

"So, no Christmas tree this year, eh?" Gideon said, as if Lara and her aunt had committed the ultimate sin.

"Nope. We'll try to think of something creative next year, but this year time ran short. We had to think of the cats. Especially Valenteena," Lara said with a giggle, "who could get herself into trouble in a plain white box. And speak of the devil..."

Valenteena bounded into the large parlor and plunked herself onto Lara's legs. Lara laughed. "You smell like a fish," she said, rubbing the little cat's head. "You're dying to help me open gifts, aren't you? Well, you're too late. We opened most of them already."

Aunt Fran had given Lara a dark green sweater with a Ragdoll cat emblazoned on the front. She'd commissioned a local woman to knit it for her, and the cat had been painstakingly hand-embroidered.

"Lara, you have to open that one from Rodney," Aunt Fran called from the sofa. "I'm bursting with curiosity."

"Okay, okay," Lara said, sliding the heavy gift out of the stack. She held it to her ear and shook it, then tore off the wrapping to reveal a festive-looking box. "Drum roll, please..." She pulled off the cover and grinned. "It's a coffee-table book of cats," she said, and flipped through the glossy pages. "Look, it has pictures of all the breeds with descriptions of each one!"

"Wow, what a great gift," Gideon said. "I'm impressed. Especially since you've never even met the man. That reminds me, have you heard from your mom?"

"She texted me about a week ago. She was kind of vague about their plans, but as far as I know, they're still in New Hampshire."

Aunt Fran lifted Dolce from her lap and set him gently on the sofa. She went over to Lara and reached down for the book. "May I see it?"

Lara gave it to her, and her aunt's green eyes lit up. "This is a very thoughtful present, Lara, and appropriate. I only hope—I mean, oh, never mind."

"You only hope what?" Lara said.

"Is that the timer on the stove going off?" Aunt Fran chirped, cocking her ear toward the kitchen. "You kids go ahead and open the rest. I'll be back later!"

"Us kids?" Gideon chuckled. "I think she wants us to be alone when we open our own gifts."

Lara's heart raced in her chest like a monster truck. Did Aunt Fran know something she didn't?

Gideon reached behind the pile and pulled out a small square box. Wrapped in gold and tied with a huge blue bow, it looked as if it came from a jeweler. "This is for you," he said quietly.

"Was that back there all this time? I didn't even see it!"

"Open it," he said. "Please."

Lara tugged the end of the bow, and the ribbon fell away. She peeled off the gold paper, then lifted the top of the box. Relief swept through her like an ocean breeze. It wasn't an engagement ring.

"Oh...Gideon, this is unbelievable."

Inside the box was a cat-shaped pendant, about an inch high, that hung on a silver chain. The pendant, made from tiny blue gems, sparkled when she held it to the window.

"They're sapphires," Gideon said, "and the chain is white gold."

"Where...how...I mean...where did you ever find this?"

"Actually," he confessed, "I didn't find it. It had to be custom-made. What's strange is that I ordered it two months ago, before I even knew about Blue."

Strange or prophetic? Lara mused.

She wrapped her arms around his neck. "It's absolutely gorgeous," she said in a hoarse voice, "and I love it. Put it on me before Aunt Fran gets back."

Gideon fastened the necklace behind her, then turned to see it on her. "It looks totally fantastic on you. So beautiful with your hair."

Lara felt herself tearing up. Gideon had known she wasn't ready for the other kind of jewelry—the kind that glittered on her left hand. Not yet, anyway. Without fully understanding why, he'd chosen the perfect gift.

She went over to where her gift to him rested against the wall. It was large and hadn't been easy to wrap. She'd lucked out when she found a festive bag big enough to hold it.

"Okay, open mine now. And handle with care, please."

"Wow. It's big." He removed the gift, wrapped in tissue, from the depths of the bag. When he pulled away the tissue, Gideon's eyes widened. His face froze, and he went dead silent.

Oh, no. Does he hate it?

"Lara, this is, I mean, I never expected..."

"Gideon, you're killing me here. Do you like it?"

Tears slid down his cheeks. He stared at the watercolor she'd painted from the photo—the one of young Gideon with his hand on his dad's shoulder, their expressions intense as they examined a legal document. "Oh...Lara. This is beyond fantastic. I'm almost speechless. Did you paint this from memory?"

"Um, not exactly. I took a picture of it with my phone that day I asked you for a bottle of water."

Lara had labored long hours to finish the painting, and then she still had to get it framed. Her favorite art shop had done a superb job, plus they'd rushed it for her. The mat was antique white, and the frame a dark cherry wood.

"It's the most beautiful gift I've ever gotten," he said. "Will you help me choose a spot for it?"

She leaned over and kissed him, just as Purrcival wedged himself between them. "You know I will."

Gideon smiled and rubbed the cat's head. "You like it too, don't you, Purrcy?"

Purrcy meowed his approval, then rested his furry head on Gideon's ankle.

As if a magic wand had been waved over the room, Aunt Fran appeared beside them. They showed her their gifts, and she hugged them both. "I feel it in my bones. This is going to be the best Christmas ever." The doorbell rang. Lara frowned. "It's too early for Daisy and crew. Who could that be?"

"There's only one way to find out," Aunt Fran said.

Lara hopped up off the floor and opened the front door. Her mom stood on the doorstep next to a pudgy man with thinning hair and a handlebar mustache.

"M-Mom," she stammered. "Why didn't you tell us you were coming?"

"Oh for heaven's sake, Lara, will you move so we can come in? It's not exactly summer out here." She smiled brightly at her daughter. "And I did tell you we were coming. I told Fran, anyway. She wanted us to surprise you."

The man squeezed Brenda's shoulders from behind. "Now, hon, give her a chance. Hi, you must be Lara," he said, sticking out a hand. "I'm Rod."

Lara opened the door wide and ushered them inside. He pumped her hand as if he were milking a cow. "Yes, I am. Please come in."

Brenda's face seemed somehow softer today. Less makeup, more animation. Lara thought it was a look that suited her.

Lara took their coats, and introductions were made all around. Brenda's eyes lit up like fireflies when she saw Gideon. "Oh my, I am simply delighted to see you again, Gideon. Do you remember me?"

Gideon smiled and kissed Brenda's cheek. "I sure do. Great to see you, too."

"Are you staying for dinner?" Lara asked.

Brenda stared at the striped orange cat sniffing her boot. "He's back," she said with a wry twist of her lips. "No, we're catching a three o'clock flight out of Manchester back to Vegas, so we can only stay a half hour or so. Enough for one drink, then we have to skedaddle. Although Rod can only have a tiny sip, since he's driving."

"One swallow and I'm done," he said, winking at Lara.

For the next half hour, they sampled Aunt Fran's creamy eggnog and munched on Christmas cookies. Cats wandered in and out of the room. Munster couldn't resist whatever he'd detected on the toe of Brenda's boot, so he curled up at her feet and rested his head on it. Rod spoke briefly of his country music career, but his subdued tone gave Lara the impression things hadn't gone well with the Greenhorn Geezers. Lastly, Lara remembered to thank Rod for the cat book.

"I had a feeling that would be right up your alley," he said, then chuckled. "Looking around here, I can see I was right."

"How about my special gift?" Brenda said with a sly smile and a glance at Lara's left hand.

"Oh, um, yes. That was lovely, Mom. Thank you." She felt a flush creep into her cheeks.

"Well, the time has flown, honeybun," Rod said, rising off the sofa. "Gotta say, I don't think I've ever seen this many cats in one place. You've done a fine job here, ladies."

"Mom...and Rod," Lara said. "I didn't even get you a Christmas present. I feel awful."

Rod helped Brenda with her coat.

"No biggie," Brenda said. "But instead of feeling awful, why don't you paint something for us? Rod and I are getting a new apartment in mid-January, so it can be like a housewarming gift."

"Oh, I'd love to. Give me an idea of what you'd like, okay?"

"You betcha," Rod said. "We'll even send you a photo."

After a flurry of hugs and promises, Brenda and Rod left.

"You know what?" Lara said. "I actually like Rodney. Something tells me he's genuine."

"I agree," Gideon said. "He's the real deal."

Lara and Gideon gathered up the glasses and plates they'd used and brought them into the kitchen. Aunt Fran opened the oven to check on her pumpkin pie.

Lara rinsed the dishes in the sink, her heart heavy when she thought about Nutmeg and Ballou. She hadn't expected them to be gone before Christmas.

A few days after Jason had been arrested, Nutmeg's owner had shown up at the shelter. The woman had left the tortie in the care of a neighbor while she went on a pre-Christmas tour of Germany and Austria. Unfortunately, the neighbor's dog hadn't approved the plan and scared the poor cat into bolting. The neighbor had been sick with worry but had no idea where to turn for help. It hadn't occurred to her to check online sources, or even local vets' offices. Nutmeg—whose real name was Swee' Pea—had somehow found her way through the woods to the back of the school, where Jason had fed her lobster. When the neighbor returned from her trip and learned her cat was missing, she was frantic. She'd immediately gone online and searched all the area shelters.

"You're lost in thought," Aunt Fran said, slipping an arm around Lara's waist.

"I know. I keep thinking about Nutmeg, I mean Swee' Pea. And Ballou."

"And you know they're both thriving. We got new pictures yesterday, remember?"

When Lara had explained to Swee' Pea's owner that the tortie had single-handedly transformed their feral cat into a playful darling, the woman immediately wanted to adopt him. Aunt Fran was unsure, but Lara had a good feeling about it. It helped that Blue had given her blessing to the match. It had taken some work to entice Ballou into the pet carrier, but once he arrived at his new home, he'd settled down with Swee' Pea and begun to explore. So far, he hadn't allowed anyone to touch him, but his owner had high hopes.

"This is what we do, Lara. You're the one who reminded me of that."

"I know."

The doorbell chimed again. Voices rang out in the hallway.

"We're here!" Daisy Bowker called.

Lara quickly dried her hands and dashed toward the front door. Daisy, Sherry, and David stood in the hallway, shedding their coats and gloves. Hugs and handshakes made the rounds.

David, who wore his ginger-colored beard neatly trimmed, couldn't take his eyes off Sherry. It was obvious he adored her. Soft-spoken and reserved, he thanked Lara and Aunt Fran for inviting him there for Christmas.

Sherry, looking terrific in a forest-green dress that accentuated her figure, her black hair fluffed around her face, pulled Lara aside. "Lots to tell you, but we're not engaged—yet. Whew! We've agreed to revisit our relationship in early July, on the anniversary of the date we met. If we still feel the way we do now...well, you'll be shopping for a maid of honor dress. Or maybe, a *matron* of honor dress?"

"Maid," Lara said firmly. She showed her the sapphire cat pendant. Sherry squealed.

"Forgot to tell you," Sherry said. "Loretta accepted your invitation, but she can't make it until later. It's so weird. Since she went back to looking like her old self, she and Mom have kind of bonded." She rolled her eyes. "Let's hope it lasts." Sherry's gaze meandered toward the cat tree in the window. "Oh...my God, is that Butterscotch?"

Lara grinned. "It sure is. He's a different cat since he met that little boy last week."

At the "read to a cat" event the Sunday before, a sweet, dark-haired boy about seven years old had arrived with his book in hand. As the boy read aloud to Munster, something about the child's voice drew Butterscotch to him. Inexplicably, Munster made himself scarce, giving Butterscotch room to curl up at the boy's side. Blue nestled up on the opposite side, and Lara knew they'd made another match.

"He stays up there all day watching the shelter doorway," Lara said. "I think he's waiting for his little boy to come back."

Sherry's face fell. "Oh, that breaks my heart." She tapped her cherry-red fingernails against her chest.

"Not to worry. The family's going to come back over school vacation. I'm almost positive they're going to adopt him."

"Lara!" Aunt Fran called from the kitchen.

"Gotta run. Be right back with drinks and snacks!"

* * * *

After everyone had stuffed themselves with ham, scalloped potatoes, steamed broccoli, and pumpkin pie, they gathered in the large parlor. Chief Whitley and Loretta had each arrived late but made it in plenty of time for dinner.

"Now that we have a chance to relax," Daisy said cryptically, "I have some news." She took a slow sip from her mug.

Everyone gawked at her.

"Okay, Mom, you're making them nuts," Sherry said, inviting Munster onto her lap. "Just spill it."

Daisy grinned. "There's a shop in Moultonborough that specializes in high-end gift baskets. They ship all over the country, and they've been looking for someone to make specialty cookies for them. Their last baker didn't work out, *soooo*...I'm their new baker."

Everyone roared and clapped and went over to hug Daisy.

"Not to mention," Sherry added, "that now we'll be able to hire someone to work weekdays at the coffee shop."

"I'm thrilled for you, Daisy," Aunt Fran said warmly. "No one deserves it more."

"I've changed my mind about using The Bakers Thryce flour," Daisy said sheepishly. "Especially since Todd Thryce is giving me a lifetime discount on all their baking products."

Lara had spoken to Todd only once since Alice's arrest. He was devastated but coping, grateful to be back in New York. And while he acknowledged that Daisy had been the clear winner of the cookie competition, he'd added that in light of Miss Plouffe's tragic death, he was donating the prize money to the local food bank.

Daisy pulled a tissue from her pocket and sneezed. "Fran, Lara, I'm afraid I need to leave. I took two allergy pills before I came here, but they're wearing off."

"We understand," Fran said. She lifted Dolce off her lap and set him down on the carpet. After another round of hugs, Daisy left with Sherry, David, and Loretta.

Gideon and Jerry had insisted on doing the dishes, while Lara and Aunt Fran put away the leftovers.

When the kitchen was spotless, the two men rolled their shirtsleeves back down. "Fran, Lara," Jerry said, "you both outdid yourselves today. That was a fabulous meal."

"And the company was top notch." Gideon swept Lara into his arms and kissed her. "But honestly, Jerry and I are going to leave. You both deserve a rest, without the men around."

A wave of relief swept over Lara. As much as she'd have enjoyed going home with Gideon, tonight her place was here with Aunt Fran. And the cats.

They watched the men's cars back out of the driveway, red taillights flashing behind them as they drove down High Cliff Road.

"Let's have a Christmas nightcap, shall we?" Aunt Fran suggested.

Lara poured them each a snifter of white chocolate liqueur, tossing a few semisweet morsels on top. They sat in the large parlor, Lara in her favorite chair with Valenteena on her chest, and Aunt Fran on the sofa with Dolce and Twinkles vying for position in her lap. Snowball hopped onto Lara's shoulder, and Lara tickled her chin. "The view is perfect from up there, isn't it?"

Lara rested her head back and closed her eyes, letting her thoughts stream freely through her mind.

Over the past year, she and her aunt had been through so much together. Aunt Fran had had both knees replaced. Lara had stumbled onto a few murders and helped bring killers to justice. Aside from that, they'd performed near miracles with the shelter. They'd rescued cats, found loving homes for most. And while they couldn't do as much as a traditional shelter, what they'd accomplished mattered.

A lot.

"Aunt Fran?" Lara said, her eyes half-closed. "Did you ever think of adding on to the house?"

Her aunt gave out a slight laugh. "You must have read my mind. I've been mulling it over for a while now." She paused. "We'd need an architect, of course."

"And a builder." Lara sipped her liqueur, letting the warmth suffuse her. "Todd Thryce gave us a pretty hefty donation. We could build out from the back porch, add a second room to the meet-and-greet area. It could be like a little library, where kids can read to the cats."

"Let's talk about it after the New Year, shall we?"

Lara looked over at her aunt. Blue had settled onto the sofa beside her, her fluffy head resting under Aunt Fran's elbow. The cat blinked once, then again.

"Yes, let's," Lara said and raised her snifter. "In the meantime, Aunt Fran, Merry Christmas."

Her aunt raised her own snifter. "And a happy New Year to you, Lara. The best is yet to be."

If you enjoyed *Claws for Celebration*, be sure not to miss all of Linda Reilly's Cat Lady Mystery series, including

The meow of death...

Whisker Jog, New Hampshire, is a long way from Hollywood, but it's the place legendary actress Deanna Daltry wants to call home. Taking up residence in a stone mansion off Cemetery Hill, the retired, yet still glamorous, septuagenarian has adopted two kittens from Lara Caphart's High Cliff Shelter for Cats. With help from her Aunt Fran, Lara makes sure the kitties settle in safely with their new celebrity mom.

But not everyone in town is a fan of the fading star. Deanna was in Whisker Jog when she was younger, earning a reputation for pussyfooting around, and someone is using that knowledge against her. After being frightened by some nasty pranks, Deanna finds herself the prime murder suspect when the body of a local teacher is found on her property. Now, it's up to Lara, Aunt Fran, and the blue-eyed Ragdoll mystery cat Lara recently encountered to collar a killer before another victim is pounced upon...

Read on for a special excerpt!

A Lyrical Underground e-book on sale now.

Chapter 1

"Oh God, I've got to get ready."

With the toe of her beaded blue sandal, Lara Caphart turned off the vacuum cleaner and pressed the button to retract the cord. The cord snaked into the vacuum with a loud snap. She jumped slightly at the sound.

Take a deep breath, she told herself. *She's only a movie star. She's only been nominated for three Oscars and a Tony. She's only Deanna Daltry...*

Lara was lugging the vacuum back to the supply closet when she bumped smack into her aunt, Fran Clarkson. Seven months ago, Lara had moved into her aunt's Folk Victorian home in the town of Whisker Jog, New Hampshire. Though Aunt Fran had lived in the house for well over three decades, as of the beginning of the year it officially became the High Cliff Shelter for Cats.

"Sorry, Aunt Fran. I'm rushing, and I— Oh good glory, you look gorgeous. Is that a new top?" She tucked a strand of her coppery hair behind her right ear.

Aunt Fran smiled, her green eyes beaming beneath the smidge of highlighter she'd swept along her upper lids. "Yes, it is," she said, referring to the gauzy, moss-colored top she wore over her pale gray capris. She did make for a stunning picture. "Lara, why are you so jittery? Ms. Daltry won't be here for at least another hour."

"But...but...she's Deanna Daltry! And she's going to be living in our town—in tiny Whisker Jog, New Hampshire!"

Aunt Fran chuckled. "I've never seen you so starstruck before. Remember, she's here to adopt, not to audition us for parts in her next movie."

"I know, I know. It's just—"

"And also remember, she has a reputation for being late. Notoriously late. So don't expect her to be here at the stroke of three."

Lara sighed. It was true. The famous actress, best known recently for her starring role in the Broadway hit *Take Me, I'm His*, had often been dubbed Hollywood's "late date." Never married, she was known for her string of leading-man lovers, as well as for her generous good works.

She glanced around the back porch. The official meet-and-greet room for the shelter, it boasted a sturdy square table over which a cat-themed runner had been draped. The ceiling border depicted whimsical cats—hand-painted by Lara—frolicking over a background of cerulean blue. A pine corkboard hung on one wall. Photos of cats that had been successfully adopted covered the board. Lara was pleased that four kittens and two adult cats had found good homes since the shelter opened in January.

A furry body leaped soundlessly onto one of the four padded chairs. The Ragdoll cat, blue eyes sparkling, gave Lara a curious look.

Lara grinned at Blue, the cat that had the knack of popping in and out of the scenery like a puff of smoke.

"You're always smiling at that chair," Aunt Fran said. "It must remind you of something."

If you only knew, Lara thought.

"It reminds me that I'd better get hustling and clean up. When our illustrious guest arrives, I don't want to look like something a squirrel dug out of a hole in the ground."

* * * *

It was the stroke of four thirty-five when Deanna Daltry arrived. The actress had driven herself to the shelter, her vintage cream-colored Mercedes spotless and gleaming under a mid-July sun.

Slender and silver-haired, Deanna wore her hair in a short, casual style combed away from her face. Clad in faded denim capris and a white halter top, she held out one hand.

"Forgive my bare face," she said, sounding apologetic. "I find that the less makeup I wear, the less recognizable I am."

"Ms. Daltry," Lara said, trying valiantly not to gush. "I would know you anywhere. And you look beautiful, with or without makeup." She took the woman's outstretched hand, holding it a second or two longer than she should have.

Deanna's gray eyes made a sweep of the room. "Is this room the shelter?" she asked Lara. "I'm loving the feline décor."

"The shelter is actually our home," Lara explained. "Three of the adult cats live here permanently. On adoption days, we outfit them with blue collars to indicate that they're in-house cats. This room"—she waved a hand at the table—"is where we introduce ourselves, tell you about our shelter, and enjoy tea and snacks with those who wish to partake. Is iced tea all right? With the heat, we figured…"

The actress grinned and winked at Lara. "'Those who wish to partake.' You're a dear young woman, do you know that? And yes, iced tea sounds like just the ticket on this sultry day."

Inwardly, Lara slapped herself. Why did she have to sound so goofy in front of this legend? Why couldn't she just be herself?

"Anyway," Lara went on, "my aunt, Fran Clarkson, will be here any second. She's—"

"I'm here," Aunt Fran's voice trilled from the doorway. Lara couldn't hide her smile. Her aunt's tone never warbled that way. Was she feeling a bit starstruck herself?

Aunt Fran set a pitcher of iced tea on the table, along with a small plate of cat-shaped cookies. "Ms. Daltry," she said, offering her hand to the actress, "I'm Fran, and we're honored that you've chosen our shelter. Please have a seat."

The table had already been set with tall glasses, dishes, and spoons. Lara poured each of them a glass of iced tea. "I hope you like cookies," she said. "Daisy Bowker at the local coffee shop made them especially for you. They're flavored with lavender."

Deanna's smile widened. "To match the iconic gown I wore in *Forever and a Century*? How sweet of her."

"That's amazing, Ms. Daltry," Lara said. "How did you know that?"

"First, I insist that you both call me Deanna." The actress flashed a brilliant smile, but Lara spied a touch of sadness in her expressive eyes. Ignoring Lara's question, she looked around. "Aside from these delightful cookies, I haven't seen any cats yet."

Lara laughed. "We close the door to the large parlor on adoption days, until we're ready to let visitors in." She pushed her chair back and left the room to open the door. Munster, an orange-striped darling, moved past her like a rocket. He knew that on days when that door closed and then opened again, he was about to meet new people.

Lara followed the cat to the back porch, where he promptly jumped onto their visitor's lap.

"Oh, what a darling you are," Deanna cooed, stroking his head. "But you're wearing a blue collar, so I can't adopt you, can I?" She pushed her chilled glass toward the center of the table.

"He's our official greeter," Aunt Fran said, then smiled at the slender gray cat eyeing them from the doorway. "But Bootsie here is ready for a nice quiet home, aren't you sweetie?"

Bootsie dipped her head forward and moved cautiously into the room. Aunt Fran called to her, but Bootsie made a circuitous route and wound herself around Deanna's ankle.

Deanna clucked over the cat, reaching down to run a hand along her soft body. "She's a doll, for sure," the actress said and then sighed. "I know I sound selfish saying this, but...well, I was actually hoping to adopt a pair of kittens." She held up a slender hand. "And I already know what you're thinking, that everyone prefers kittens over adult cats because they're so cute and frisky. But for me, coming back here represents a new beginning, and—" She paused and gazed up at the ceiling, the fingers of one hand lightly touching her throat.

Aunt Fran spoke first. "Ms.—I mean, Deanna, you don't need to explain. Your feelings are fully understandable. And, as it turns out, your timing is excellent."

"Three weeks ago," Lara said, "someone left a cardboard cage on our front porch. No note, no explanation—just a shy mama kitty and three very hungry kittens inside."

"The kittens are about fourteen weeks old," Aunt Fran explained, "so they're definitely ready for adoption. We've already approved an application from a woman who wants to adopt the mom and one of the kittens. As soon as the woman's recovered sufficiently from her hip surgery, she and her daughter are going to pick them up."

Deanna's gray eyes beamed. "So, the other two are still available?"

"They are," Aunt Fran confirmed. "They've both had their vaccinations, but they're due for a second round in a few weeks. We'll give you a referral to our preferred vet, who will also do the neutering and spaying when each one is ready."

Lara couldn't suppress a smile. "They're predominantly white, but the male has two black stripes above one paw that make him look like he's wearing an armband, and the female has a brown, diamond-shaped mark next to her right eye. We've been calling them Noodle and Doodle, but of course you can name them anything you'd like."

Deanna clasped her hands together. "Oh, I can't wait to see them."

Lara rose from her padded seat just as the elusive Ragdoll, Blue, slipped onto the vacant one. Blue set her chin on the table and gave a slow blink, her gaze coming to rest on Deanna. From the cat's expression, Lara saw that she approved of the woman.

"I'll get them for you," Lara said. "Last I saw, they were napping on the cat tree in the large parlor."

She scooted out of the room, returning a minute later clutching the kittens to her chest. Lara handed the male kitten to Deanna. Munster sniffed the kitten's tail but didn't vacate his comfy lap space.

"Oh, they're absolutely angelic." Deanna nuzzled the male kitten against her cheek, smiling at the female tucked under Lara's chin. "They're perfect," she declared. "I promise to give them a loving home."

"We do have an application that needs to be filled out," Lara said carefully. She didn't want to risk offending the actress, but anyone wanting to adopt had to be approved. It was part of the process designed to give their feline residents the best homes possible.

A noise from the large parlor drew Munster's attention. He leaped off Deanna's lap and went off to investigate. Lara set the female kitten in Deanna's lap.

Deanna bit down gently on her lower lip, then curled her free hand around the female kitten. Her voice grew soft. "I wasn't sure about coming back to Whisker Jog," she murmured, a pained look dimming her eyes. "But you've both made me feel so very welcome. I'm glad I'm here, and I'm grateful to both of you for giving me a private appointment. I know you're not normally open on Thursdays." She laughed. "Application process? Good! Bring it on. I assure you that once you check me out, you won't have any reservations about letting me adopt."

"Excellent," Aunt Fran said.

The kittens had gotten antsy, so Deanna set them down. Their mom appeared suddenly and sat watching them from the doorway. Her other kitten hovered behind her.

"Here's mama now," Aunt Fran said. "We've been calling her Catalina and her other kitten Bitsy, but her new owners will probably change that."

All white with one black ear and one black forepaw, Catalina looked up at Deanna. Her tail curled around her feet as she assessed the newcomer.

"So that's the mama kitty," Deanna said with a smile. "What beautiful markings."

Bitsy, slightly smaller than her sibs, padded over to Deanna and sniffed at the toes of her purple sneakers.

"I think she's checking me out." Deanna winked at Lara.

Catalina was clearly comfortable around the actress. Deanna reached down and stroked her head, eliciting a soft purr from the cat. The kittens immediately went over to their mom. Introductions over, Catalina turned and strolled from the room, Bitsy, Noodle, and Doodle following in her wake.

After that, Deanna seemed to relax. She began regaling Lara and Aunt Fran with tales from her early days in Hollywood.

"Do you ever get tired of people intruding on your privacy?" Lara asked. "I'll bet people are always trying to take selfies with you."

The warmth in Deanna's expression cooled, and her eyes narrowed. "You've hit the nail on the head, as they say, Lara. You can't imagine how many times I've wanted to hide, to disappear. How often I've wanted to seek out a place where no one can bother me or hurt me." Her thin nostrils flared slightly.

"I'm sorry," Lara said. "I shouldn't have asked. I didn't mean to pry."

The actress' smile instantly returned, as if prompted by a cue card. "Don't be silly. It was a fair question." She swallowed the last of her iced tea, then pulled her cell phone out from the tiny purse she'd brought with her. "By the way, you're both coming to the reception on Sunday, right?" "Reception?" Lara asked.

Aunt Fran piped in. "I saw something in the paper about it. The Whisker Jog Ladies' Association is holding a welcome tea and reception for Deanna this Sunday afternoon at the historical society. I'm not a member, so no, we've not been invited."

"Bummer," Lara said.

Deanna waved a hand. "Never mind that. You *are* invited, because I'm inviting you. I'll speak to Evelyn Conley, the coordinator. Besides, I fully intend to support your shelter, and I want to make that known to everyone attending this little shindig."

"Oh, that's so kind of you. Thank you," Aunt Fran said.

Lara's mind instantly flitted to her wardrobe. As a watercolor artist, she spent most of her days working in paint-splattered T-shirts and denim. She had no idea what to wear to an event like the one to which Deanna had invited them.

But that got her thinking. Gideon, the local attorney she'd been seeing for a few months, had asked her to dinner the following Saturday at a new restaurant just outside the town limits. She'd planned to splurge on something summery to wear, but hadn't had a chance to shop. Maybe she could find something that would fit the bill for both events.

"Yes, thank you, Deanna," Lara said. "I'd love to attend."

"Fine. I'll see that invitations are hand-delivered to you by tomorrow. As for that application, is it something you can send to my private email address?"

"It sure is," Lara said. "If you give us your email address I'll get it right off to you."

Deanna's smile was genuine. "I'm so pleased that I came here today. You've both been gracious and lovely. And I promise, those kittens will have a wonderful home."

About the Author

Photo by Harper Point Photography

Raised in a sleepy town in the Berkshires, **Linda Reilly** has spent the bulk of her career in the field of real estate closings and title examination. It wasn't until 1995 that her first short mystery, "Out of Luck," was accepted for publication by *Woman's World Magazine*. Since then she's had more than forty short stories published, including a sprinkling of romances. She is also the author of *Some Enchanted Murder*, and the Deep Fried Mystery series featuring fry cook Talia Marby. A member of Sisters in Crime and Mystery Writers of America, Linda lives in New Hampshire with her husband, who affectionately calls her "Noseinabook." Visit her on the web at lindasreilly.com.

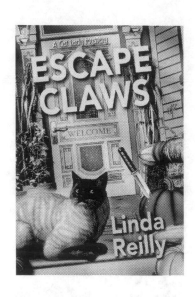

Here, killer, killer, killer…

For the first time in sixteen years, Lara Caphart has returned to her hometown of Whisker Jog, New Hampshire. She wants to reconnect with her estranged Aunt Fran, who's having some difficulty looking after herself—and her eleven cats. Taking care of a clowder of kitties is easy, but keeping Fran from being harassed by local bully Theo Barnes is hard. The wealthy builder has his sights set on Fran's property, and is determined to make her an offer she doesn't dare refuse.

Then Lara spots a blue-eyed ragdoll cat that she swears is the reincarnation of her beloved Blue, her childhood pet. Pursuing the feline to the edge of Fran's yard, she stumbles upon the body of Theo Barnes, clearly a victim of foul play. To get her and Fran off the suspect list, Lara finds herself following the cat's clues in search of a killer. Is Blue's ghost really trying to help her solve a murder, or has Lara inhaled too much catnip?

Printed in the United States
by Baker & Taylor Publisher Services